Thomas' 100 Cat Tales

The Cat Who Came in from the Cold

Dwayne Sharpe

Thomas's 100 Cat Tales / Dwayne Sharpe -- 1st ed.

Print Edition ISBN-13: 978-1726448130

DEDICATION

Dedicated to my wife Linda, for her wonderful support and encouragement.

Humans can be very helpful, when trained.

—THOMAS

CONTENTS

Tale 1 - My New Home 1

Tale 2 - The Intruder 3

Tale 3 - Legos 5

Tale 4 - Round-Up 6

Tale 5 - Taxes..8

Tale 6 - The Box 10

Tale 7 - Presents..12

Tale 8 - Black and White 14

Tale 9 - The Visitor..16

Tale 10 - The Little Girl...18

Tale 11 - The Yarn...20

Tale 12 - The Birthday...22

Tale 13 - Sick Day 24

Tale 14 - Getaway 26

Tale 15 - Ping Pong..28

Tale 16 - Cat Fight 30

Tale 17 - Puzzling 32

Tale 18 - House Sitter 34

Tale 19 - House Guest..36

Tale 20 - Poker Night...38

Tale 21 - Black Bird..41

Tale 22 - Flowers 43

Tale 23 - Fireworks 45

Tale 24 - The Photo Shoot 47

Tale 25 - Take Out 49

Tale 26 - The Cable Guy...52

Tale 27 - The Accident..54

Tale 28 - Arts and Crafts..56

Tale 29 - The Nursery 58

Tale 30 - The Baby...60

Tale 31 - Trick or Treat...63

Tale 32 - The Big Bird 65

Tale 33 - Tree Tops Glisten 67

Tale 34 - Rain...69

Tale 35 - Rock, Rumble, and Roll 71

Tale 36 - BBQ Time..73

Tale 37 - Valentines 75

Tale 38 - A New Toy 77

Tale 39 - Kitty Company 79

Tale 40 - The Eggspert..82

Tale 41 - Vacation Day 1 84

Tale 42 - Vacation Day 2 86

Tale 43 - Vacation Day 3 89

Tale 44 - Magic Cleaner..91

Tale 45 - Grandma 93

Tale 46 - Grandma and the Dog...96

Tale 47 - Grandma and the Kitten..98

Tale 48 - Observations 100

Tale 49 - The Vet 103

Tale 50 - Super Cat 105

Tale 51 - Cat Show - The Leash 107

Tale 52 - Cat Show - The Walk 109

Tale 53 - Cat Show - The Show 111

Tale 54 - Ride Along..113

Tale 55 - Tiger Visits 116

Tale 56 - A Day of Terror 118

Tale 57 - A Winter Holiday 120

Tale 58 - Home Alone..123

Tale 59 - Looking Pretty 125

Tale 60 - Office Life 128

Tale 61 - Puppy Love..130

Tale 62 - Sick Time..133

Tale 63 - Beyond My Backyard...135

Tale 64 - Something Fishy 138

Tale 65 - Baby Walkabout 141

Tale 66 - The Farm - Jake 143

Tale 67 - The Farm - Big Animals...145

Tale 68 - The Farm - Night Sounds 147

Tale 69 - Home Protection 149

Tale 70 - Hot Dog 152

Tale 71 - Trapped..155

Tale 72 - A Cry in the Night 157

Tale 73 - A Vet Checkup 160

Tale 74 - A New Home 162

Tale 75 - Yard Sale 165

Tale 76 - Catnip..168

Tale 77 - Lost Part 1 - Truck Ride 170

Tale 78 - Lost Part 2 - The Little Boy..172

Tale 79 - Lost Part 3 - Grandma 175

Tale 80 - Lost Part 4 - Homeward Dreams 177

Tale 81 - Lost Part 5 - Home Again...180

Tale 82 - Cookies 182

Tale 83 - Porch Pirate...185

Tale 84 - An Artistic Touch 188

Tale 85 - Day Care 190

Tale 86 - Camping...193

Tale 87 - Camping - The Campfire 195

Tale 88 - Camping - The Hike 198

Tale 89 - Cat Door 200

Tale 90 - Baby Rescue 202

Tale 91 - A Visit From Lucky..205

Tale 92 - Smoke Alarm...207

Tale 93 - The Dog 210

Tale 94 - Max...212

Tale 95 - Ride 'em Cowboy..214

Tale 96 - Can You Dig It?..216

Tale 97 - Ghost Image..219

Tale 98 - Max Meets Lucky..221

Tale 99 - Street Repairs..223

Tale 100 - Past Tense 226

ACKNOWLEDGMENTS

Several people have provided many hours of copy editing including Ginnie Wilcox, Elizabeth Dennis, and Norma Schumow. Thank you for your valuable time.

Besides my wife, Tim and Trina Darcy have been my most vocal cheerleaders and I thank them for their enthusiasm.

Special thanks to Paul Sharpe for his copy editing and maintenance of a website to host my short stories including the preview for this book. The site is located at http://paulsharpe.us/PaulSharpe/Dwayne_Stories/Dwayne-Sharpe-Stories.htm

Thomas' 100 Cat Tales

Tale 1 - My New Home

My name is Thomas, and I rule over this kingdom. After all, this is a king's purpose. As I cleaned my white furry boots, I thought back about how I arrived at this location. I lived off the street and back alleyways for all my life. Food from trash cans, fast food begging, and other cat's bowls provided my basic needs, and I figured it was time to change this lifestyle. After many days of exploring a good neighborhood, I found a house where two humans lived. I hid in the bushes and watched them. They seemed to come and go every day. My hopes were high I could move in and have them provide me with food and water. Conditions seemed right to take a chance with them. After careful consideration, I decided this is where I would put down my paws.

Once I made my decision, I parked myself on the front porch, waiting for the female human to come home. Based on my observations, there were two humans living here and I felt the female would be an easy target. While waiting, I groomed myself while catching the last rays of the sun for the day.

The female human arrived, and I figured this would be an easy entry. When she opened the door, I strolled in like I owned the place. She seemed to put up a small fuss at first, but when I rubbed my smooth black body against her legs, she picked me up and said, "You must be lost." I think I might have even turned on the purr motor for her. I'm sure the sweet music convinced her to let me stay.

It took time to train these humans. They tried to feed me some dry food. While I was hungry, I had to ignore dinner a few times before they brought something fit for a king. I sat next to my bowl and stared away from it. I showed them the offering was unsatisfactory. The cardboard tasting kibble was as bad as scrounging for food on my own. It took three days before they opened a can with a tantalizing aroma. After eating this,

I rewarded these humans by letting them pet me. The training paid off, and they have brought me this fancy food every day since then.

During the daylight hours, such as today, I sit on one of the window sills enjoying the sun and catching up on my rest. I have two favorite windows, one in front for the morning sun and the other in a back room to catch the afternoon warmth. When the humans arrive, I allow them to pet me, and I turn the purr motor on. They seem to enjoy the sound. At night, I wander around my kingdom making sure there aren't any strangers present. In the mornings, I run and jump on top of the bed and wake the humans up. The routine is part of the training to remind my humans it was time to feed me.

One night, while patrolling the house, I detected an unhealthy smell. I traced this down by using my sniffer. The smell came from the kitchen. I found a burning odor, I think the humans call it smoke. There wasn't a lot, but it burned my eyes. To save my house, I had to wake the humans.

I ran into the bedroom and jumped on the bed. At first, this didn't work, but I tried jumping and walking back and forth on top of the covers. I even turned on my siren, a big meow. This is used rarely but worked in waking up the humans. I jumped off the bed, thinking they would follow me. Unfortunately, they ignored me. I started up my siren again, and this time, my male human got out of bed. Once he was up, he must have smelled the smoke. He yelled something to the female human, and they both followed me into the kitchen. One of their electrical devices was doing a slow burn. Whatever it was, they removed it from the countertop and set it outside on the back steps. This stopped it from stinking up my house any further.

The humans held me and stroked my sleek black body. They even talked and thanked me. My female human said, "What a brave kitty." At first, I wanted to get down and wander around, but this petting felt wonderful, so I turned on my purr motor and put it into high gear.

Then my female human said, "We need to give you a name."

My male human said, "Let's call him Thomas. He's been a tomcat for too long to change now."

And that is how I adopted my humans and new surroundings.

Tale 2 - The Intruder

Today started out pretty much as usual. My nightly prowl around the house ended, and it was time to eat. I pounced on the bed where my human hosts were sleeping. Their training is incomplete as they are still slow to rise and prepare my morning meal. I needed to remind them daily to set out fresh water and food for me. My being a king carries the responsibility for protecting this kingdom, and my human subjects need to provide regular feedings.

I finished my morning meal and waited for my humans to leave for the day. I then strolled to the front window where the sun provided warmth. Grooming is an important aspect of being a king. I needed to maintain my royal appearance. I cleaned one white boot at a time. When I finished all four paws, I rewarded myself with some well-earned rest.

Around mid-day when the sun had shifted, I heard strange noises at the back door and investigated. An intruder pried the door open and was coming inside. Scraggly hair covered his unfriendly face. Anyone disturbing my kingdom had to deal with me. I stood my ground and let out a long hiss followed by a growl. The man ignored me, so I hissed louder. A swift foot came my way, and I skirted it in time. He entered my kingdom without permission, and it was my job to fend him off.

I've been in many scrapes in my life, something necessary for survival, but repulsive. It is one reason I settled down and made this my private kingdom. This intruder was an insult to my royalty and a disturbance to my personal space. I needed to drive him from my castle and teach him a lesson.

He passed by me and entered the large living room. I leaped on his back and sank my front claws deep into his neck. His hand came up to pull me off, and I bit hard into his soft skin. His other hand reached up and pulled me off, but not before my claws dragged across his neck. He threw me hard across the room. I would have landed on my feet, but there was a wall in the way. I hit hard and slid to the floor.

The intruder went down the hall and out of sight while I caught my breath. My side ached from hitting the wall. A few minutes later, the man returned, carrying a bulging pillowcase. I was ready for round two.

He stood facing me, and I raced toward him and clawed my way up the pillowcase, leaving a few minor tear marks as I gathered speed. I bit down hard on the hand holding the case. He tried to shake me loose as my sharp claws sunk in deeper. The case dropped, and his other hand grabbed for me. He cried from the pain I inflicted upon him. I bit the hand trying to grab me while keeping my claws secured in his other hand. He twisted and turned trying to knock me loose. When I let go, he dashed for the door, drips of blood trailing behind.

My fur was a mess, and I worked my grooming magic to restore my regal looks. My side still hurt, but I figured a long nap would make me feel better. I laid in the back window and soaked up the sun.

When my humans arrived home, they saw the jimmied door and then the pillowcase filled with their shiny objects. They also noticed the blood and claw marks on the case. The humans wanted to hold me. Maybe they were checking if I cleaned off all the intruder blood. That night, they gave me an extra bowl filled with milk. It was a real treat, but I couldn't let them know how much I loved it.

I curled up in my female human's lap and started my purr motor. She enjoyed my company as her hand caressed my long black body. I left my purr motor on longer than normal.

Tale 3 - Legos

My name is Thomas, and I live with two humans who seem to want me to exercise with them. They have these games and want me to take part. Today, they dragged a little gray stuffed mouse around on a red string in front of me. I chased it for a while hoping this would satisfy their exercise need. After a while, this became boring, and I stopped to clean my white furry boots and sleek black body. Being a king, I require regular grooming to maintain my noble appearance.

The stuffed mouse got me thinking. Maybe my humans didn't want to exercise. Maybe they wanted me to bring them a mouse, and they were trying to show me what they wanted. I have caught a few in my day. I wondered whether the mouse should be a dead one or a live one? If I capture a live one, they can play chase with it around the house and get their exercise. I will remember this the next time I see a mouse.

The next day after the humans left, I looked around and spotted a toy they hadn't given me yet. I think they called the little blocks Legos. I have watched my humans sit for several hours playing with them, stacking them up higher and higher. They spoke the words Eiffel Tower to describe the structure they were building.

I jumped up on the table where all the colorful play pieces laid. The small pieces all had round indentations perfect for my nails to hook into. While sniffing a pile, I pushed a whole stack down onto the hardwood floor where they scattered around. On the floor, I tested one with a bat of my paw. It is amazing how far they slide when hit like a hockey puck. I played a while and even scored when a couple went under the stove and a few more under the refrigerator. I even moved a few into the big room with one going under the sofa. Now, why hadn't they given me these toys to play with earlier?

Now about that stuffed mouse, I think they liked to play with it, so I picked it up without sinking my teeth into it, and carried it back to the table with the Legos on it. I placed it right in the center so they could find it easier. I think I knocked a few more Legos down while doing this. Maybe they could build a house for the mouse.

When my humans arrived back home, they discovered the gray mouse. Their loud voices showed me how happy and excited they were. I watched their facial expressions. They kept pointing to the table with the stuffed gray mouse on it. Ah, I thought, that was the perfect place. Maybe they both wanted to play with the mouse, and they debated whose turn it was first.

My male human must have lost the debate as he gathered up the little play pieces I knocked on the floor and placed them in a box. I figured I could play with them another time. It was so nice of my humans to keep them all in one place.

That evening, when they picked me up to pet me like they always do, I turned on my purr motor to thank them for providing the entertainment. Maybe they will play with the mouse and take turns chasing it. I will stick with the Legos. They spin fast across the floor, and there are so many!

Tale 4 - Round-Up

Thomas is my name, and I'm the king around these here parts. While I don't ride a horse, today I felt it was round-up time at the OK Corral. I sat in my back-window perch cleaning my beautiful white furry boots when I spotted one of those large pesky dogs coming into my backyard. He received my full attention when he invaded my backyard, which is part of my kingdom.

The dog had long legs and short brown fur reminding me of a horse. He's a dog, so he stinks and attracts flies too. The dog kept his sniffer pointed to the ground like he was looking for something or trying to pick up a scent. I reckoned he was a true Bloodhound, with those long ears and oh my gosh, he was drooling all over the place.

My yard backs up to a hilly area with many trees standing tall. This makes it easy for him to wander about and track animals. I have seen deer, rabbits, and even a few field mice on the hillside. I might have to trap a mouse for my humans to play with sometime.

Now the dog's sniffer was up in the air, and he was breathing heavily to pull in the various scents. I saw movement about 30 feet back towards the other side of the yard. I couldn't make it out but looked like another cat. Wait, I thought, the only thing worse than a dog in my backyard was a stray cat trying to take over my territory.

My body was stiff except for my head which pivoted back and forth between the dog and the cat. I was hoping the dog would chase the little cat out of my yard. What? Me root for a dog? What's this life coming to, anyway? The dog continued a slow back-and-forth movement around the yard. The cat had stopped all its movement. I knew the dog would sniff him out. What a revolting situation this is!

The brave cat crept along the hedge. It was a strange walk for a cat. In the distance, I could barely make out a little white mixed in with the black fur. I realized the coloring was like mine. A little closer now and... That's not a cat. It's a skunk!!

By this time, the dog had zeroed in on the scent and was moving closer. I figured if he gets too close, he will get a snoot full of an unexpected aroma. When the dog looked up, he caught sight of the skunk and howled. That was an ugly sound, and it gave his position away. The noise alerted the skunk to run for cover. The hedge was perfect for this as he could crawl under and around it. When the dog ran for where the skunk had been, he let out another series of howls. His sniffer was in the air and worked hard.

I had to find another window for my vantage point as I could not see all the action. On the other side of the house, there is a big garden window my humans don't seem to like me in. I don't know why, just because the small plants make tasty treats. From this window, I could see a little of both sides of the hedge. The dog worked my side, and I could see the skunk on the other side waddling away towards the trees.

The dog wised up and jumped over the hedge and sniffed there. A few moments later, he caught the scent and let out more awkward howls. He then took off towards the trees. I thought all these intruders were out of my hair and I was about to go back to my comfy perch when to my surprise, I saw the dog come running out of the trees howling with his tail tucked between his legs.

I tired from supervising this rodeo and glad they left for parts unknown. My right paw was clean, and I worked on another one. When finished, I stretched my regal body out for a well-earned siesta.

Tale 5 - Taxes

It seemed like a normal day. The morning routine started when I pounced on the bed to wake up my humans. They greeted me with a "Not now Thomas, it's the weekend." That didn't mean a lot because it was breakfast time and someone needed to provide me with my kingly nutrients. I let my tail drag across their noses, and they must have received the message. My male human filled my bowl and refreshed my water.

My male human sat down and began work at the large table. He muttered the word taxes several times, but I didn't know what it meant. I jumped up on the table to investigate. He petted me down my back, and it felt so good, my hindquarters arched up for the full effect. He must have had snake charmer in him as my tail stood up straight. After a few well-earned moments of petting, he picked me up and gently placed me on the floor.

I sat there minding my business grooming myself when I heard him say, "I can't find any deductions." I think I heard it right, de-DUCK-shuns. He must be looking for the duck that hides. I will help search for any ducks. With my detective hat on, I went about the house, looking for the missing duck.

I started with the big bedroom and looked all around there. Then I moved off to the bathroom and checked the sink area. No ducks here either. From the counter, I could see into the corner of the bathtub. There I spied a duck hiding. I jumped down and peered into the tub. The tub was dry, but I made sure. I try to stay away from big bodies of water as I do my own grooming. I then hopped in the tub and went over to the corner and gave that pesky duck a swat. It jumped down at me and rolled into the tub.

Now how am I going to get this duck out to my human? The little yellow duck had funny white ears on its head and a short cotton colored tail. I wondered if this was a duck or an Easter bunny pretending to be a duck. It would have to do. I clamped down on those long ears, jumped out of the tub, and headed for the big table.

My human wasn't there, but that didn't stop me. With a tight grip on the duck's ears, I jumped up on the table and released the duck. Now, where was my human? He should be here to reward me for finding his de-duck-shun.

While waiting, I spotted a shiny object on the table; it was a paper clip. I crept up on it and with a big pounce, landed on top, ducked my head down, and rolled over with it clenched between my forepaws. It was a fight to the finish. The clip came loose, and I attacked it again. I was oblivious to all the neat stacks of receipts, bills and other statements surrounding me. These merged into a large pile on the table with others falling over the edge. The clip had enough and gave up. I was victorious and defended my kingdom once again.

After all of this hard work, it was time to bathe in the warmth of the sun. I found my favorite window and sprawled in the sunlight coming through. There was some loud talking in the other room. I could barely make out the word duck. Ah, I thought, he has found his de-duck-shun. I swished my tail a few times feeling great satisfaction of a job well done.

Tale 6 - The Box

I was sunning myself in the noonday sun when one of my humans came home. I thought this was strange as she returns closer to sunset. She carried a large cardboard box, something I was familiar with in my earlier life. I usually found these near dumpsters where I would seek my evening meals. I am so glad I now have regular meals of tasty treats.

She placed the brown box in the large room and then went about doing something else. My curiosity got the better of me, and I checked the box out. The box was upright with the flaps hanging out. I stood on my hind legs and stretched up to the top and peeked in. It was empty and inviting. With a short hop, I was up and over the edge and came down inside. The box created shadows as the sides blocked most of the light coming in from outside.

I climbed out, and when I did, the box fell on its side. While this gave me a start, it made it easier to enter and exit. I did so several times, claiming this new territory as part of my kingdom. This was enjoyable, playing in the box. My human entered the room and said, "Thomas, we have to go to the vet now for your shots."

I didn't understand this as she picked me up and stroked my back a few times. She then stood the box back up and placed me inside. At first, I thought she wanted to play, but the flaps were closed, and it became dark except for the crack at the top. I stretched up and tried to open the flaps. I fell backward as she lifted the box which threw me off balance and I let out a big meow.

My human said, "It's okay Thomas, we're just going for a short ride to the vet."

Being enclosed, I can't say for sure what happened next, but the box, with me inside, rocked from side to side for what seemed like an eternity. Once stopped, my female human lifted the box and carried it. I hoped this was the end of this trip. When she opened the box, I found myself in a brightly lit room. It had many strange smells, one of which I recognized as something used for cleaning. My human said to the vet, "Doctor, will these shots hurt Thomas?"

Hurt? What was going on I thought? Then some lady stroked my back. It felt enjoyable, and I relaxed, except for my long tail. It had a mind of its own and was reaching for the sky. The Doctor was petting my head, looking at my ears and trying to look inside my mouth. That part didn't sit well with me. Then from behind, I felt a pinch which didn't last too long but was uncomfortable. I think they were trying to be sneaky about something.

As I was being placed back in the box, instinct kicked in as my four legs spread out wide trying to stop this box torment. I lost the battle and let out another big meow. The box was closed and carried again. I experienced the same sideways movement as before. At last, someone carried me into my home. I know because once the flaps opened, I bounded out and ran to find a safe, quiet place under the bed.

Later that night, my female human picked me up and petted me for some time. I rewarded my human with some soft purring as it still upset me about the box. My other human took over and rubbed under my chin and then more behind my ears. The purr motor reluctantly kicked into high gear. Things were back to normal in my kingdom.

Tale 7 - Presents

My humans were laughing again at my expense. They somehow controlled a little red dot that raced around the room. Normally, I would not chase these toys, but this one had me fooled. I ran around the room chasing the little light until my tongue hung out. This made me think about dogs that let their tongues hang out and drool all the time. Royalty does not pant. Because this running exercise wore me out, I didn't even have enough spit to groom myself. I held my head up high and strolled off towards the kitchen where the humans place fresh water for me daily. I lapped up a lot of water.

That evening while I was prowling about, I thought about how I should thank my humans for bringing me gifts. Maybe I should bring them a plaything too. My mind was pondering the situation when I spotted the door to the garage open. Usually, it is closed, but when it is open, I include the garage area in my patrol. This area is also part of my kingdom and needs guarding. I strolled into the garage, my padded paws silently leading the way.

After a considerable amount of time wandering around all the boxes, shelves, appliances and work areas, I was about to leave. Something near the big garage door caught my eye, so I strained my eyes and focused hard as the room was dim. There was a slight movement, a trespasser to my kingdom. I needed to move closer.

From the workbench, I jumped down ever so gently, careful not to scare this prey away. I hunched my body up and kept close to the cement floor. I took four quick paces and then paused. There was no movement from the intruder; perhaps it hadn't spotted me yet. The soft pads on my paws were noiseless as I moved closer. It was a lizard, trying to creep in on my territory.

The lizard was unaware of me and made a quick dash, stopping within pouncing distance. I leaped and landed on top of him. He squirmed for a moment and then froze in fear. I captured this invader. I thought this would make a nice present for my humans. It will show how thankful I am for receiving their gifts!

I carefully picked the lizard up to prevent squishing him and carried him into the bathroom where I knew my humans would come by and see their present. I dropped the lizard on the floor, and after a few moments, it tried to crawl away. My paw reached out and dragged the lizard back. I couldn't let my present leave on its own. I repeated this process a few more times as the lizard tried to escape.

The lights came on in the bathroom as my female human entered. She looked down at me and then at the lizard. She let out a loud scream and ran out of the room still screaming. I thought, she's so happy with my present she's screaming with delight. My male human entered, and he also saw the present I had brought them. The lizard tried to make another move, and again I dragged him back.

My human left and returned with a small food container. He bent down and pushed the lizard into the clear plastic box and then placed the lid on tight. That was my cue to leave as I had delivered the present. I wondered if they would play with it or have it for dinner? Regardless, it was time for me to groom myself as I had been out in the dusty garage guarding my kingdom.

That night while I was being petted, my female human said, "No more lizards, Thomas." I guess she was happy with the one I brought her.

Then again, maybe it didn't taste good. I was glad she liked the gift. My purr motor volume increased.

Tale 8 - Black and White

It must have been the weekend as my humans call it. They constantly disturb my daytime slumber while I bask in the sun. The big noise maker, I think they call it a vacuum, chased me around the big room. It seems I had to move from place to place to keep my tail from being sucked in. I looked for a room where I could find a quiet time alone. I tried the kitchen and the bedroom with no success. My male human kept banging the connecting door to the garage, and I figured I would try my luck in the garage.

I waited for an opportunity for the door to open as they usually keep it shut. When it opened, my male human came out carrying something and didn't see me as I slipped by and entered the big garage. This was a great hangout as there are many places to explore and check out. Sometimes I even spot intruders, like the lizard the other day.

I started my tour across the workbench and checked the stuff out. There was a yellow pencil in a coffee mug, and when I swatted it with my paw, it went around and around. I did it again. This play toy was new. I moved around the room, jumping from the workbench to the big white washer and dryer. I noticed a large table set up in the middle of the floor where they normally parked the car.

My male human entered the room, but he didn't see me. I watched him as he bent over the big table and played with some black and white objects. The pieces were lined up in little rows down one side of the table and circled up and around the middle. It reminded me of a long snake curled up. The black and white colors were just like me, lots of black with a little white on the underside and paws.

I watched as he seemed to line up the objects. My female human entered and said, "Honey, it's time for lunch. Stop playing with your dominos and come in and eat." They both left, and I checked the dominos out.

I jumped down from the washer and moved closer to the table determining the best place to hop up. The table had lots of dominos on it, and I didn't want to mess any of them up. I settled on the corner furthest from the door and sprang up.

The dominos filled the table, all standing up on their edges and in line like little soldiers. I sniffed a few, but there wasn't anything interesting. There was an area in the middle of the table where there weren't any dominos, and I cautiously stepped over several of these objects and sat down there. I couldn't figure out why my human had all this interest in them.

I was grooming myself, as I take pride in looking good all the time when suddenly, the door opened, and my male human entered. He saw me and seemed to get very excited. Perhaps he was happy I found these toys, I wasn't sure.

I remained frozen, watching him dance around the table waving his hands and arms. He kept saying something excitedly, but I didn't understand. For a moment, I thought he wanted me to get down. While I cleaned another paw, he bumped the table. That seemed to trigger something as the dominos cascaded down on each other. I had to stand up to watch as they circled the table and ran around me. The clicking noise from the falling dominos worried me.

I jumped down from the table and ran over to the door as my female human had come in to see what all the racket was about. She asked, "What's wrong, dear? Did your dominos fall over?"

I went back to the living room. She had put the big noise maker away. Maybe now I could relax in peace while catching the afternoon rays.

After dinner, my female human picked me up and stroked my back. I relaxed, secure in my human's arms. The petting felt good and with the house silent, you could hear my purr motor from a distance.

Tale 9 - The Visitor

I was basking in the sun when my humans came home and interrupted my relaxation. They were talking loudly and disturbing my opportunity to catch up on some sleep. Oh well, I thought, I am awake now, so I had better check out what all the chatter was about. I took my sweet time and stretched way out before jumping down.

I crossed the soft carpet in the large room to find them in the kitchen. They were holding something furry. As soon as it let out a juvenile meow, I knew it was an unwelcomed guest. My humans looked down at me and must have recognized my disapproval. My female human said, "Thomas, this is Boots. He will visit with us until his owners return. You two can play together!"

Play, she had said, play? I don't play. I can see it already. This Boots character will try to make me run hard. I save my energy for when I need it the most. An example of this is when that intruder came into my kingdom. With Boots here, I knew this would be a long week.

Boots had stripes like a tiger with black paws. That must be why they named him Boots. I needed to show him who was boss of this household, so I strolled over with my tail high in the air just showing him he wasn't any big deal!

Boots wasn't far behind as he was checking me out. Being the king in this house, I needed to keep up my regal look, so I stopped and groomed myself. This also provided cover while I watched to see what he would do. The humans had stepped into the big room to watch. Boots made it over to the sofa, stretched up and sunk his claws into the flowered fabric on the front corner. He sharpened his paws until my female human shrieked. That startled Boots, and he ducked for cover. Score one for the good guys.

I went over to the scratching post and performed a minor manicure of my nails. I had to show Boots the right way to do this. Besides, I wanted to impress my humans. I might get extra petting out of this. Afterward, I went over to my window and sat perched waiting for the show to continue.

The humans tried that gray mouse trick with Boots where they drag the mouse around hoping they could get their exercise and have Boots exercise with them. They tried it with me before, but chasing a stuffed mouse wasn't my thing. Boots watched the mouse being dragged back and forth. His eyes tracked it, and then he hunched himself up and pounced upon the mouse digging his nails in deep. He followed up with sharp teeth that pulled at the head.

The toy mouse was no match for this rough treatment as half of the head, along with some stuffing separated from the rest of the body. That only seemed to encourage Boots more. Once Boots tore the mouse open, he pulled out its remaining stuffing and scattered it about. He raised his head looking for applause like he was the gladiator that won supreme in the Coliseum.

It was a good show, but you could see how displeased the humans were with their exercise toy broken and strewn all about in little pieces. I could see Boots was rapidly losing points. I continued to watch from my perch.

The male human picked Boots up and stroked him while talking to him. I couldn't make out all the words, but a few were you destroyed that toy. Maybe Boots understood this, then again, maybe he didn't. The petting relaxed Boots, and he stretched out his nails to make bread on the human's leg. The male human yelled "Ow." I think I scored more points on that maneuver.

That evening, my female human picked me up and placed me on her lap. I did a slow dance, crossing back and forth across the legs of my human. My tail was erect, and my purr motor cranked out sweet music. Maybe it was good Boots was here. I think my humans appreciated me more now.

Tale 10 - The Little Girl

I can't believe it. A little girl and I were playing together. Now, I don't want this to get around as people might think I'm a sissy. Let me tell you what happened, so I have my side of the story out.

I was enjoying the peacefulness of an empty house and dozed off in the front window while catching the morning sun. I heard the garage door open and within a minute or two, knew my humans had arrived home. My female human called out, "Thomas. I have someone I would like you to meet." The last time something like this happened, the visitor was a furry mischievous cat I had to steer clear of.

I jumped down from my window perch to investigate this newest visitor. My human introduced me to a little girl by saying, "Thomas, this is Susan, my niece. She will play in the living room while she visits today. Susan, this is Thomas. He is smart and friendly."

Did she have to say smart and friendly? Now I had to be on my best behavior. Susan looked about 4 years old with cute blond curls. She was toting a big bag on wheels decorated with dolls. What do I know about little girls and their things?

I sat off to the side while Susan opened her case and pulled out dolls, doll clothes, and doll furniture. She set the dolls around a little tea table. I think I made the mistake of walking over to get a closer look when she reached out to me and stroked my back. Wow, I thought, that feels good. My purr motor started without my help. Something about the chemistry between this little girl and me made my tail stand upright. I laid right down in front of her and let her pet me more.

That was the turning point. I should have left then, but this felt so enjoyable, I wanted it to continue. Susan was jabbering away, saying things I didn't understand. I could tell she was enjoying my company as much as I was enjoying hers. She continued playing with the dolls while I stretched out and watched her.

Susan then changed the clothes on the dolls. She tried out various outfits and several color combinations. She said, "Thomas, with your black coloring, you need to have a happy color." I wasn't sure what that meant, but she pulled out a soft pink colored bonnet and placed it on my head. She ran her hand down my back and across my tail. This frilly bonnet should have been history, and I can't tell you why I wanted to continue lying there and keep her company.

Maybe it was because my human said I was smart and friendly, maybe it was because the petting was so gentle, maybe it was because I was getting old. Old, I thought. Oops. That will never happen. I eased myself up and shook my head, letting the little bonnet fall to the floor. I was about to step away when Susan wrapped her arms around me and picked me up.

"Thomas, I love you," she said. She kissed me on the head and then let me go. I ambled away and found a place in the sun where I could rest and keep an eye on my new friend. I kept asking myself, why do I feel this way?

While the sun felt good, I rose and headed back over to where Susan was playing. I looked up at her and let out a soft meow telling her I liked her.

She rewarded me with some gentle petting on my head, around my ears, and under my chin. I had chills running through my body. How did she know all the places where I liked to be rubbed? My purr motor sounded like a motorboat that wanted to be a ski boat. Really, I wasn't a sissy!

Tale 11 - The Yarn

I sat on my front window ledge enjoying the view out the window. It was a nice sunny day, and the little birds were walking around on the grass looking for bugs to eat. That didn't bother me as long as they stayed outside my kingdom. They were fun to watch as they hopped around and pecked here and there. It upset me when a big black bird swept in and scared all the little ones away.

My female human came home from shopping, and I jumped down and went into the kitchen to see what was happening. She emptied one of the brown paper grocery sacks, and it laid on the floor. I needed to explore this. I peeked inside and then scrambled in. It was cozy.

When I turned around, I could peek out. This was like a fort, and I could defend my kingdom from here. I ran out, turned around, and ran back into the fort and performed a somersault inside. This made the sack flip over to the other side where I could peek out and look around from the other side. After a while, I tired of this, and my human picked the sack up, folded it, and put it away.

The next day, my female human had a visitor, I think she called her Mother. Anyway, they were chatting on the sofa, and the Mother was doing something with all these colorful strings she referred to as yarn. There was a paper sack sitting on the floor, and the Mother reached in and pulled out a red ball of yarn and tossed it on the floor near me. This looked interesting.

I pretended this yarn was an evil king trying to invade my territory. I hunched up and then pounced upon this evil ruler, rolling with it clenched between my paws. The evil king escaped, and I chased after him, batting him across the room. I could see I was winning as the ball's tail grew longer and laid out across the floor. A few more attacks and I declared victory.

The humans went into the other room while I continued to protect my kingdom. I looked into the fort where the evil king had come from. There were more knights and foot soldiers inside. I jumped in and turned the bag over knocking these defenders about. I batted them around, and they rolled this way and that way, each one trailing a length of yarn. The huge battle left the big room covered in a colorful mosaic of yarn showing where each defender boldly fought. I was victorious once again after freeing everyone from the dungeon of the evil king.

I stood in the hallway when the humans returned to the big room and discovered the battlefield. The Mother let out a shriek. I'm glad she recognized the hard work I put in to defend the kingdom. However, I thought it best to retire to another room as their chit-chatting was more than what I wanted to endure. Besides, they might want to care for all the casualties I left behind.

I laid down in a window looking out on the backyard. A large bird rested on the fence. It looked like the one that chased the smaller ones away earlier today. He looked like an evil king trying to invade the territory of the peaceful ones. One day, I might have to show him who rules this kingdom.

That evening, I jumped up on my female human's lap. She said, "You have been busy today, Thomas. Mother thinks you are very destructive, but I know you were just playing. I thought it was funny."

I had no clue what she was talking about, and the gentle strokes down my back, up my tail, and around my head were positively delightful. Her lap made the perfect runway for me to strut back and forth, letting her continue with this petting. My purr motor was in high gear and was probably loud enough to scare that large bird away.

Tale 12 - The Birthday

I can't say I have experienced anything like this before. I chose this house for my home because of the calmness associated with it. Today, it seemed like anything but calm. It started early this morning right before breakfast. Someone picked my bowls up, and they swept and scrubbed the floors in the kitchen. There was even a strong odor associated with this. I think my human called it bleach. I didn't even have my breakfast delivered until the floor was clean. By then, even my food smelled bad.

I thought by lying in the front window, I could rest peacefully. My female human started up the big noise maker and pushed it all around the room, sucking up the hair I shed since the last cleaning. It's hard to believe there could be that much hair. Does royalty shed? I then moved to the rear window, but that area did not escape the cleaning team either. Finally, the noise stopped, and there was peacefulness throughout my kingdom, even if it was for only a short time.

People arrived carrying many things, trays of food, colorfully wrapped boxes, and balloons. They left most of these in the big room, except for the food. I found the ribbons on the boxes were the most interesting. I swatted a few of the curly ribbons, and they danced on the packages.

The balloons had long strings tied to them with little thing-a-ma-jiggers at the bottom to keep them from flying away. These were fun to play with too. One caught on my nail, and when I tried to shake it loose, the balloon came down and chased me. I tried to run away, but the balloon kept chasing me, and this thing-a-ma-jigger prevented me from escaping. With a quick twist of my paw, it came loose, and I escaped the inflated monster.

I checked out the kitchen where all the food smells were drifting around. While I like the smell of my special food, this one smelled sweet with something mixed in I couldn't identify. I located the source of this on the kitchen table. The smell was enticing, and I jumped on the chair near the table. My sniffer pulled in the sweet smells, and my head moved from side to side trying to identify the specific item.

I spotted a large flat object in a pink box. The aroma was stronger, and I had to get closer. Using one paw at a time, I stepped onto the table. I was about to get a nose full when someone came in, yelled at me and then pushed me down. I don't know who it was, but they were lucky my humans had invited them. Otherwise, when that hand retracted, it would have done so with some deep scratch marks.

I waited a while. Someone came in and opened the pink box and set the object on the table. I think they referred to it as a cake. They put these little sticks in the cake and took a match to them. Maybe the cake needed more cooking. The lighting created a little smoke, something I didn't like. I went back to the room with the ribbons and balloons.

From the kitchen, I heard the words Happy Birthday several times. It seemed like an attempt at singing and sounded more like moaning. Maybe they couldn't stand it either as the people came back into my room. Someone unwrapped the birthday boxes, wadded the paper up and threw the paper balls onto the floor. Maybe this was a game. I pounced on a couple but there were too many, and there were a lot of feet I had to avoid. People stared at me, and I realized a king would not humiliate himself in front of this large of an audience. I strutted out with my tail high in the air.

A minute or two later, I arrived back in the kitchen, and I again checked out the table. The fiery sticks must have finished cooking the cake as someone removed them and only part of the cake remained. I put my nose up close and sniffed. I reached my paw out and swiped at it. A lot of sticky stuff was now all over my paw. I tried to lick it off, but it had a nasty sweetness I didn't like. I left the kitchen.

It was late before everyone cleared out. My humans stretched out on the big sofa looking tired, and I curled up next to them. I agreed, it had been a long day. I was glad it was quiet again, and my purr motor sang a sweet melody.

Tale 13 - Sick Day

I had a rough night. My humans were both coughing and sneezing all night long. I even got bounced off the bed, so I found a quieter room to sleep in. The morning came, and I was checking my bowls; both were empty. This was not normal, so I went to check on my humans. I saw the mechanical gizmo flashing that told them when to get up, but I knew it was past my feeding time and I was feeling famished.

They were still in bed, sleeping. I jumped on the bed and walked back and forth. After a few passes, I added my high-pitch little siren, meow. That seemed to get their attention. Suddenly, it became a madhouse. Both humans jumped out of bed and hurried to the bathroom. They acted like something was chasing them. I kept hearing the words late for work and electricity off being repeated between the two. My female human was still coughing and sneezing. Her pale face was white and she constantly used a tissue to wipe her nose.

My male human rushed by me and headed to the garage. Most of the time, he provides my breakfast. Sometimes my female human does this. I know the routine, feed me, feed themselves, brush the teeth, and then out the door. The male brushed his teeth and ran to the garage. I could see my female human was about to do the same.

I figured she needed to stay home and get well enough to feed me and not keep me up at night. Now, what to do? I remembered their routine when they head off to the garage. They pick up some shiny metal objects hanging on a hook next to the garage door. I checked, one set of keys was gone, picked up by my male human. I would have to hide the remaining keys so she will stay home, feed me, and get well. Someone needs to take the initiative around here.

I jumped up on the counter and walked over near the door. The hook was just out of reach. There was something soft attached to the ring. I didn't know what it was, but it looked like one of my paws. Maybe this is in their plans for me!

I studied the hook board and then prepared myself by hunching up, trying to get my hind legs as close to the counter edge as possible. I leaped to the board and grabbed it with my claws. While hanging there, I opened my mouth and clamped down on the fuzzy something. I pulled and shook several times trying to make it come loose. My paws were tiring, and I was about to fall as I shook the shiny objects loose. I dropped to the floor with the fuzzy in tow. A spot near the trash can looked like a good spot to hide the keys. Just behind it, I spit the fuzzy thing out. After a careful inspection of the fuzzy object, I determined that it wasn't a cat paw. I felt a little better now.

I then went over to my empty bowl and waited. My female human came through the kitchen door and headed toward the garage. Her hand reached for the empty hook before realizing her fuzzy key ring was not there. "Where're my keys?" she said.

She raced all around, looking everywhere for her keys. I figured it was time to give her a hint, so I let out a long meow to let her know I was waiting for my breakfast. She took a few minutes for the message to register. Perhaps she damaged her ears from all the coughing she suffered. Still, it took too long for her to understand my need for food.

She walked over, pulled a can of my favorite from the cupboard, and emptied the contents into my bowl. While I was eating, she then washed my water bowl and filled it. Another coughing spell hit her like she had for most of the night. She said, "Thomas, I don't know what happened to my keys, but I think I will call in sick today. You can keep me company."

I finished my breakfast knowing I had done a good deed. When my humans are healthy, they can feed me on time. I then went over to where I hid the keys and pulled them out so they could find them. I strolled into the bedroom with my tail flipping at the end. My human was getting cozy in the bed. I curled up to her for some daytime rest. I even played her one of my bedtime songs in purr-fect harmony.

Tale 14 - Getaway

I wouldn't say my life is boring, I have this great house to live in and two humans whom I have trained to feed me every day. I have the pleasure of dozing in the windows soaking up the sunshine during the day and a soft, warm bed to lie on at night, even if the humans roll around sometimes and push me off.

My female human brought a small box like contraption into the house. I inspected it as my human seemed to think it was for me. It had a door and bars all around. It looked like a jail. I think I heard her call it a carrier.

There was a lot of commotion in the bedroom today. The humans were putting their clothes in suitcases and taking them to the car. When they picked up my food bowls, it concerned me as the morning feeding had been on schedule.

My female human picked me up, petted me a few times and then said, "Thomas, we are going on a little getaway, and you get to come with us. You can ride in your new carrier." At that point, she placed me in the carrier, closed the little door, and lugged it out to the car. I remember the last car trip in a box, and that was very unpleasant. I let out a meow to let her know.

We arrived at a large house, and my male human hauled the carrier into the house, with me still inside. There were new smells all around. There was an older female human they called Mother. Funny, this wasn't the same Mother that visited my house some time back. After a while, they released me and showed me where my food bowls sat. They even had fresh water, and an early dinner meal set out for me.

I explored the large house. There were many rooms and doors. I knew it would be easy to get trapped behind one of these doors. There was even a staircase leading up to more rooms. I was content to check out the first floor. Once things seemed to settle down, I found the Mother in a room where the late sun was shining in. I found a warm spot on the carpet and tried to recuperate from the trip.

The Mother worked two sticks together pulling yarn slowly from a ball. Occasionally, she would look down at me and smile. When the sunlight moved from the floor, she patted the sofa cushion next to her, letting me know it was okay to sit on the sofa. I accepted the offer, and once I was comfortable, a hand reached out and petted me.

That night, my humans were in a room upstairs, and the covers looked inviting. I jumped up there and snuggled down. I could protect my humans right from this spot. It was difficult to sleep as there were strange sounds that seemed to come from every direction. These didn't seem to bother my humans, but I was on the alert, none the less.

Wow, I thought, I didn't even have to remind my humans to feed me. Everyone seemed to go downstairs in the morning at the same time. The Mother opened a can of my tasty food for me. I will have to thank her for that.

Later that day, I found her again in a room with the sun shining in. I jumped into her lap, and she gave me a nice gentle rubbing around the ears and under my chin. It felt good, and I stretched my neck out to get a little more. I started up my song of purr and let the music play. She seemed to enjoy it and I laid down next to her.

The next day, all the commotion associated with the packing of suitcases repeated itself. When my female human picked up the carrier, I was afraid of what might come next. She picked me up and stuck me in the carrier again. The ride home was uneventful, but I let them know with a few meows that I wasn't happy about it.

I was glad to be back home, especially because it was dinner time. Back to my kingdom and routine. This time, the sounds of the house were familiar and relaxing. I curled up on the bed between the two humans to let them know there weren't any hard feelings about the trip. My female human stroked my back, and I repaid in kind with a low volume purr.

Tale 15 - Ping Pong

I was soaking up the warm sun, sitting in my window. I daydreamed about the time I had this horrible fight with this big long-haired cat. He had tried to move in on my turf and push me out. I tried to avoid the fight, but I guess he wanted me out of the way more. The fight was bad. I kept knocking him down, but he would get back up again and again. I even walked away twice, but he came after me. His long fur prevented me from sinking any deep wounds, but he tired from being knocked down several times. It was enough for him to quit and saunter away.

My humans were in the kitchen where I heard this funny sound over and over. How can you get any rest with this racket filling the house? The two were at each end of a table with wood paddles trying to clobber this little white ball. I jumped up onto the chair seat to get a better view of this torture treatment.

They batted a little ball back and forth until it could escape. One human would then pick it up and beat on it more. I watched the action, mesmerized by the swift movement. The phone rang in the other room interrupting the play. Both humans rushed to talk at the little device that demanded their attention.

The little white ball lay still on the table. For a moment, I thought they had finished it. I placed two paws on the table and stretched out to sniff the ball. It didn't move. The rest of my body hopped up, and I then used my paw to give the ball a good batting. It must have had wings as it flew off the table. With all the beatings the humans gave it, there was still life in the ball. The humans hadn't defeated it yet.

I jumped down and chased after it. When I caught up, I gave it another big swat. The ball flew over and hit the oven door and bounced back hard at me, hitting me in the side. I hadn't expected it would be on the attack. When I spun around, the ball lay still for a moment. I leaped straight up and came down with all four paws surrounding the ball and then went into a roll.

I now had the advantage as the fight progressed. The ball escaped my grasp as my claws would not sink in. It reminded me of that big black cat with the long fur, hard to get a grip on it. The ball rolled, and I attacked it again and again, but it kept coming back for more each time it ran into a wall. The harder I swatted it, the harder it came back at me. I now understood why the humans were using the paddles. This was a feisty little booger that didn't know when to quit.

The little ball was wearing me out. I had put the little guy into a corner while I lapped up water from my bowl. It was time for round two. I stayed close to the wall and made my approach, inching ever closer. It never knew what hit him as I swatted it across the room with a high-flying throw. Wonders of wonders, it took one big bounce and then landed on top of the table next to the wood paddles. It had given up the fight! Obviously, the ball would rather be beaten up by the humans than to take another licking from me.

While I contemplated this, the humans came back into the room and picked up their paddles. They once again attacked the little white ball. I felt victorious and decided I had earned myself a grooming. I worked on my legs and head, all the while keeping an eye out for that little booger in case the humans let him escape again.

That night, I felt so proud of myself I had to perform a special lap dance for my humans. They were on the sofa, and I moved from leg to leg and back again across each lap. It was almost like that little ball, going back and forth, but this was much slower as each human ran their hand over my head and back. My tail was straight with a little flip at the end, and my purring seemed to be turning on and turning off with each round trip I made. I was thinking how lucky these humans were to have me around.

Tale 16 - Cat Fight

The small brown sparrows were in the yard again. Their heads moving up and down like a bobble head pecking at the bugs in the grass. They entertained me, and I enjoyed watching them. A big black bird came swooping in targeting one of the small birds. At the last second, the little bird hopped and took flight just missing the claws of the larger bird.

This made my blood boil. I wanted to go out there and teach that big bad bird a lesson, but it was too late. All the birds flew off to parts unknown. I could have hidden in the tree and waited for the big bird. Alas, I laid my head down and dozed off thinking about how I would hide somewhere and wait for the big bird to return.

I was sitting in another tree, and a light breeze was rustling the surrounding leaves. I was as cool as a cucumber. Speaking of which, it was nearing time for my evening meal. The tree overlooked the alley behind this fancy sushi diner. It was one of my favorite hang-outs. In the evening hours, the waiters would bring out big plastic bags and drop them in the huge green dumpster. I would then jump into the dumpster, use my claws to open the bags and find all the tasty treats.

The sun was setting, and I knew it was about time for dinner. The waiter brought out a bag, right on schedule, and deposited it in the garbage bin. As I approached, I spotted another cat making its way towards the dumpster. I let out a long hiss to let him know to back off as these sushi offerings were for me.

The tiger-striped cat only paused for a moment and then continued over to my personal food bin. I raced over and leaped to the rim of the receptacle and perched precariously on the edge. I looked down at this scavenger and let out another warning hiss with a low growl to back it up. This didn't seem to deter him as he jumped up on the other side and let out a growl. He was ready for a showdown.

I increased my growl volume and let out another hiss. The fur on my neck and back was already standing on end. I extended my claws, and my tail twitched. These tactics scare most other would be scavengers away, but this guy was a hard case. I looked in the dumpster at the bag holding my dinner, thinking tonight, I would have to fight for my dinner or else go hungry. I prepared to defend my food source.

The black and yellow striped cat's tail was twitching, and he continued to growl. My teeth were bared, and I hissed and growled. He stepped forward to where I was standing. His long front paw reached out with shiny nails and swatted the air in front of me. He took another step and another swing. I stepped back and lost my balance. Down I fell in front of the dumpster with a thump.

It was at that moment, my eyes opened, and I realized I had been dreaming and fell from my window perch. The dream was so real about my younger years. It was long before I found these humans to fill my bowl twice a day. I consider myself lucky compared to the old days when I had to fight for food. It was evening time, and I heard my female human in the kitchen. I wandered in to see if she brought me any sushi today.

That night, I curled up to my female human to thank her for providing my daily nourishment. While it wasn't sushi, it tasted good, and I didn't have to fight off any competition to eat it. My human rubbed under my chin, and I stretched my head up high to get more. That led to some nice rubbing around the ears. I rewarded her by cleaning her arm with my rough tongue and letting my purr motor run.

Tale 17 - Puzzling

Did you ever have someone ignore you? Now, I like the peacefulness my home has to offer but occasionally feel the need to be recognized as royalty. I know the training I have given my humans about filling my food and water bowls has paid off, but there is something extra needed, like a good rub around the ears.

The evening had come, and my two humans seemed engaged in something on the table. It had consumed the entire afternoon and darkness was about to fall. Typically, about this time of day, they are preparing their meal and fixing mine. Nope, their concentration was on this table, and they hadn't moved for hours.

I figured it was time to investigate this, so I wandered over to the table. Looking upwards, I saw their arms move occasionally. I picked my opportunity and jumped up onto the table. This startled them for a moment as they seemed to be in a trance. My male human was the first to react.

He said, "Hey, Thomas. Careful. We almost have this side of the puzzle completed."

My female human reached out and picked me up. She stroked me a few times and then she said, "You must be hungry. I will get some food for you." With that, she set me down on the floor and went over to the cupboard where they kept my food. She said, "Thomas, it looks like we need to go shopping. We ran out of your food."

This definitely was not what I wanted to hear. I let my humans know of this revolting development with a long meow. They needed to be better prepared. The only thing they did today was work on that puzzle. They didn't think to pick up more food for me. I will have to give my female human some credit though. She found a can of tuna and used it to fill my bowl. It was tasty and a change of pace. However, it made me wonder what my breakfast meal would be like.

She then fixed food for herself and the male human, sat and ate, and then went back to the puzzle. With my hunger pangs dissipated for now, I decided to help with the puzzle. I jumped up on the table at the other end to see better. Their hands picked pieces up, moved them around and then set them back down again. They repeated this over and over. After a few tries, they would connect one piece to another filling in a picture. I became bored and found a nice soft place on the couch and curled up for the night.

In the morning, my bowl was empty again. The humans had started their day with food, but my bowl remained empty. Empty I say! I brushed up against the legs of the humans, first one and then the other. They needed to know I was hungry and wanted my breakfast. I would not tolerate being ignored! I carried this on for a few minutes and then went over to my bowl, sat down, and let out a meow.

My female human said, "Thomas, I will go shopping today and buy you more food. I only have left-overs for you to eat."

Left-overs? I don't do left-overs. I left my last life because I didn't want left-overs anymore. Then again, the sushi was tasty. My human put something into my bowl. It did not smell good. I ignored it and let out another meow. I think they got the message I did not like left-overs. After a while, my female human picked my bowl up and washed it out. They then both left the house, leaving me hungry.

While they were away, I inspected the puzzle again. They had assembled the outline of a picture, but there were still a lot of gaps. I found connecting pieces and worked them into the gaps. At last, I filled in the corner with a picture of a fat cat. I guess he had his food bowl filled to the top every day.

When my humans returned, they filled my bowl with my favorite food. I reconsidered my opinion of these humans, and when they climbed into bed for the night, I laid next to them. They needed thanking for bringing my food home, so I rubbed my head against one hand and started up the purr motor.

Tale 18 - House Sitter

My female human had one of her friends over visiting. They were chatting away in the other room. I think I heard my name, Thomas, come up in the conversation a few times. This didn't bother me as people always talk about royalty. I ignored them both while sitting in the front window, watching the kids walk home from school. It was about snooze time when I heard the cupboard doors where they store my food, open and then close. I listened and these sounds were followed by my food bowl being moved about.

It was too soon for dinner, but hey, if they are offering food, I better check it out. I performed my royal strut into the kitchen with my tail straight up. My bowl was on the counter, and the friend was preparing my dinner. My human reached down, picked me up, and said, "Thomas, this is Joan. She will house sit while we go on vacation."

I wasn't sure what that meant, but if someone would prepare my meals for me every day, who was I to complain? The sitter placed my bowl on my blue mat, and I had dinner. She even put down a fresh bowl of water to accompany it. To think, I didn't even have to train this human!

Early the next morning, my two humans packed their suitcases. I was on the alert to see if they would try to stuff me into the carrier again. I was thinking about hiding. However, the two humans were in such a rush with their bags, they forgot about me. I realized at that point they had left without setting out my food. They had abandoned me!

I contemplated what to do about this situation when the sitter arrived. She came over stroked my back a few times and then said, "I bet you're looking for breakfast." I didn't know she read minds. After feeding me, she left, and I had the whole house to myself. It was quiet, and I could move from room to room soaking up the sunshine.

That evening, the sitter returned and filled my food bowl. This was a real treat for someone to be trained so well. I needed to reward her. While she was sitting on the sofa, I jumped up and laid on her lap. Her hand automatically stroked my back. This was okay, but when she rubbed behind my ears and under my chin, it had my purr motor racing.

Later, the sitter said "Goodnight, Thomas," and left. Again, I had the whole house empty and all to myself. I walked all around several times. Without my humans around, I seemed to have lost a little purpose in my life. I was used to protecting my humans and my house, but now, it was an empty house.

The next day, the sitter came again in the morning, fed me, left, and then returned in the evening. While I was happy my nutritional requirements were being fulfilled, there was still something amiss. She repeated this routine for what seemed like an eternity, but I think it was only for a few days. Each night, this strange feeling came over me, and it seemed to grow in intensity.

On the last day of this strange routine, my humans arrived back home in time to fix my evening meal. Their leaving had upset me, and I wouldn't even give them a leg rub, let alone eat my food. I sat at the top of my tree house with my back to the room. My humans would come over, pet me a few times, and say something like, "I'm glad to see you, Thomas." At last, I relented and walked into the kitchen and had dinner. I wouldn't want to waste this food.

At bedtime, I jumped on the bed and laid down between them. This act lets them know I wasn't mad at them. I even let the purr motor run at half speed. Could it be I somehow missed my humans? Was it loneliness I experienced? Nah, a king is royalty and can never be lonely. I even had a loyal servant come daily to prepare my meals. I shrugged off that silly feeling and dozed off curled up between my two humans.

Tale 19 - House Guest

I seem to have my routine established. Life is good. Unfortunately, something always comes along to change the status quo. Today, the exception was a new house guest. From my front window, I watched a man come to the door carrying a large suitcase. My male human invited him in, and they spoke for a few minutes. There was even a hug exchanged, and I knew to be on my best behavior. My human picked me up and said, "Thomas, we have a guest staying with us. Be nice to Cousin Al."

I looked the man over; he emitted a strange, unpleasant odor. He didn't offer a hand to pet me either. The man said, "I'm not too fond of cats." That set the stage for the week ahead. He could go his way, and I would go mine.

I decided the window perch was the best place to watch everything and get fresh air with the window open. The man settled on the sofa, a place where I curl up sometimes. I even leave a little hair to mark where I have been. This hair seemed to bother the man. He rubbed his nose and sneezed a lot. His hanky hung from his pocket, ready for use.

My female human got out the big noise maker, which she calls the vacuum, and ran it over the sofa and floor. It picked up a lot of my loose hair in this process. The man stood around watching and didn't even offer to help. Not only was he ignoring me, but he was rude to my humans. I could see this would be a long week.

At dinner, the man went into the kitchen and kicked my food bowl across the floor. He mumbled something to my human who retrieved it, washed it out, and filled it with my dinner meal. This man would not win any nice awards from me. There was no respect for my things.

After dinner, I went to lie on the sofa. After a few minutes, I realized this smelled like Al. I was about to leave when he entered the room and mumbled something. His words made little sense, but he reached down and pushed me off the sofa. I almost turned to take a bite out of him but held my temper. I went over to the tree house and sharpened my nails for later.

That night, he left his suitcase open. I checked it out, and it had fresh smelling articles inside. It would make a good bed for the night, and I curled up there. I even left some of my beautiful black hair behind, just for him. I was up and prowled around several times during the night and kept returning to the suitcase to curl up in. Each time, I had to rearrange the clothes so I could find a comfortable position.

The next day, I heard the man shouting a lot from the room where the suitcase laid. I was minding my own business having breakfast when this happened and assumed he was unhappy with the hair I left on his clothes. I thought it would be a great fashion statement or at least some kind of statement. The man sneezed a lot more now.

The man and my two humans were in the kitchen, and I heard the man say several times something like the word allergic. I think it meant he didn't like me. Then again, it went both ways. He smelled and wasn't very nice. Doesn't he know royalty demands respect?

Perhaps I triggered his leaving, then again, maybe his stay was over. Regardless, he packed his suitcase and left. Maybe the bad smell would leave too. I felt relieved I could now go back to my normal routine and watch the birds from my window.

That night, I curled up on the bed with my two humans. They petted and talked while rubbing behind my ears and under the chin. In return, my purr motor was running like clockwork. I even cleaned my human's hand. It smelled good.

Tale 20 - Poker Night

I watched my female human clean the house again. Maybe it was because of the last house guest, then again, she seems to do this every week or two. They set a round table up in the big room with chairs all around it. Something like this meant people were coming to visit today.

I needed to look my best, so I prepared with some grooming of my paws. Being a king requires maintaining my royal look. Then there was a little manicure over at the scratching post. I polished this off by brushing my top knot down. This took time as I had to wet my paw and then use it to brush back some unruly fur centered on my crown.

After dinner, people arrived, and I strolled through the crowd showing my royal walk. Some people were rude by not moving aside as I sauntered along. Someone nearly stepped on my paw, and it was necessary to take a few dance steps to avoid being hurt. After a while, they all sat down at the roundtable. I felt it best to retreat to my cat tree. It is high enough I can see all around the room.

The people at the table made a lot of clicking noises but I could not figure out what was causing the noise. It sounded like they were playing with the Legos, but those had been boxed up and hidden. I watched from my perch and saw all these round pieces being thrown into the middle of the table. The men dealt cards out and then tossed round pieces into the center. Someone would then rake it all up in front of themselves. I heard one player say "I'm in the chips now." Maybe that is what they call them. This routine seemed to repeat over and over. There was a lot of laughing and talking around the table.

My female human yelled something from the kitchen, and everyone at the table got up and left the room. I hopped down from my perch to investigate the round things up close. I leaped onto the big table and moved to the center and looked around. In front of each chair was a pile of these little chips they used in their play. The stack in front of my human's chair was smaller than everyone else's.

I didn't think it was fair, so I used my paw to play hockey with a few of these things and slid a few over to my human's pile. The blue colored ones were my favorite. I moved around the table and hit a few more blue ones from different stacks around the table. This was fun, like playing hockey and hitting the puck into the goal. My human's stack was now bigger, and it had more blue chips than all the other stacks. I then jumped down to see what all the commotion was in the kitchen.

The people were eating again. This time it was something on a stick. They coupled it with a bottle in the other hand. They all laughed and enjoyed each other's company. I left and went to sit on my perch again. Soon, they all returned and sat down at the table.

There were some strange looks at first as everyone was trying to straighten out their stack of play toys, but they dealt the cards, and the playing continued. I must have dozed off because when I opened my eyes, the game was breaking up. The players were all counting their chips. It seems blue chips were worth more than the red and white chips. I had good taste. They opened their wallets, and money changed hands. I noticed several people were handing money over to my male human who seemed happy with a big smile on his face.

He must have appreciated my moving the chips even if he had most of the blue ones. Maybe I should have pushed white chips into his stack? The night wrapped up, and people said their goodbyes.

After the guests left, my humans were talking. My male human was telling my female human how his luck had changed. He had almost been out of chips, but he must have miscounted. My male human ended up winning the most. He was putting all the chips in a chip rack when he noticed some of my hair on the table. He said, "Honey, wasn't this a new tablecloth for tonight?" She said it was. He replied, "I guess Thomas checked things out again. Do you think….? Nah."

That night, I curled up on the bed between them again. This nightly practice was habit forming. It felt good to have loyal servants take care of me. As I settled in, the petting and the purr motor began.

Tale 21 - Black Bird

The big bad black bird was on a stakeout again. I could see him in the tree while looking out my open window. The last time he was here, he attacked one of the little birds. I like to watch the little birds. They are cute as their heads bob up and down pecking at the bugs in the grass.

The black bird needed a life lesson, and I'm the self-designated teacher. I worked the latch on the screen until I could open it. After sliding out, I made my way towards a bush near where the little birds land. I waited until the small brown birds arrived. Up in the tree, the black bird surveyed the small flock. His legs were bent in a crouching position ready to leap out of the tree. I was ready too.

The black bird dove straight down at one of the small birds and I leaped out from under the bush. He hit one small bird with a crushing blow, and I sprang on top of the black bird trying to find a foothold for my sharpened claws. The black bird let go of the smaller bird, and we rolled over several times. His wings were very strong, and he got one loose. He flapped that wing hard causing us to twist and turn in the grass. He somehow freed his other wing and took flight.

I figured the big bird learned his lesson and would not come back here again. I didn't see the little brown bird that had been attacked. It was gone too. He must have been okay and flew away.

I now needed to get back into the house. I went to the window and saw the screen ajar. The gap was small, but if I could poke my nose in, I could work the rest of my body through it. It was a short jump, and my front paws clung to the sill while I worked my nose and then my head under the edge of the screen. The gap became larger, and I pulled the rest of my body through.

My once beautiful black fur was a mess from rolling in the grass while fighting off that big bird. Grooming would be a priority now to regain my royal appearance. I looked back at the yard, but no one was there. My paws picked up the most dirt, so I cleaned them first, followed by my head and body.

I then saw the man that comes everyday approach the house. He wears shorts, a large-brimmed hat and carries a bag filled with papers and stuffs some of them into the box right outside my window. It is my job to keep him from proceeding any further. I stare him down, so he no longer approaches any closer. I stand erect and look at him. He even has a symbol for a bird on his shirt. Maybe he is a friend of those big black birds. He left papers in our box and then turned away. Success! I drove him off again. With the screen open, I could have shown him I meant business.

When my humans come home, they always go out to this box and empty it out. Most of the time I hear the words more bills in an irritating tone. Someday I might have to figure out how to stop all this paper from being left. I like to have my humans happy.

After dinner, my female human closed my window to keep the cold air out. She noticed how something had pushed the screen out a little and then latched it. She said to her mate, "The front screen was unlatched and pushed out. Thomas could have gotten out." Little did they know I could leave anytime I wanted.

Today was gratifying for me. I saved the little bird from further injury, gave the black bird a lesson he won't forget, and stared down the man that brings the bills. I strutted around the house doing my happy march.

My human was looking me over and said, "Thomas, it looks like you have grass in your fur. Let me brush it out." Here I thought I had done an excellent job with my grooming, but I wouldn't object to the royal fur being brushed again. While she was grooming my body, she said, "Now where did you pick this up from?" I relaxed and turned on my purr motor while I received the royal spa treatment. I even let a little meow escape.

Tale 22 - Flowers

I trust everyone knows how I like my undisturbed peacefulness. Having my food bowl filled twice a day is another priority. My humans are trained well, but there have been slip-ups. I laid in the window and enjoyed my time in the sun when I heard a racket in the other room. The two humans were yelling at each other. By the tone of their voices, I didn't think this was something good.

Last night, I heard similar high-pitched exchanges between the two. The loud sounds were unpleasant, and I left the room. I sought refuge in the back window and stared out at the stars. The sights were peaceful and so relaxing that I spent the night there.

This hostility can't continue if I'm to have quiet in this house. I don't know who started it, but I know one of them needs to make up to the other. Flowers seem to have a special magical power when men give these to women, at least that is what I have heard. They go a long way in helping to resolve conflicts. Maybe these humans needed a little help to bring harmony back into their lives. If they can't agree between themselves, I won't have a happy and quiet home.

I went into the office and found the computer still running. I checked it out. They had what they called a mouse attached to it, and I figured anything using a mouse, had to be simple to control. I have done my fair share of chasing them and making meals in hard times.

I reached my paw out and pushed the mouse about testing the feel. Its hard shell slid across a little pad. There were grooves in the top that allowed me to press the front left and right sides down. I remembered batting a few mouse ears down, so how hard could this be?

There were many images on the screen, and I had to push one button a lot of times until I found flowers. The yellow and red flowers are my favorite. Blue ones are nice too. A bouquet made the most sense for the situation to improve in this household. I saw a picture of a van next to the flowers. It must mean they will deliver; I clicked on it. There was a long form to fill out. I guess I was lucky the human had pre-filled all the forms, so I only had to click on the order button. When I completed the order, I hit the power switch so the human wouldn't know what I did.

My front window allows me to relax, watch the birds, and keep an eye on things. There was activity on the street today. Little humans were kicking a ball around. I then heard the music from the ice cream truck. It was getting louder. The kids all seemed to line up waiting for it to stop. I waited for the music to stop too. This was another thing to disturb my peace. After the kids got their frozen snacks, they seemed to melt off into the sunset.

My eyes closed and I was ready to doze off when the big lawn mowers started up. The lawn men pushed these big noisemakers back and forth on the lawn and cut the grass. Then another noise maker scratched against the edge of the concrete cutting the ends. They used a third noise maker to blow the trimmings out to the street. The men used a rake to sweep the gutter. This still left a lot of trimmings in the street.

The afternoon sun was showing its age as the shadows were creeping across the yard. A van pulled up in front, and it had a picture of flowers on the side. I think this is just what the cat ordered, I thought to myself. A young woman opened the van and pulled out a beautiful bouquet and walked up to the house. When the doorbell rang, I waited and hoped my female human would answer. She had been in the kitchen, and it had been quiet for some time.

She opened the door and saw the flowers. I could tell by the tone of her voice she was pleased and excited. She took them and set them on the table. I watched all of this with my all-knowing eyes. Her eyes dampened. Afterward, she left the room and looked for the male human.

I followed and when she found him, gave him a big hug and said, "I'm sorry."

The surprise hug bewildered him at first, but then said while embracing her, "I'm sorry too Honey."

I had dinner in a very peaceful environment and later curled up between them. I figured the purr motor would help provide soothing music, unlike the ice cream truck, so I provided a lot of romantic purring.

Tale 23 - Fireworks

Last night, it was tough to sleep. Loud noises seemed to occur each time I was about to nod off. So today, I looked forward to the peace and quiet of my window. My humans were talking, and the word celebration kept coming up. It seems when they celebrate, they make a lot of noise. I can do without the racket.

The humans packed their ice chest and loaded it and a small barbecue into the car. This pattern of packing the car leads to them leaving the house. Soon, I would have the house to myself.

My female human filled a second food bowl for me and set it down. She filled it with dry kibble. Were my humans expecting me to eat that? Chunks of cardboard are not on my diet. That bowl will just sit there. I ate my regular food and licked my lips afterward. My training has paid off as the water was fresh, and I did not have to remind them today.

The humans left, and I had the house to myself. I saw more kids on the street today. They liked to play with a funny shaped ball that bounces unpredictably. They then chase whoever has the ball, and when others get too close, they throw it to another person.

It was time for the pesky man that stuffs the bills in the box to come by, but he didn't come. Maybe he knew I was ready to stare him down. The little birds pecked away in the grass. It relaxed me, and I enjoyed the view. Even the sun shined and brightened my spirits. It was time for a long nap.

Darkness was falling while I slept. A large boom woke me with a start. I hopped down from my lookout, ran to the middle of the room and turned towards where I thought the sound came from. Nothing! I waited and then cautiously returned to the window and looked out again. There wasn't anything different.

I was still on the alert, sitting and looking out. A loud whistle blasted in the distance. It started with a low pitch and moved to a shriek. It made my ears hurt. Loud popping sounds and some other flash bangs followed this. I left the window perch and looked to see where I could go.

The bedroom looked the safest, and I jumped on the bed. My humans have a nice little towel for me to curl up on when they are away, and I used it now. When I am nervous, I find that grooming takes my mind off the problem. This relaxed me.

I was in a light doze when a huge boom seemed to shake the whole house. A reddish light lit up the room and crackling sounds followed. I crouched down ready to fight or hide. Another boom came, and I jumped off the bed and ran under it.

More booms rattled the house and shook the windows. The reddish glow was not as bright under here. The house seemed to shake a little after each blast. My eyes were wide open, and my ears kept twitching, not knowing which way to turn. I was under attack, and I couldn't see the enemy. The door to the bathroom was almost closed, but I pushed it open and squeezed through, hoping it would be quieter inside. The room muffled the sounds, but it felt like they were getting closer.

Then there was a big crescendo of many booms, crackles, and lights of varying colors coming from all directions. It sounded like they were coming for me through the front door. My back was against the wall as I crouched down and prepared to attack anyone who might come through the door. I focused on the door for any movement. Then it all stopped, except for a few pops. They must have turned away, knowing I was ready for them.

It was late when my humans returned. My stomach growled although I didn't notice this during the bomb attack. I ran to the kitchen and let out a long meow. Nothing happened, so I did it again. Didn't they know my food bowl was empty? Could they hear anything after all that earsplitting noise? My ears twitched at the slightest sound.

My female human came to the kitchen and studied my bowls. She said, "Thomas, you didn't eat. One can of your favorite stuff coming up." While she opened a can, it slipped out of her hand and crashed to the floor making a loud noise. I took off for the bathroom again.

My female human came in, picked me up and nuzzled me. She made soothing sounds and said, "You're okay. I guess the fireworks terrified you." My eyes still darted left and right as we walked back into the kitchen. She set me down in front of my bowl, and after a moment, I ate.

That night, I curled up close to my humans to protect them from the beasts who made all the booming noises. I had trouble getting my purr motor to start.

Tale 24 - The Photo Shoot

Being a king is hard work. To maintain my good looks, I require regular grooming which includes manicuring my nails. This is something I take pride in doing, but I let my female human brush my sleek, handsome body to remove any loose hair. When you are of royal blood, you must hold your head up high and strut most of the time.

I finished my breakfast meal and gave my paws and face a good cleaning. My human arrived with this little noisemaker she calls a phone. Seems that every time it makes a noise, she runs over and talks at it. Today, she was pointing it at me as it made clicking noises. She said, "Thomas, I'm only taking pictures of you. Nothing for you to be scared about."

I gave her my royal walk and paraded back and forth in front of her. While she snapped pictures, a pesky fly came into view. I hated flies and took a swat at it. It flew up, and I leaped up to try swatting it again in mid-air. With a series of aerodynamic twists and turns coupled with leaps and swats, I did my best to knock down the fly. The fly must have known it was unsafe, for it left the area. I didn't know until much later that she recorded the entire episode.

I was relaxing when I heard my human say to the phone, "I just took some fantastic pictures of Thomas. You have got to see them. I posted them on Facebook." Being of royal blood, I know I'm handsome and photogenic. With that in mind, I ignored the rest of the conversation and headed out to my window perch.

That evening, my two humans were talking while my food bowls were being washed and filled. My male human said, "Darling, I saw the pictures of Thomas you posted. They are great. Did you see how many likes there were? The last count was over 3,000."

As she opened my food can, my female human said, "Really? I think I will post the video on YouTube." Talking to her mate distracted her. I patiently waited until she set my food down, and I enjoyed my evening meal.

The next day, my female human was cleaning the house, and her phone made a noise. She talked about the pictures again, something about the number of likes skyrocketing. I didn't understand everything and tried to ignore the conversation. If people saw pictures of me, they would recognize royalty.

After supper, the two humans huddled around the computer. My female human was holding me and stroking my back. They were talking, and my male human said he wanted to watch the Thomas video again. Video? I thought. My human just took my picture, didn't she?

The video played, and I saw my image dancing around on the screen. It looked like I was in a circus performing an acrobatic act. I recognized it but could not see the fly I chased. The performance made me look like a crazy animal! The worst part of it was that both my humans were laughing all the while the video was playing.

My male human then said, "Honey, you know this video has gone viral. It has over a hundred thousand views already, and the number is still climbing. I can't believe you took this video of Thomas." They both chuckled again as they started a replay. I couldn't stand it anymore, so I jumped down and headed for the bedroom for some peace and tranquility. I felt humiliated.

Later, my humans joined me in bed, and both petted me. They rubbed my head, ears, and chin along with gentle stroking across my beautiful body. How could I resist all this attention? My purr motor started. Maybe royalty could take a day off and show the physical prowess of oneself. Then again, if they point that phone at me again, I will run like the dickens to get away.

Tale 25 - Take Out

It seems every day is a new adventure. Whether it is the birds playing in the front yard or that old Bloodhound that can't seem to find his way home. The days pass with new things that look like the old things.

Today, I relaxed in my window seat enjoying the early morning sun. My humans were late in getting up, and this occurs a couple times a week. I think they call it the weekend. I call it a poor excuse for not feeding me on time. Oh well, they're only human I guess. I think I hear them now.

The noisemaker started up again which signaled that guests were coming over. I figured this routine out a while back. Clean the house and then invite people over to dirty it up. It seems this should be reversed, but then again, humans. I saw the back door open and strolled out. There is a picnic table where they seat guests when they have a big party. I sat on it and watched while the humans ran around. It didn't take too long before my female human spotted me and went a little crazy. Maybe she thought I would run away. If I had wanted to do that, I would have been long gone.

I let her pick me up and carry me inside. She gave me lots of strokes, almost to the point of me wanting to purr. If this is the treatment I get, I think I will go outside more often. Perhaps being royal has something to do with it. Then again, maybe she thinks she is protecting me. Either way, I can accept that.

After a while, little people arrived. This was not what I was looking forward too. It was a birthday party for a neighbor's child. I had to scramble to avoid sticky little hands from petting me. I wasn't fast enough for one little girl. She picked me up, and I hung over her arm like a wet dish towel. If I had been a napkin, you would have thought she was a waiter walking around chatting with the other kids while I was hanging there.

At last, the big people came back and rounded up their kids and took them away. The sun was going down, and I knew supper time would be just around the corner. My male human said something about picking up takeout food and left. Maybe my cupboard was bare, and he would refill it. I needed to be patient as this was the weekend.

He returned with a sack that was letting delicious smells out. Normally, I ignore these as I have my own canned food, but this reminded me of my sushi days. I followed the sack to the table and sat on a chair watching carefully. They got out plates and then opened these little boxes and dished out food onto each. None of that looked good until they uncovered a platter with a nice fish on it. I let them know with a soft meow that this not only looked good but smelled good.

This reminded me of the old days when I had to perform dumpster diving for my dinner. Outside that sushi restaurant, I had plenty to choose from. The problem was, I had to compete with other cats for the food as they wanted a good meal too. What did I say before, what's new is like old all over again?

My humans devoured the food on the plates. They avoided the fish head, and I hoped it might make it into my bowl. I patiently waited for them to finish their meal. They were about to clear the plates from the table when I let out a big meow and stared at the fish head.

My female human said to her partner, "Do you think Thomas wants the fish? I know he is particular with what he eats."

My male human said, "It won't hurt to see if he wants it. Let's put it in his bowl and see if he eats it."

My mouth watered and I licked my lips. Sushi! I jumped down from the chair and spun around in tight little circles, nearly tripping my male human. He placed the fish head in my food bowl, and I made one little sniff before biting into it. Memories flooded my brain of times past. Those were the good old days, or were they? I didn't like the fierce competition nor the cold nights. I quickly forgot about them and enjoyed eating the fish.

That night, I curled up to my humans and thanked them for a nice treat and a warm home. My purr motor was running. I even got a few strokes which put the icing on the cake.

Tale 26 - The Cable Guy

It seems there is never enough rest time in a day. Interruptions seem to be the norm. Whatever happened to just enjoying the little birds out my window? Every day I have to stare down the man that wears the big bird patch as he stuffs the mailbox full of bills. And then there is the water delivery man who comes and refills the water dispenser. Did I leave out the newspaper guy that tries to hit my window every day?

Well today, a man pulled up in this van with all kinds of equipment strapped to the top. He wore a big belt with lots of things hanging down that swayed when he walked. After ringing the doorbell, my male human answered and they talked. I could tell he was friendly, so I didn't pay attention at first. Then the guy came into my territory and walked around. They talked some, but the word I heard the most was TV. Maybe this guy would hook up the PET channel.

Soon this guy was climbing up on the roof and making some terrible sounds. I was wondering if he was setting something up to scare the big black birds away. The next thing he was doing was entering one of the hall closets. He climbed up through a big hole in the ceiling. I never knew it existed before and I thought I knew this house inside and out. There were more noises, some silence, and then more noises again. How was the king supposed to get any rest with all this racket going on?

I retired to my front window hoping it would be a little quieter. Nope, this time a truck playing awful sounds attracted all the kids in the neighborhood. It blasted out the words, "Ice cream. Get your ice cream here." Of all the places to stop, the truck had to park in front of my yard.

Soon all the kids around the block formed a line to get their ice cream. I knew what was to come next, a lot of discarded paper wrappers.

About this time, the man came down the ladder and was moving a big piece of furniture that the TV hung over. He was making a hole in the wall and was playing with some wire. Once he had it, he pulled the wire out of the wall and laid it on the floor. He hooked something up to the wire and then went outside. I checked out the wire by batting it around a few times. Whatever the man had hooked up to the wire came off. I went back to my window and looked outside again.

The man came back in and saw the wire was free from his instrument and hooked it up again. He looked around, and I let out a little innocent meow. He went outside again, and I checked the wire out again. I swatted it and watched it swing back and forth. It kept coming back for more so I hit it a few more times. The wire came apart again. Maybe it was defective.

I could hear the man outside saying loud things to himself. It sounded like something upset him. Maybe he saw all the papers from the kids blowing around creating a big mess. Then again, maybe the thing wasn't scaring the birds away. It didn't take long before the man came back in the house and found his wire loose again. He mumbled something to himself as he hooked it up again. This time he put some sticky tape on it.

That must have worked because he returned from the roof with a big smile on his face. He then hooked this wire up to a box which connected to the TV. He played with the remote control a lot. My humans do that at night sometimes. After he hooked everything up, he pushed the big piece of furniture back against the wall to hide the hole he made. I wondered if any mice might find their way in through that hole. I will have to watch at night.

Both humans came in and stared at the TV and talked to the man. He then collected his tools and ladder and left for the day. I figured the day would end, now that all the commotion was over. I retreated to the back window to catch the setting sun and looked forward to some peace and quiet.

It was now supper time, and my humans remembered to feed me. My rest time was so interrupted that it left me tired. I was glad it was over as I climbed into the lap of my female human while she and her partner watched TV. I thought about starting my purr motor as I was being petted and rubbed, but I didn't want to interrupt their enjoyment of the TV.

Tale 27 - The Accident

I love my home, and by extension, I love my humans that provide these necessities of life—Shelter and Food. I know I can provide for myself, but being a king has its perks. This morning, after a nice breakfast, I laid about soaking up the sunshine. The carpet provided a soft place for me to stretch out and relax. Maybe this would be a relaxing day for the household.

Around mid-day, my humans were busy preparing food. I ignored this as my feeding only occurs in the morning and evening. However, I noticed more work going into this meal. In the backyard, I saw the old rusty black barbecue being dragged over near the picnic table. I try to avoid it because of the heat and smoke it creates when they have a fire in it. It looked like that is what they would do today.

I sat in the back window and enjoyed the fresh cool air coming through the screen. The window provided a perfect view of the backyard and hills beyond. There was a stillness in the air. In fact, it was a beautiful day, just the kind I like. The puffy white clouds floated high overhead.

The back door opened and closed several times which interrupted my peace. They carried out food trays along with things to put on the table. The two humans reminded me of ants moving back and forth carrying stuff in one direction. I heard my male human say, "Honey, I'm going to take a shower. Why don't you fire up the grill?"

Her reply was, "Sure. I'll have the barbecue ready for you to cook the steaks when you're done."

I didn't think too much about this. It was more conversation that didn't involve me. I closed my eyes and was about to doze off when I heard a large noise. The blast sounded like a boom and almost knocked me out of my back window. There was a cloud of dark smoke surrounding the barbecue, and my female human was lying on the ground. Something bad had happened, and I let out a big meow to let her know I was here. She didn't move. Many thoughts raced through my mind trying to figure out how to help my human.

I jumped down and turned on my meow siren. "Meow. Meow." I ran through the house and into the bathroom. I kept my siren on, hoping to find my male human. He asked, "What's wrong Thomas?" I meowed again and started for the door. He didn't follow. I repeated this, and he stepped out of the shower and slipped a robe on.

In the bedroom, I let the siren hail again, and he followed. I ran to the kitchen door and let my siren run until he arrived. He said "What is it Thomas?" as he looked out the window and saw his partner on the ground. He pulled open the door and together we ran outside to see what we could do. Black soot covered her face, and she wasn't moving.

I remembered that thing she talks to people on, the phone. The back door was still open, and I ran into the house and hunted around for it. I found the small phone on the counter. A case protected the phone which had a little chain with a fuzzy ball attached. I sunk my teeth into the ball and jumped down carefully. The phone was heavy, but I somehow managed to carry it outside and drop it next to my male human and let out a meow.

He saw the phone and tapped numbers while I inspected my female human. Besides her face, one of her hands looked red, perhaps a burn. I let out another meow, this time a cry. My male human said, "Help is on its way, Thomas."

What had started as a peaceful day now had a truck with its own siren alerting the neighborhood of a problem. Men poured into the small backyard. Two were taking care of my female human, and some others inspected that old barbecue. Over the sounds of people talking and moving about, I heard the sweetest sound of the day, my female human coughed.

The men loaded her onto a stretcher and took her away. My male human followed in his car. They left me alone. It was late that night when he returned. After he fed me, he held me for a while and petted me. He said, "Thomas, you were very helpful today. I don't know how you knew to get my attention or to bring the phone out, but you did. I'm very grateful. She's okay, but they need to keep her at the hospital tonight."

I sensed deep gratitude in him toward me, along with concern and loneliness for his partner. I relaxed and curled up next to my male human. My purr motor was warming up knowing my subjects were okay.

Tale 28 - Arts and Crafts

It must have been another weekend as they fed me late this morning and my humans did not leave the house. I stretched out in my window and looked out. Alas, it was already too late to see the little birds. Knowing it was the weekend, I knew the street would be noisy and busy with all the kids in the neighborhood playing there.

My female human was busy around the big table. She spread out newspapers and brought in a lot of small items. Some of these smelled musty and others like new. I was curious, so I found a comfortable chair next to the table. She was using the scissors to cut colored paper into small shapes. If I were doing this, I would have shredded them with my sharp nails. It would have been faster than using the scissors.

She had a large flat paper she was arranging the little-colored pieces on. She moved them around and around. Maybe this was a new way of being entertained. I kept watching and waiting for something else to happen. She then moved all the pieces off to the side and picked up a can which she shook. When she pushed on the button, a sticky spray came out, and she covered the large paper with the stuff. She then picked up one of the colored cut pieces and was about to place it on the paper when her phone rang in the other room.

I decided that while she was away, I would check all of this out real close. I strolled across the table and stepped on the large white paper. It was sticky. I then put my paw out and touched one of the colored pieces. It stuck to my paw. I set my foot on the large paper, and the colored piece stuck there. I then touched another colored piece and did the same thing. This was like playing with Legos only it was with bits of paper, and they didn't slide around. It was fun but slow. I then swatted the whole stack of colored pieces onto the large paper.

The stack was in a heap, so I moved the pieces around, making them flat. The sticky stuff on my paws was wearing off, and I needed something else to do. I jumped down to the chair and turned around to admire my work. My male human came into the room and looked at the mosaic I created. His partner came into the room about then, and he said, "Honey, this is a great abstract you have made."

She looked down at the paper she had left only minutes before and then looked at her partner suspiciously. She said, "I didn't know you liked to make abstracts."

He said, "I didn't make this."

Both sets of eyes turned toward me. That was my cue to check out the window. As I walked away with my tail high in the air, I heard a roar of laughter from both of my humans. Were they laughing at the collage? Were they laughing at me? As I strutted along, I glanced back and saw one of those little red pieces of colored paper stuck to my tail. It waved back and forth with each swish of my tail.

I quickly twisted around to perform an emergency grooming on my tail. This red flag ruined my noble appearance. With the flag removed, I retreated to the front window where the air was cool. There were a few kids in the street tossing a ball back and forth. It was quiet, and I dozed off, dreaming about those colored pieces of papers sticking to my paw.

I had an early dinner that evening. Maybe my humans felt guilty laughing at me. Once I finished, I looked around and found something new in the room. There was a picture frame set on the table. It looked like the paper I had played with earlier in the day. At the bottom of the picture, someone had drawn a paw print with some letters next to it. I couldn't read, but the letters were T-H-O-M-A-S. Maybe they were giving me credit for the artwork.

That night, I curled up to both of my humans and started my purr motor. To think they were framing my artwork. How nice of them. They rewarded me with gentle strokes down my back and a nice rubbing around my ears. The purr motor sounds grew louder.

Tale 29 - The Nursery

I like to know what is going on in my kingdom. Today, workmen came in and moved stuff all around in the back room. That is where I have my backyard lookout. They moved all the furniture to the big room. The men laid large sheets of material down to cover the floor. They opened a large can, and I was about to check it with a sniff when my female human said "Thomas! Stop! That is paint. You don't want it on you." It didn't smell good anyway, so I went to my front room perch to get fresh air.

That pesky mailman was early, and I stared him down again, but not before he stuffed the bills into the box. This house is my kingdom along with what I can see outside. My job is to protect it. I heard my female human say a few times to the workmen, "Keep the door closed, or Thomas might get out." Hey, I could get out anytime I wanted.

The next day, different men came. They brought carpeting and laid it down. It was soft, and I enjoyed stretching out on it and letting the sun warm me. The room still smelled of paint, so I didn't stay long. My window was open, but something blocked me from climbing in. The paint there must still be wet, and my humans are thoughtful enough to prevent it from sticking to my fur. I wondered what these changes were leading up to.

Another day passed, and this time a truck pulled up in front of the house and men unloaded new furniture. They carried the stuff in the house, and my female human directed the workers to place it in the back room. One item looked like a big dog carrier on stilts. I hope they weren't planning on getting a dog. If they do, I'm out of here.

That evening, the humans were in the room. My female human was sitting in a big rocking chair holding her stomach. I had to be careful as the big rockers could pinch my tail. She seemed content looking around the room and talking to her mate. I heard her say, "The Nursery is looking very nice." I'm not sure what a nursery is, but I guess that is what they will call this room.

I found my window perch now open, so I parked myself there and looked out. The sun was setting, and I knew it was close to dinner time. I gave my humans more time before reminding them of supper.

They brought in a big box from the garage containing stuffed animals. They placed these around the room. I guess they thought I would like them. There were more items added that required pounding nails into the wall. I think they will hang stuff there, but I didn't like the noise, so I departed and waited in the kitchen. I knew they would be along soon.

At last, the two came into the kitchen, and they opened a can of gourmet food and spooned it into my bowl. They refreshed the water too. I have trained my servants well, but they have to get the timing down better as it was past my feeding time. Maybe I should have reminded them with a big meow. Nah, they seemed to have enjoyed themselves in the nursery.

The next day, another truck pulled up, and more workers came to the door. This time, my two humans pointed out the old furniture in the big room that had been removed from the nursery. The two workmen carried these items out to their truck. I now had more room to run around in.

After the smell left the back room, now called the nursery, I liked it. It seemed fresher, more open, and ready for me to lie on the soft carpet and soak up the sun. To think, they did all of this for me. I even have large stuffed animals to keep me company. I will have to thank them.

That night, I curled up with them on the big bed, and when they stroked my soft, beautiful fur, I provided them with a sonata of purring. That earned me some additional petting under my chin and around my ears. Life was good.

Tale 30 - The Baby

My humans have spent a lot of time in the nursery. This had my curiosity piqued, so I hung out there too. My window perch was ideal as it gave me a great view of the backyard and all the activities in the nursery. It seemed every trip the humans took, they brought back a few more items for the room. The closet had several boxes with pictures of tiny humans sitting without many clothes on. The hangers had lots of small colorful clothes.

I noticed my female human was getting bigger around her middle. She seemed to hold her stomach more, as it protruded. This made the lap space smaller when she sat down. I tried lying in her lap but felt I was being crowded out. There were also strange sounds coming from her stomach. A few times, it felt like I was being thumped. She seemed to like my company more, so I stayed with her, providing comfort. Besides, the additional petting and rubbing around my ears felt good too.

The big noise maker was being pushed around the house by my male human today. This was unusual as my female human always does the vacuuming. There was extra cleaning being done, and they placed colored tablecloths on the table. I knew what this meant; people would come by and create a lot of racket. I heard the words baby shower but didn't know what that meant. By early afternoon, people arrived. They carried boxes covered with bright colored wrapping paper and ribbons. I like the long curly strings. They are fun to bat and then watch them spring back.

I tried to stay out of the way. I figured by going into my room, the nursery, I would be safe. Nope, it seemed every partygoer had to come in and see me. They would come into the room and look around. I guess they didn't see me right away as I was in my window perch. The chit chat they had while trying to find me was interesting. I heard one person say, "The baby will have a very nice room to sleep in."

Baby? What baby? What is a baby? I thought. Were they referring to me? The people would then come over to my window and stroke my soft fur. That felt good, but why did they refer to me as a baby? I'm the king, and my name is Thomas.

Two weeks later, I understood. My two humans came home with a third human they called the Baby. I figured it all out then. The boxes in the closet were clothes for the baby. They had to buy these in bulk because the baby kept dirtying them. My female human spent a lot of time in the nursery with the baby, and I recognized the love she had for it. That meant from now on, this baby was under my protection. I would protect it along with the rest of my kingdom.

I noticed the baby needed feeding every few hours. This became a routine. It would start in the early morning, then late morning, early evening, and then a late-night feeding. I realized my twice a day feeding was not a big deal. If they missed a feeding for me, I might remind them with a soft meow a few times, but when the baby was hungry, cries carried throughout the house.

I thought my female human was becoming a zombie. She seemed to be up at all hours. She needed my comfort to help relax her so she could rest. I would curl up to her and let my purr motor run to help her unwind. I listened for the baby and let her know when the baby needed something. It was the least I could do to help protect my kingdom, my servants and the baby.

My male human tried to help too. He had the job of changing the baby's clothes. I think he called them diapers. After changing the baby, he would run outside to throw the old diaper away. I didn't blame him, they smelled bad. He seemed to be the one to set my food out more often too. When he went to bed, I would lie next to him and help him settle down too. I became exhausted with all the baby watch duties I had along with helping my two humans. Then again, I received food, companionship and a lot of petting. What more could a king ask for?

I wondered if this is what they call a family? Well, as long as I am king, I will protect my family and my kingdom. I guess a new emotion, called love, is the driving force behind this.

Tale 31 - Trick or Treat

It seemed to be that time of the year again when it gets dark earlier and cold outside. This reminded me of some old times when I was on my own. Just when you thought humans were nice to you, they would chase and try to capture you. Seems my beautiful black coat was in high demand at this time of the year. I was lucky enough to avoid any bad things, but I still remember how close I came to being caught.

Times are a lot better now. I found two humans that are very nice and I have trained them to put food down for me in the morning and evening each day. I allow them to pet me and stroke my lean body. However, today, my female human exceeded the limit of my patience. It was more than I could bear. Let me tell you about it.

I suppose you heard about the third human who arrived. The baby is precious, and I have made it my duty to protect this beloved child the best I can. I found the female human dressing the child in a strange outfit. It was orange and big around the body. A hat which looked to have a handle sticking out topped it off. She told me, "Thomas, we're having a small Halloween party today. I will carry the little one in a pumpkin pouch, and I will carry you as my familiar spirit. That way, you won't have to hide."

A familiar I thought. What is a familiar? She would carry me as a familiar. At that point, I wasn't sure what was happening, but the infant was tucked into this pouch my human had and then she picked me up. There was a side pouch she tried to push my back legs into. My tail would not go down the same time as my hind legs. This was getting weird, and I let her know this wasn't the thing to do.

She stroked my head and said, "Thomas, it is okay. You get to ride next to the baby for security." I looked over at the little one, it was helpless in the pouch, same as me. How could I protect this child if half my body was stuck in this tight little contraption? She kept talking as I

63

sank lower into the hole. My hind legs slipped through holes at the bottom, and I could not get any traction to extricate myself without causing harm to either her or the baby.

The doorbell rang, and all three of us went to the door. My human greeted the visitors and one by one they had to talk to the baby and then reached out to pet my head. This wasn't going well, but at least I could see all the action and knew if anyone tried something tricky with the baby, I still had two front paws with sharp nails that could wreak damage.

More people came, and the scene repeated itself. They all seemed nice and paid tribute with a gentle stroke or rub behind my ears. Maybe this wasn't so bad, but I was still on high alert. I couldn't wait for this to stop.

It seemed like an eternity until my human carried us to the nursery and closed the door. It was feeding time for the baby and escape time for me. While they settled in, I stood guard by the door. It wasn't necessary as no one tried to enter. They must have sensed a familiar was on guard.

She put the baby down to sleep, and my human and I rejoined the party. I was free from the pouch, and everyone knew to keep their distance. My tail was straight up as I walked amongst these strangers, sniffing out any danger. The party was about over, and some guests left. I found the front window a great spot to observe this and keep from being stepped on.

Later that night, my humans and I curled up in bed together. I was being stroked, and my purr motor was working overtime. Everything worked out well, although I could have done without being carried around in a pouch.

Tale 32 - The Big Bird

I was feeling satisfied. They filled my bowl early this morning, and I had fresh water. Training my humans to provide for me has taken time, but the rewards keep coming. My female human fed the baby and the two were now having a morning nap. That left the house quiet. The day was starting off on a perfect note, that is until my male human came home. He made a lot of noise and carried endless bags of groceries into the kitchen. It was enough to wake everyone in the house. He rarely brings home the groceries. I then remembered something about a grocery list given to him this morning.

Once both humans were in the kitchen, I heard them chatting about a good bargain he got on a big bird that weighed a lot. I wondered if this was like the big black bird I fought off in the front yard. That bird attacked my little bird friends, and I taught him a lesson. Maybe this bird would be in a cage or something. I then heard they were putting the bird in the oven. The bird can't escape from there, but I would be on guard in case he gets out.

Then there was the usual racket when they get out the big noise maker and push it around on all the carpets. It seems to emit a lot of dust into the air. I found my window perch was great to get fresh air from outside. There was more cleaning which meant more humans would invade my territory later.

As the day progressed, a savory smell came from the kitchen. I usually ignore those smells as I have my satisfying bowl of food, but this was different. Two more people arrived, and they helped in the kitchen. I figured there would be too many cooks in there, so I retreated to my window where I watched as a more people arrived. The house was crowded, and more people were coming.

The baby was up, and my female human was in the nursery providing nourishment. That is a fairly quiet room, so I laid in the window there to keep guard. I have a great view of the backyard from this position and could see all the activities there. My male human and another person were setting up two large tables. They even put decorations on them. A few kids ran around in the backyard playing tag. I was glad I was away from them.

The doorbell rang, and a few more people arrived. Where were all these people coming from? One partygoer helped my male human carry more chairs from the garage and place them around the tables. Large dishes of food were being carried out to the tables. The smell from the kitchen was so enticing, I had to go peek. My male human opened the oven and pulled out this large thing. He called it a turkey. I then realized this was the big bird he talked about and he had cooked it. I guess that bird won't be flying around here anymore.

He used a large knife and cut the turkey up. While I didn't like the big black birds, cooking and eating them was not something I had thought about. However, the cooking smells tantalized my senses.

As people sat down outside, I went out to watch the festivities. Before they ate, they gave reverence to the food and everyone there. My male human was thankful for their baby and health. After that, everyone ate as if they hadn't eaten for a week.

It took a while for this gathering to finish and clean up, but they hung around and talked. It was my feeding time, and I worried they might forget about me. Then my male human picked up my bowl up and said, "Thomas, this is a special day when we give thanks for everything we have. I am very thankful you came into our lives. You have saved the house from fire and theft. You helped my wife when she was injured. We are both grateful."

I had been staring at the bowl in his hand the entire time. I didn't understand everything he said, but my appetite was growing. When he placed the bowl down, it wasn't my regular food. It was some of this bird. I tasted it and then devoured it. Now I'm thankful for turkey!

Tale 33 - Tree Tops Glisten

I knew it was winter. When I laid in my window, the cold air would give me a chill. Most of the time, the window was closed, so I didn't have this problem. However, today it was open, the sun was shining, and I looked out at the trees. One tree had lost most of its leaves shortly after changing colors from green to yellow to brown. It was a pleasant view. Another tree had tiny leaves called needles which were green all year long. I liked climbing these trees.

There was a disturbance in the garage, and I went to check it out. The humans had returned, and there was something strange on top of their car. It looked like part of that big tree in the yard, the one with the needles. My female human carried the baby inside. With all the covers, you could hardly tell there was a baby wrapped up in the carrier. My male human untied the green tree from the roof of the car and pulled it into the front yard. From there, he carried it through the front door and into the big room. He bumped up against the doorway, and some needles dropped behind him leaving a trail. I smelled a few, and they were like the ones from the big tree in the yard.

He set the tree up in the living room. It was nice of them to think of me. He filled a big pan with water, and the tree sat in it. It had legs to keep the tree from falling over. Maybe if I tired of running up and down the tree, I would have a ready supply of water to quench my thirst. The tree was an ideal play toy because even when it is too cold out, I can still climb up and down for fun. I am very fortunate to have a family that is so thoughtful. They are well trained in setting food out for me each morning and evening and now, bringing home a tree makes things even more enjoyable.

Before I could check the tree out any further, they carried small boxes into the room and opened them. Bright colored bulbs and long wires filled these boxes. The two humans pulled these wired things out and wrapped the tree up in them. I was beside myself. They were making my tree prettier.

Next came the round balls that hung on hooks which attached to the tree. The larger ones were near the bottom and smaller ones near the top. Just when I thought they finished, they opened another box and draped the tree with silvery foil-like stuff. The lights reflected off of this all around the room. This was too much. How was I supposed to climb up and down with all these wires, balls and foil? I sat back near the window, observing their continued antics while cleaning my sleek body.

They moved the bulbs and other decorations around, and there was a lot of talking about certain balls that hung on the tree. I know they made a big deal about one as she said, "Baby's First Christmas." Finally, they stepped back, and the male human turned a switch. The whole tree lit up and sparkled. It almost looked like it was on fire. I cautiously took a few steps back.

Apparently, they still had more things to do. They pulled boxes with brightly colored paper with bows on top out from various hiding places around the house. They placed these under and around the tree. There was a big stuffed Teddy Bear that took up a lot of room. It was so packed that I could not see how I was to even get to the base to climb up. I decided the curly ribbons on the packages would be my limit.

My humans curled up on the sofa with the baby and watched the tree. I wondered if something else would happen. If they were sitting back protecting the baby, I should take the same advice and stand clear. I jumped up on the sofa and laid close to my male human. He stroked my back and around my head. The two were talking quite a lot, but I could not make out most of the words. The two words I heard repeated the most were Merry Christmas.

My purr motor was on, and I was humming along with whatever spirits made the evening special.

Tale 34 - Rain

The weather depressed me. My window was closed, which was a good thing, as it had been raining off and on for several days. I hadn't seen any of the small birds in days. In fact, water covered the grass in the front yard. The view from the nursery wasn't any better. There was a depression that ran behind the houses, and it had turned into a large stream. The gloomy weather seemed to make everyone cranky.

Take today as an example. I woke up and expected them to clean and fill my food and water bowls. My humans were moving in slow motion and ignored my dietary requirements. I couldn't stand it any longer, so I let out a hefty meow. That got their attention, and soon I was having breakfast.

I saw my male human staring at some paper on the table, so I jumped up to see what took so much of his attention. He had a pen in his hand and was marking on the paper. My female human asked him in one of those unpleasant tones, "Aren't you done with that crossword puzzle yet? You have been working on it all morning!"

I knew it was time to leave. If it hadn't been for the rain, I'm sure she would have helped him finish it. As it was, tempers were likely to flare, and I didn't want to be around for that. I scooted off to check on the baby.

The baby has been growing fast over the last few months. Rolling over and peeking out between the bars was an easy task. I would walk back and forth showing off my sleek body and letting my tail rise high in the air. Occasionally, I would flick it back and forth, and this would elicit a little laugh. A small hand would reach out and try to touch me, but I knew to stay just far enough away to avoid any hair pulling.

A few hours later I finished my mid-day nap. The rain had stopped, but the dark clouds promised more to come. A knock on the door interrupted my rest. I scrambled to my front window to see who was making this noise. It turned out to be the man wearing the big bird symbol on his coat. My male human opened the door and spoke to the man. When the door closed, my human held a package which he carried into the kitchen. My curiosity made me follow along.

He yelled out, "Honey, the mail came, and we have a package." This prompted my female human to come into the kitchen too. She said, "Is that the box with the new Lego building? I know how much you wanted it. Open it up and let's see."

He took a knife and slit open the package and removed an inner box. It had bright colors on it with a picture of a leaning building. He said, "Look, it's the Tower of Pisa." Together, they removed several small packages from the box and placed them on the table. He said, "Honey, let's put this together while it's still raining and the baby's sleeping."

I observed them looking at a diagram and moving the small Lego parts around. I could remember playing with these before. Once on the floor, I played with them like hockey pucks. There still might be a few under the stove or behind the refrigerator. Maybe they will give me a few so I can play with them too.

The evening had come, and my humans had missed the subtle clues I dropped letting them know it was dinner time. I figured I needed to remind them, so I let out a nice little meow. Their heads turned towards me, and they both laughed. They had been so intent working on this Lego building they forgot about the rain and the time. My female human then took care of my food.

Afterward, I climbed into their laps and started up my purr motor. I could see why they were so engrossed. The Lego building was leaning over. I guess they were trying to figure out how to make it straight. Maybe the pieces under the stove would help.

Tale 35 - Rock, Rumble, and Roll

Something was bothering me. The weather was colder, and it reminded me that choosing this place as my home was the best decision I ever made, even if it took a while to train my humans. But, that wasn't it, and I couldn't put my paw on it.

My humans put out my food on time today. My male human left for the day on his daily ritual. I think he referred to it as work. My female human busied herself preparing the baby for traveling. Once bundled up, she placed the baby in the carrier, and I wouldn't see them for the rest of the day.

I roamed around and checked the view from all my windows. I still had this funny feeling, but nothing seemed out of place. It was time for my morning nap, so I laid in the front window and started to sleep. At least I tried to. I was about ready to doze off when the house shook. Then there was a rumble and another violent shaking. Noises came from several directions. The shaking threw me out of the window and onto the floor. I remained standing but could not run for fear of falling down. My nails held me to the carpet.

When the rumbling stopped, I ran to the nursery and then to the bedroom. I made sure the humans were not there. Then there was some additional shaking, but it wasn't as bad. This caused the blinds to bang against the wall which added noise. I crawled under the bed and laid still for several hours until I felt it was safe to move around again. It was time to investigate what happened.

The bedroom seemed okay. A lamp in the nursery had fallen over but hadn't broken. The kitchen had the most damage. One cupboard had opened, and some dishes had fallen, scattering the broken pieces about on the floor below. My water bowl was empty, and there was a little water surrounding it. Overall, I felt like some spooky monsters had invaded my kingdom with strong mystical powers that could shake up the whole house.

I relaxed somewhat and sat in the window of the nursery. Something strange still nagged at me as I looked out. One of the big poles with wires attached was leaning at a funny angle. It looked like it was ready to fall and crash down on my house right where the nursery window was. I stared at the pole watching for movement. I heard the garage door. This was my female human returning from her errands, and she would bring the baby in here. I had to make sure that didn't happen.

I stood in the doorway to the house from the garage, blocking the entry. My human opened the door with one hand and held the baby in the other. I let out a big meow to let my human know something was wrong. She looked at me and said, "What's wrong Thomas?" I let out another big meow as she took a step forward. That didn't seem to stop her, so I gave her a big growling hiss. I even put a paw in the air. That seemed to get her attention. She backed up and set the baby carrier down and then looked around. I continued my stance. She tried to enter, and I hissed again. I even raised my hackles. She said, "Okay Thomas. I know you don't want me in the house. I don't know why, but I will wait."

She tapped on her phone, and I heard her talking with her mate. I heard the words Thomas and blocking several times. I scrambled to the window and looked at the pole. It looked like it had leaned over even more than before. I needed to keep them out. My male human arrived, and I stopped him from coming in too. He then walked around the outside of the house and came back yelling to his mate about a pole in the backyard.

It took several hours for repairmen to anchor the pole. They mentioned the word earthquake and said it was limited to a small area. It was late in the evening when the workmen gave my humans the okay to enter the house.

My humans served me an extra-large portion of food and gave me a lot of strokes. My purr motor must have been on the fritz as I was still nervous from all the shaking that took place today. At least my humans are safe from harm, and my kingdom is not in too bad of shape from the monsters that attacked it.

Tale 36 - BBQ Time

The sun has been shining for several days now. The warmth of it has made my beautiful sleek body feel like spring is in the air. I was thinking about basking in the light outside when I heard a commotion in the house. The big noise maker was being pushed around on the carpets. That meant other humans would invade my domain later.

I checked out the window in the nursery and saw my male human outside with another noise maker going back and forth across the grassy backyard. I felt like I was watching a slow tennis match as he passed back and forth in front of the window. After he put that machine away, he pulled a big picnic table out into the center of the yard. It looked inviting, so I went through the kitchen door and jumped up on the table. Yes, the sun was right here as I stretched out. My male human came over and softly petted my head and rubbed my ears. I felt a slow purr begin inside me. Contentment had set in. He pulled out the barbecue, and my male human was trying to make a fire in it. I decided it was time to leave as the last time they used it, it exploded. I retreated into the house.

There were more humans in the house than I expected. I checked on the baby in the nursery, and the room was full. The bedroom was unoccupied, and I found a soft place on the pillow to relax. As I was about to doze off, someone threw clothes on the bed and startled me. What the heck? I thought. I figured I had better check out what was happening.

In the big room, some kids were running around with balloons. One of them had the idea to chase me with a big yellow balloon. His idea didn't last long as I stood my ground and when the balloon came up to my face, I swatted it with my nails extended. It burst with a loud noise, and the kid stopped in his tracks. It was a good time for me to leave.

I strolled out the kitchen door and saw the backyard filled with humans. The noise from so many people talking hurt my ears. I needed a quiet space and walked around to the front of the house. There is a big tree there, the same one that old big black bird liked to hide in. A large branch jutted out and looked like a good resting spot. I raced up the tree and checked it out. The view of the house and yard were great, and it was very peaceful with a gentle breeze blowing. I stretched out the best I could and laid there.

I must have dozed off, because the next thing I knew, one of those balloons was right next to me. The kids overflowed from the backyard and now invaded the front yard where they were laughing and playing under the tree. Before I knew it, the balloon popped. It must have hit a sharp piece of bark on the tree limb. It scared the heck out of me, and I wasn't sure whether to jump down or run up the tree. The kids below laughed even more. I'm glad the tree was tall, as I climbed up further.

It was getting dark, and the humans were leaving. My stomach was telling me it was past dinner time, so I moved down the tree, checking to make sure the kids had left. My last few steps were a big leap onto the grass below. Remnants of the balloon were still there. I cautiously walked around to the backyard. The kitchen door was still open, and I went inside.

The house was empty except for my humans who were cleaning up the place. I stood by my bowl and waited. I was about to let them know it was time for my feeding but my female human opened a can of some delightfully good smelling food and scooped it into my bowl and then refilled my water.

After satisfying my nutritional requirements, I found my male human on the sofa relaxing. I heard him say "That was a great barbecue with all the family and friends. We should do it again sometime."

Barbecue? I thought. That was not fun. It was noisy, and I had balloons pop all around me. Regardless, I jumped up into his lap and started up my purr motor. At least he wouldn't push a balloon near my whiskers.

Tale 37 - Valentines

Another beautiful day was in the works. My humans placed my morning food and water on a fresh red mat, ready for me to enjoy. I savored every bite. I noticed my female human wrapping something up. It was red wrapping and had a big red bow tied on the top. I sat in the kitchen chair watching her, and she said, "Thomas, it's Valentine's Day, and I have a surprise for the man around the house."

This box might be something special, but the significance was beyond my understanding. I sniffed the box, but there was nothing to give me a clue as to the contents. Maybe it's another box with some Legos in it. If so, I hope all the pieces are there. That last thing they made leaned over like it was missing pieces.

My male human came into the kitchen and asked, "Sweetie, may I fix you some breakfast?" Hmm, he rarely seems to do that. I wondered if this change of routine has anything to do with Valentine's Day. I left them alone and checked out my front window.

The sunshine felt good across my body as I looked out across the front yard. My eyes were only half open when I spotted another cat. It looked mangy, nothing like my beautiful, well-groomed body. The cat was nosing around and getting closer. I then recognized this gray cat, it had given me a bad time in my early days.

I used to hang out in alleys behind restaurant row. My favorite was the sushi bar. They tossed out the best food in town, and I tried to be the first in line to get my evening meal. This gray cat was a competitor for the handouts, and sometimes he would put up a fight to get at them first. He was mean and a bully around me.

The little birds had come out to play, and the gray cat looked like he was sneaking up on them. Maybe he thought one of them would make a tasty meal. I wanted to warn the little birds with a meow but the window was closed, and I knew they wouldn't be able to hear me. The gray cat moved up closer, as more little birds joined the group.

I hoped the birds would see the gray cat and fly away, but they kept pecking in the grass as the gray cat moved closer. Suddenly, the stinky dog, that runs by once in a while showed up on the sidewalk. He stopped short when he saw the gray cat, and then like a bullet, shot across the yard right towards it. If the dog hadn't let out a howl, I'm sure he would have had the gray cat for breakfast, but the noise warned the cat just in time. The gray cat leaped out of the way and ran down the street. The dog continued the chase.

I never saw that old gray cat again. As for the stinky dog, while I don't like him much, he protected the little birds that are my friends. I will have to give him a kind thought someday. All of this excitement required a long nap.

Towards evening, my humans returned from an outing and gathered in the kitchen. I followed them in. My female human said, "Honey, thank you very much for a lovely day and for the romantic dinner. I have something for you." With that, she handed him the red package.

He opened it carefully and inside was a framed picture of my female human, the baby, and me. I had forgotten she had taken a picture the other day. This picture brought him joy, I could tell by his bright smile and glistening eyes. I guess he needed a picture of me to remind him of all the good things I provide. He said, "This is very nice. I will put this on my desk at work so I can think of our family and Thomas." He then gave her a big kiss. I hope he wasn't planning on giving me a kiss. A little rub around the ears would do nicely.

Finally, they filled my food and water bowls and once again and set them on the red mat. I felt like a king, and on some days my humans actually treated me that way. While they sat on the sofa, I crawled up and laid down across their laps. I got the two for one treatment with a rub around the head and ears by one and soft petting down the length of my body by the other. My purr motor worked overtime.

Tale 38 - A New Toy

I was up early, sitting in my window watching the little birds peck in the grass. It was very relaxing. I was hoping my humans would rise soon and fill my food bowl. One can only hope.

After the morning rituals, my humans left, and I had a peaceful home all to myself. I stretched out where the sun shone on the carpet. It was a nice warm place to doze for a while. I must have been sleeping soundly when I heard the door to the garage open and my humans returning from wherever they went. They seem to always be up to something, so I stretched, put a few hairs in place and then sauntered about the house.

My first stop was the nursery to check on the baby. The ride in the car must have tired the baby out. The baby seemed calm and rested comfortably in the crib. I checked the nursery window to make sure nothing was happening in the backyard.

My next stop was the kitchen. This seems to be the hub of most activity. Two sacks and a box were on the table, and my humans were hovering about talking up a storm. While they were opening the box, my male human said, "I hope this new Roomba doesn't frighten Thomas."

What is a Roomba? I thought. And me scared? That never happens. They placed the empty box on the floor, and I sniffed it. I jumped in to prove that I'm no scaredy-cat. There wasn't anything special about the box, and I looked up at my humans for approval, but they were ignoring me as usual. A strange sound started up, like a deep hum and then it stopped. I watched my male human take this round black object into the big room and set it on the carpet. He then pushed something, and the hum started up again, and the object moved around the room.

My female human said, "The Roomba seems to be working. Look, it seems to cover the floor in straight lines. Let's see if it picks up Thomas' hair."

Now I was scared. Is this thing going to pull my hair out? I stepped behind the legs of a big chair, just to distance myself. The thing went back and forth, each time moving a little closer. I thought this was a big mouse, and it needed taming. I waited for a few more passes as it would bump into something and change direction. Maybe this overgrown mouse had poor eyesight.

I then saw my chance. The thing came close to the chair, hitting one leg. I stuck my paw out and got in the first blow. I knew I had to show it who the boss was around here. The thing changed directions again and left without a fight. I guess it learned fast that this is the king's home and I'm the king.

I still kept my eye on it. After a while, it came my way again. I watched it approach and judged the distance. I leaped on top of the strange thing. It kept moving, but it was slower than before. It was heading towards the wall, and I jumped off. I figured if it likes to bang its head against the wall, it could do that without me. When it started back, I hopped on it again. Now that it knew who the boss was, I made this into a game. It still bothered me it might try to pull my hair, but I was ready to swat it if it tried.

The game became tiresome, and it didn't take long before I had enough. I left the thing still running in the big room. It had crossed the patch of sunlight where I liked to lie, and I would not give it a chance to sneak up on me and pull my hair. I headed back to the nursery to check on the baby.

The baby was standing up in the crib holding onto the top railing. I hadn't seen this before. It must have been one of the firsts my female human keeps describing to everyone that will listen. Maybe she would like to see this. I let out a big meow to let my female human know. She hurried in and saw the baby standing up. She said, "Wow! Aren't you getting big? Standing there all by yourself."

After dinner, I found a warm lap to lie in and thought about the day. My humans brought me a new toy I could ride around on, and the baby is getting bigger. My family is growing. I let contentment settle in and my purr motor start. Of course, the gentle rubbing around my head and the strokes down my beautiful sleek body helped my motor hum. I wondered if the Roomba hum came from the rubbing it gave the carpet.

Tale 39 - Kitty Company

The patch of sunlight on the carpet was just right. I had my breakfast, and it was time to soak up the sun with a little catnap. Seems I had only closed my eyes when there was a knock on the door. I hoped it wasn't that pesky mailman with more bills.

My female human opened the door and greeted a friend of hers. They talked, but the only word I could make out clearly was the word kitten. I thought maybe they were talking about me when suddenly, the friend set this little furball down next to me. I sniffed the kitten, trying to make sense out of the situation. The tiny kitten was so small, it could fit into my food bowl. I watched it take wobbly steps. I decided there wasn't any danger here and moved closer for a better examination.

The two humans were watching to see what would happen as I put my paw out and touched the little one. I heard this very tiny meow come from the kitten. And then it surprised me by leaping onto my paw. I backed up, and the little kitten leaped forward again, attacking my paw. My paw was the target of more playful assaults. I turned around, which was a mistake. My tail was unprotected, and the little ball of fur jumped on it, trying to catch it. I moved, and this furball followed me around the room.

The humans were laughing, and then the friend said her goodbye. I was hoping this kitten would not be a permanent resident. The little kitten found a piece of lint and during the attack, rolled over. I was unsure of how to play with such a small little feline. The patch of sunlight was inviting, and I laid down in the warmth. As I did so, the little furball followed. For what seemed like an eternity, the little ball of energy climbed over me, attacked my tail, played with my paw, and tried to chew on one of my ears. This became tiring, and I needed an escape. My window was open, and I jumped up there to lie down.

The kitten could not reach me here, and I could watch the antics below. It pulled one of my old toys, a little red stuffed mouse, out of a box below. The kitten batted it around the room and chewed on it. For once, I was glad my humans had gotten that toy as I never played with it. However, it seemed to be a good distraction for this little kitten.

The sun had shifted, and I went into the nursery as the sun created a warm patch of carpet in there. The baby wasn't there, so I had the room to myself. I stretched out and tried to get an afternoon nap. After I had closed my eyes, I felt a tug on my tail. The kitten had found me and was attacking my tail again. This little kitten had an endless supply of energy. I turned around and stared at this innocent looking little face. Maybe it needed a little big brother help. I put my big paw out and pushed the kitten down. It was nap time and this cat needed one. I repositioned myself, so I could hold the kitten and catch the fading sun.

My female human came in and placed the baby in the crib. She said, "Come along Thomas, and bring your little friend with you." I rose obediently and followed her out of the room. The furball was close behind.

A knock on the door caused us to move in that direction. My female human's friend had returned. They chatted some, and the friend picked the little furball up. There was more laughter, and I heard my name spoken several times. The friend then left, taking the kitten with her.

I was glad the kitten left as I did not want to share my evening meal. Running around all day with that ball of energy created a real appetite. The little red mouse lay on the carpet with minute little puncture wounds from the tiny kitten's teeth. I think my ear received a few punctures from those teeth too. I sat near my food bowl watching my human move back and forth in the kitchen. She only had to look down once to get the hint it was time for my feeding.

That evening, the baby was on the carpet. It had learned to move its body. I think my humans called it crawling. I had missed seeing one of these moves once, and the baby had reached out and grabbed my tail. The baby has a strong grip, and I had to tug hard before I could pull my tail away. The little kitten was like the baby, both wanted to get my attention and pull my tail. Of course, my tail is beautiful like the rest of me, and that would give them reason enough to pull it. The lap of my human was a good place to lie, and if they wanted to stroke my tail, then I might even start up the purr motor.

Tale 40 - The Eggspert

Another day and contentment has settled in. My humans filled my food and water bowls without me reminding them. I guess all that training has paid off. Now I can stretch out my sleek furry body and soak up the sunshine coming in my window. It was a beautiful day outside, but the birds had left. I'm glad I scared the big black bird away, but I still check to see if he has returned.

The family interrupted my peaceful rest by coming into the big room. I had a great view from my window, so I turned my head and watched. My humans were carrying what appeared to be a large basket in colorful wrappings. The baby was being held and was trying to reach for the basket. They set both the baby and the basket on the floor.

The wrapping paper let out a lot of crackling noises each time the baby yanked at it. After a few minutes, my male human worked on it and pulled it free from the basket. I thought the noise would go away, but he crushed the wrap, and it made more noise.

The baby could now touch the basket and its contents. I wasn't sure what these brightly colored objects were, but I heard the word eggs several times. They weren't like any bird eggs I have ever seen, and if they are eggs, then the birds that laid them must be huge. It would be best to avoid those birds. I wondered if any of them knew their eggs were in this basket?

The mother birds must not worry the humans as the baby pulled an egg out of the basket and was pushing it around. It intrigued me, so I jumped down to investigate. I didn't want any big bird to hatch out of one of these. I sniffed around and decided these were safe to play with.

My humans are careful around the baby. I swatted one egg to be sure it was safe, and it rolled over by the baby, and the baby hit it back.

The baby giggled, so I pounced on the egg and sent it flying right past the little hand of the baby. I didn't realize how fast the baby could crawl as it went after the egg. Upon reaching the egg, the baby sat up and then threw the egg in my direction. Being a quick feline, I avoided a direct hit. I swatted it on the first bounce, and the egg rolled back to the baby. The room seemed to explode with laughter as the baby giggled and the big humans laughed.

I then looked in the basket and found a couple more eggs in it. I warily snuck up in case there was something I was missing and then stretched my paw under one. It was smooth and slid easily out of the basket with a sweeping arm. I did the same with the next egg, and it rolled off near the baby. Having multiple eggs to play with seemed to keep the baby occupied.

I stepped into the basket thinking this might make a nice little bed. There was some stringy stuff in it that reminded me of the soft grass outside. I worked this a little and then laid down. I could peek over the rim of the basket and see the baby playing. Maybe my humans got the eggs for the baby and the basket for me. That was nice of them, I thought.

The baby corralled all the eggs and pushed them toward where I sat. With one in each hand, the baby tossed the eggs in my direction. I was under attack, and my fort might not protect me. I ducked below the rim of the basket as one egg sailed over my head. Another egg hit the side of the fort. Ha Ha, I thought. I'm safe from the artillery barrage.

The next egg came down on top of me. I knew it was time to retreat, so I moved off to the window to sit in the observation lookout. The baby continued to throw the eggs at the basket and then crawled over and emptied the basket out. Obviously, this kid knew how to reload its ammunition.

The evening meal was on time, and I double checked there weren't any eggs in my bowl. I knew someone had fed the baby and it might be on the prowl again soon. Later in the big room, I found the basket with all the eggs in it. I flipped the eggs out of the basket and crawled into the fort. I was safe from enemy attackers again.

After my female human tucked the baby into the crib for the night, I found the lap of my male human and made myself comfortable. His hands smelled a little like salt, and I licked them to make them clean. He rubbed behind my ears and under my chin. The purr motor was working eggs-tremely well.

Tale 41 - Vacation Day 1

My humans disrupted the morning routine by filling my food and water bowls so early, it was still dark outside. I ate anyway, no telling when they would feed me the next time. The humans scurried about, packing suitcases and bags and then carrying them out to the car. When they take the baby anywhere, they pack a lot of stuff, but this seemed like a whole lot more. My male human picked me up and petted me as he carried me to the garage where they stored my carrier. He said, "Thomas, we're going on vacation, and you're coming with us." He placed me inside the cage and then loaded the carrier into the car. There wasn't anything I could do about it as I was now going on vacation.

My carrier was next to the baby's car seat. Small fingers tried to push through the metal cage that held me. I wanted to keep all my hair, so I laid against the far side of the carrier, away from the little fingers. I tried to sleep as there was nothing else to do. It seemed to be late in the day when we made our final stop.

We arrived at our destination, and my humans carried the luggage inside along with more stuff for the baby. On one of his trips, my male human carried me in and set the carrier on the floor. When the front door was closed, he lifted the slide on my carrier, and I stepped out to look around. Sensing no immediate danger, I began a long stretch to limber up my muscles. I heard the humans talk about this place and they called it a cabin. It had a different smell from the home I'm used to.

I checked the cabin out. There were a lot of wooden floors polished smooth. I would have to be careful not to run too fast on them, or I might slide. There was a big window near the door where I found a sill to rest on. I could see a lot of trees and the car. There weren't any other houses nearby. I was relaxing when I heard the can opener grinding. I figured it was meal time and went to take advantage of the opportunity.

They had placed my sleep bed near another window, and that is where I went after everyone else bedded down for the night. All kinds of sounds kept me on the alert. Several times, I checked the windows, but it was too dark to see anything. I was about to close my eyes when I heard a new sound in the kitchen. I had to investigate what caused this.

My soft padded paws allowed me to sneak towards the kitchen door. The sound was of a small animal moving about. I peeked around the doorway and spotted a mouse. I froze and stared at it while it devoured crumbs on the floor. When it turned its back, I advanced several steps. The last time I chased a mouse was in the old days before I settled into my new kingdom. This brought a lot of memories back.

The mouse was ready to move on. It turned in my direction, not knowing I was ready to pounce. When it scampered across the floor, I made my move. My sharp nails reached out, but the momentum of my body kept me going as I slid across the slick floor. I quickly regained my balance and ran back. I caught only a little movement as the mouse disappeared through a small crack in the baseboard.

For only a fleeting moment I thought I might have lost my touch. In the old days, the mouse would have been my dinner, but since I have my humans trained to provide me with some great tasting food, making the mouse my snack did not appeal as much as when it was necessary for survival.

While I drove that mouse away, I was sure it would be back. The slippery floor would be a challenge, but I would be more prepared next time. I also knew where it might stick its nose out from. Tomorrow would bring another opportunity for me to eliminate this pesky rodent.

I heard early morning activity from the room in which the humans slept. My bed was warm and comfortable, and I figured I could doze for a little longer. My female human came into the room, saw me and picked me up. She said, "Thomas, you're such a good cat." She then petted me most lovingly, causing my purr motor to kick in. I'm glad she didn't know I missed catching that mouse. However, it was entertaining in the attempt. Maybe this is what they called a vacation.

Tale 42 - Vacation Day 2

I think I can get used to this vacation. The cabin is big enough to roam around in, and there is entertainment at night with the mouse. The sun was up, and I laid in a warm spot. My humans had somehow stuffed the baby in a backpack and were heading out for what they called a hike. It looked like they were going on a walk in the woods.

The cabin was quiet, and I was at peace. I couldn't see any other humans or houses from my windows. Looking out, I glimpsed a lot of trees. I thought some of these might make a climbing challenge. The window in the bedroom was open, and I pushed the screen until I could squeeze out.

I sniffed around the first tree and avoided it. There looked to be a lot of sticky sap on it and I wanted to keep my beautiful fur coat clean. While I studied the trees, I saw movement on one a little ways off. It somewhat looked like a cat, but it had a big bushy tail. I have seen some of these before, and I think they call them squirrels. It busied itself with picking up little things and sticking them in his mouth. I strutted towards the squirrel in my most regal manner as I wanted to impress upon this squirrel my royal stature. I guess he didn't want to be honored with my presence as he ran to another tree and disappeared.

Another tree caught my attention. It was huge. With a running start, I ran up the side of the tree and stopped when I was several branches up. From this vantage point, I could see further than what the cabin windows allowed me to see. Obviously, there were a lot more trees, but in the distance, I could see a few cabins. I thought about how I would need a lot of time to explore this new territory. In another direction, I could see my humans heading back towards the cabin. Maybe their hike was over. I ran down the tree and headed to the cabin's porch to await their arrival.

They greeted me with, "Thomas, how did you get out?" I licked my paw and ignored the question. We all went inside, and my humans set the baby on the large rug. It looked like the baby had slept on the hike and was now ready to have fun. They placed a small ball down for the baby to play with. When the big humans left the room, I swatted the ball over to the baby. The baby giggled and knocked it around. I chased the ball and using my left and right paws, scored a goal in front of the baby. There were a lot more giggles, and the two humans returned to see what was happening.

I enjoyed this vacation in the woods. My humans seemed more relaxed, and they fed me early each day. I was also looking forward to the nighttime entertainment. This time, I found a spot to lie near the kitchen door. There was just enough moonlight so I could see. After a while, the mouse appeared. It scampered about looking for crumbs. I watched carefully and prepared myself to make my move. Suddenly, there was a motorized sound. I think it came from the refrigerator. This scared the mouse, and it ran for cover.

I froze, hoping the mouse hadn't seen me. I laid still for what seemed like an eternity. To my surprise, another mouse appeared on the other side of the room. It ignored the deep hum coming from the refrigerator and scurried about looking for bits of food. This mouse became my new target, and I prepped myself. My shoulders rose first, and then my body arched. The first mouse came out of its hiding spot and ran under the table. I had to decide which mouse to chase.

The first mouse was closer, but I would have to dodge the legs of the table and chairs. The other mouse was in a straight line of sight. I made my decision and raced across the slick wooden floor. I was within striking distance and needed to slow down. The next part was tricky and difficult. On my approach, I would have to reach out and grab the mouse as I slid past him. My sharp nails dug in as I continued into a slide. I bumped up against the baseboard with the mouse firmly in tow. In the excitement, I must have sunk my nails in deep as the mouse didn't move anymore.

One down and one to go. I looked around, but the other mouse must have left. I protected my territory once again from the evil vermin wandering about. The trophy needed to be placed on display to show my humans how well I protected the house, so I dropped the mouse in the doorway leading to the kitchen. My humans would find it in the morning. I returned to my sleep bed knowing the house was safe once again.

In the morning, a loud scream came from the kitchen, waking me up. Did I miss something when I closed my eyes? I rushed in to see what happened. My female human had found the present I left her. It must have been a scream of delight. She picked up the dead mouse with a rolled piece of newspaper and tossed the critter outside. Maybe she thought it would get up and run.

I'm sure she was proud of my accomplishment as she picked me up and stroked my back. It felt great for her to reward me this way. She said, "Thomas, I'm glad you stopped that little mouse from running around." This started my purr motor. After a minute or two of this, I remembered that food was an important part of my diet, so I jumped down and stood next to my food bowl. I worked hard last night.

Tale 43 - Vacation Day 3

Last night was freezing. I curled up on my sleep pillow in a tight position to keep warm. This morning I stretched several times, but still felt sluggish. I wanted to find a warm spot in the sun, but heavy clouds prevented the sunlight from shining in. Maybe this vacation time is not as wonderful as I originally thought.

My humans seemed to be moving slower too. Everyone stayed up late last night playing with the baby. Both humans took turns giving the baby various toys to play with. The baby had a lot of energy and batted the toys around constantly. At home, the baby has a special chair it can sit in and play with different gadgets attached to it. The humans left that behind, and I think the baby missed it. With all the noise and late-night activities, I think the mice stayed away too. I stayed up even longer watching and waiting for enemy combatants to show themselves.

My stomach was telling me it was breakfast time and yet, there wasn't any movement in preparing this. I sat patiently by my bowl and looked at my humans as they passed by many times. They prepared coffee for themselves, but nothing for me.

On the next trip to the kitchen, I let out a small meow to remind them my bowl was empty. That prompted the required response, and they soon fulfilled my quest for food. I think the baby was catching up on its sleep as the cabin remained fairly quiet. My male human put on his coat and opened the front door. I thought it would be a good opportunity to check the outside, so I slipped past him as he closed the door. He stood on the porch and looked around. I did the same. He strolled out by the small wooden fence near the car, and I jumped up on one railing to see what he was doing.

A big animal was standing in the woods some distance away. I could see my human had also spotted it. The animal had horns coming out of the top of his head and seemed wary of his environment. After a moment or two, another, smaller version of this animal, stepped into view close to the first one. I was peering closely at both animals. My human said, "Do you see the deer, Thomas?"

I saw nothing like this before and decided my perch on the fence was as close to these deer as I cared to go. Something seemed to startle them as they darted and disappeared into the woods. I think my human was ready to go back inside, and I knew with it being so cold, I had better follow.

The baby was up and being fed, and things seemed to be back to normal. Once my humans took care of the baby, they seemed to move into high gear and packed everything up. I heard something about a storm coming in, and they did not want to be in the cabin when it came.

My male human set me in the carrier and again placed it on the seat next to the baby. We were on our way home. The first part of the trip was bumpy as they drove over some dirt roads. Before we were on some smoother ones, some rain fell. It pounded on the car roof, and I even felt a chill in the air as the rain eased up, and bits of the white stuff fell on to the car. I heard the word snow several times.

It was dark when we arrived back home, and my humans carried all the stuff from the car into the house, including me. I ran to my cat tree and used the scratching post to stretch and work off excess energy. I then ran to each of the rooms checking everything was secure. The last place I checked was the kitchen. My female human was washing my bowls and preparing my food. Ah, it felt good to be back home.

There were several firsts for me on this trip. I now knew what a vacation was, what a cabin was, what a deer was, and now, I knew what snow was. The big animal and the cold snow I could do without. The vacation gave me a chance to catch a mouse and show my humans the value I provide in protecting the household. It also gave me a chance to improve my skills while having fun at the same time.

Once my humans were under the covers, I jumped onto the bed and curled up between them. They have a very warm bed. They talked excitedly about the vacation and how great it was to get away for a few days. Their hands naturally had to stroke my beautiful fur. I even got a rub around my ears. While I was happy to be home, the vacation was good too. My purr motor was humming right along.

Tale 44 - Magic Cleaner

After breakfast this morning, I noticed something upset my female human. She kept fiddling with the buttons and knobs on some device in the kitchen. I know she places my bowls in it periodically and when they are removed, they are clean. Maybe it is some sort of magic cleaner. Maybe the magic has left as it doesn't seem to work anymore. My human washed my bowl in the sink today, so I'm happy. The sunlight coming in through my window enticed me to stretch out and doze for a while.

Later that day, a knock on the front door revealed a man carrying a bag. My female human led him into the kitchen, and I followed. She talked to the man and used her finger to point at the magic cleaner. The man nodded his head several times in acknowledgment. Maybe he understood more than he let on. After a few minutes of this, the man fiddled with the knobs and buttons. Maybe he didn't believe what my female human said.

In the man's bag was a computer which he worked on for a while. He then went out to his truck and retrieved a small box. After using his tools on the magic cleaner, he opened the box and took something out. I couldn't see what it was as his body blocked my view. He continued to fuss around on his knees trying to reach under the machine. This was getting boring, so I checked on the baby.

The baby was in its own little machine. It was round with wheels on it, and the baby could push itself about. These movements were sometimes fast and erratic. I had to keep my wits about me when I strode past. One time, the wheels ran over my paw and it hurt. This gave me an added incentive to stay clear of this device. There were several noise makers on the machine the baby could push, pull, or hit. I noticed my female human sometimes flipped a little-hidden switch which silenced these little annoying sounds. Today was not one of those days. The baby knew which buttons to push to make the most annoying sounds, and it was more than I could take. Whatever happened to peace and quiet?

I heard the man yell in the kitchen and I ran to investigate. The man was sitting on the floor shaking his hand. I think he somehow hurt it. He then stuck his hand under the magic cleaner and then yanked it out fast. This time he gripped his two hands together. He was muttering something softly, but I did not recognize the words. From the tone, I didn't think they were happy words. Maybe there was some magic still in this device, and it would not let this man touch it.

I noticed he had brushed dust and dirt out from under the device into a small pile. In the middle, I spotted a Lego piece. I wondered if it was the missing piece that would make the leaning tower stand up straight. When the man left to go out to the truck again, I pulled the Lego piece out. I swatted it over towards the table where I knew my humans would find it.

When the man returned, he carried another box. He opened this box and began fiddling with the magic cleaner again. From the way he jumped before, I knew to stay away. I went to check on the baby again.

The baby had played and ate an afternoon snack. Now it was time for a restful couple of hours. I decided the nursery window, where the sun was shining in, would be a good place to hang out.

I heard a big clang in the kitchen and followed my female human. The man was finishing up with the magic cleaner. While he was talking to my human, I walked over and sniffed the machine. It was humming, and I wondered if it was trying to purr. It must have gotten its magic back. Maybe the boxes had magic in them, and that is what the man pushed and poked into the machine. The man left, and it was peaceful once again.

That evening, the baby crawled around and headed towards the kitchen table. I remembered the Lego I had retrieved from the pile of dust and knew the baby would try to eat it. Once in the mouth, it might become stuck. I raced to beat the baby to the Lego and reached in time to swat it away. The baby crawled after it like it was a game. I guess the old leaning tower would have to continue to lean as I swatted the Lego back under the magic cleaner. It probably would never be seen again. It's a lot of work keeping the baby safe. I led the baby back into the big room by swishing my beautiful tail back and forth. I then jumped up into the lap of my female human who petted me. The purr motor, like the magic cleaner machine, hummed.

Tale 45 - Grandma

My breakfast was on time. I think I have trained my humans rather well. I'm still working on the baby. A knock on the front door interrupted my rest and relaxation in the windowed sunlight. My female human came running and opened the door. There was a lot of excitement and hugging taking place. My male human came into the room and repeated this routine. I was glad this doesn't happen to me when my humans come home each day. I think they would squeeze me to death.

My female human left for a few minutes and returned with the baby. The hugging routine continued. They called the visitor Grandma several times. My male human carried a big suitcase in from the porch and rolled it to the guest room. I think she will stay for a while as there was a second suitcase that followed the first. I remembered a smelly old man visited once, and I enjoyed playing in his suitcase. Maybe I will have the same opportunity again.

There was talk going on constantly. I couldn't follow what was being said, but at one point, my female human pointed at me, and I heard my name, Thomas, repeated several times. Thinking this was a cue for me, I paraded around showing off my royal body. The alternative was to find another place to hang out at, but I stuck around to see what other surprises were in store.

After a while, I wandered over towards Grandma and gave her an opportunity to stroke my sleek black fur. I even flipped my tail a few times to gain her attention. She couldn't resist touching my beautiful black fur. A gentle hand reached down and stroked my back. I even had a little rub around my ears. I think I can accept this human into my home for a while.

There was more talking, and I found this to be dull. I went to the front window and looked out. I was in time to stare down that pesky guy who brought the bills. He was wearing a shirt with the big bird on it again. Once he put the bills in the box outside, he left. He must have known he was being watched by me. My male human opened the door. He was too late as I had already chased the guy away. My male human retrieved the bills along with a small package left by the big bird man.

I noticed the bills were once again tossed onto a small desk where bills from previous days were stacked. My male human stared at the package for a few moments before opening it. Some paper from the package fell to the floor. I crept up and pounced on this and performed a roll at the same time. I was keeping the paper in the air as my paws batted it around. When I heard my human laugh, I stopped. Maybe he found something funny, and I didn't want to miss out.

He said, "Thomas, I didn't know you liked paper that much."

He then dropped the rest of the package wrappings on the floor as my female human walked in. I ignored these as she gave him the eye. He sheepishly bent down and picked them all up.

She then asked, "Honey, what's in the box?"

I had been wondering the same thing myself. The floor was a poor vantage point to watch all the action, so I jumped up onto the desk to get a better look. The big wad of paper wrappings were in my way, and I gave them a swat, sending them back to the floor. Both humans seemed to think this was funny as they laughed.

He opened the box and revealed a shiny piece of jewelry. My male human said, "I had that old broach cleaned, and the clasp repaired. It has arrived just in time to give it to Grandma for Mother's Day."

The next day, my male human wrapped that same box in pretty paper and gave it to Grandma. She was pleased as she pinned it to her clothes. The baby must have thought it was beautiful too as the little hands kept reaching for it and trying to pull it off. Grandma must understand a lot about babies as she knew to give the baby a little toy to play with instead of the broach.

My female human sat in the rocking chair with the baby. Once the baby fell asleep, my human set the baby in the bed with the bars. Back in the big room, I crawled up next to Grandma. She rubbed my head and ears. I even had my chin rubbed. This felt good, and my purr motor hummed rather smoothly.

Tale 46 - Grandma and the Dog

I was up early checking on the baby and my house. It surprised me that Grandma was up and washing my food and water bowls. She made fast work of filling and setting them down. I didn't even have to give her any subtle hints. Maybe she was trained by another cat. I think we will get along well together.

Grandma opened the back door and said "I think we need some fresh air in here. What do you think Thomas?" I strutted up to the threshold and looked out. The fact she asked for my opinion gave her a couple more brownie points. The sky was blue with some puffy white clouds scattered about. I thought the air smelled good and acknowledged her with a meow.

The sun was shining on the picnic table in the backyard. I took advantage and ran out and jumped on it, stretching out so I could keep the house in sight. The fresh air would have to wait until after my morning snooze.

The entire yard was in full daylight when a sharp bark woke me up. I was on full alert looking around. My priority was to check on the baby, but the back door was closed. At least I knew the dog could not get in there. The dog must have wandered in from the street and was coming around the house into the backyard. The fence in the front should have kept the dog out. Maybe that mailman left the gate open. I would look into that later. Right now, this dog was on my turf, and I was ready for battle.

I watched from my vantage point on the picnic table in the attack position. My front paws had nails extended for a firm grip, and my fur was ready to stand up straight. I can look ferocious when I need to. My tail was down, but the tip twitched from side to side as the dog moved closer. He hadn't seen me yet as his head was moving across the grass sniffing.

I hoped the smelly dog would keep moving and leave my yard. I didn't want the hassle of removing his fur and messing up my yard. While he was still wandering around, I heard the back door open. Grandma must have opened it again for some of this fresh air. Well, it wasn't as fresh as it was earlier with this stinky dog walking around. The dog turned and looked at the door. Maybe it thought it could find something to eat in there. I knew I would have to intervene and show this dog who the king was around here.

I snarled at him to get his attention. He spun around, not expecting to see a dark knight ready to defend his kingdom. At the door, Grandma appeared holding the baby. No way was I going to let this dog come close to the baby. All I knew was the baby, and now Grandma too, needed protection.

With a huge leap, I sprang from the picnic table, and in a moment, I was between grandma and this ugly intruder. My paw was in the air, and I hissed at the dog. He barked and then made a slow approach. I hissed again, but he did not get the message because he moved in closer. I raised my hackles, and my front paw stretched out with the nails extended and swiped at his muzzle. He made a yelping sound, and I knew I had scored. The dog backed up and barked again. I advanced and then stood my ground with my paw raised. The hair on my neck and down my back felt stiff while standing on end. I snarled once more, and he turned and ran towards the trees in the back. My eyes followed him until he was out of sight.

I turned to check on Grandma and the baby. Both had moved back into the house. I went up the steps and into the house. The door was still partly open, and I pushed against it with my strong royal body until it closed. I heard the latch click and now knew the dog could not get in. Grandma said, "Thomas, you are very courageous." I rubbed my body against her leg in acknowledgment.

It felt good to be recognized for deeds done well. I decided I would spend the rest of the day in the nursery window that looks out over the backyard. I will deal another blow to that dog if he ever comes back again. The day passed, and the sun was setting. There were no further signs of the dog. My kingdom was safe for another day.

That evening, Grandma had my dinner ready when I was. I think we will have a harmonious relationship. I found her lap on the sofa and laid down on it. Her gentle hand stroked my lean, sleek body. I couldn't help myself as the purr motor engaged. Then there was a little rub around my ears I leaned into. The purr motor was running at high speed now.

Tale 47 - Grandma and the Kitten

It worried me that pesky dog might come back. He trespassed into my kingdom and threatened my humans. I decided it was time to inspect the neighborhood and check out potential problems. My backyard extends into a wooded area. There are quite a few trees back there, and I have seen a few animals. I remember when another dog chased a skunk back there. He had gotten a snoot full on that romp.

My search started in my backyard, which extends along all the neighbor's homes. Two houses over, I heard a soft sound. The bushes were tall enough for me to drop down and hide. My head peeked above the weeds to make sure it was safe and then approached. I spotted a yellow striped kitten that looked abandoned and was crying. A nearby tree offered a good vantage point, and I climbed up it. I hoped the mother cat would return and find her baby. Maybe that dog had chased her off. Maybe the mother cat led the dog away from her baby and lost her way. Many thoughts raced through my mind. I heard the intermittent cry from the kitten as the day passed. It was time to act.

I advanced again and found the kitten alone. It looked scared and frightened. I reached down and clamped my mouth on the scruff of the kitten's neck. The kitten drooped in a relaxed position as I carried it back to my place. I wasn't sure what would happen next, but I couldn't leave this little one without protection.

I let the kitten down on the back step of my home and let out a big meow. This usually has the desired result of a door opening. In a few moments, the door opened, and Grandma was standing there. After she looked down, she said, "Thomas, what have you brought home? It looks like a little tiger."

Grandma picked up the kitten and took it into the house. She offered it some milk in a bowl, but the kitten did not know how to drink it. Grandma used her finger and dribbled milk into the kitten's mouth. This seemed to work. Grandma then found something that looked like what my humans write with, but different. Grandma filled it, and the kitten sucked on it. I could see the kitten was in good hands, so I left to find a sunny spot.

I worked at cleaning my sleek and handsome body as I had been outside padding through the dirt and weeds. My white paws needed the most work. When I finished grooming myself, I took a little nap. It would be dinner time after my snooze.

My other two humans arrived home for the day, and there was a lot of talking. I heard the word kitten many times. They passed the kitten from one person to another. It was getting a lot of attention. I was not envious as I knew I was still king around these parts. Besides, Grandma had my food ready for me without my needing to remind anyone.

That evening, Grandma made a small box into a bed for the kitten. I figured I had better keep an eye on it to make sure it didn't get into any mischief. A few times in the night, I heard a tiny cry. I gave the kitten a few licks on the top of its head. This seemed to settle it down.

The next day, Grandma repeated the feeding process using that thing filled with milk. The kitten was much more active because of this food and a good night's sleep. This routine continued for two weeks until the kitten could drink out of a bowl. Grandma was a pro at keeping us fed.

I had a companion to play with although I preferred simple peace and quiet. Getting my tail pounced on each time it moved can be annoying. Even when I playfully swatted the kitten away, it returned for more. Sometimes the kitten would curl up next to me and sleep. When I wanted to get away, I escaped by jumping up into one of my windows and relaxed in the sun.

One day, I saw Grandma packing her two big suitcases. I jumped up on the bed to check them out. Grandma must have known I would do this, and she picked me up and said, "Thomas, this is not your playground." She then set me back down on the floor. I knew what the suitcases meant and was hoping she would not leave.

Grandma placed the kitten into a small carrier and set it alongside the two big suitcases by the front door. Grandma picked me up for the last time, gave me a hug and said, "Thomas, I love you. I'll see you again someday. This little kitten will remind me of you. I will call him Tiger."

That evening, the house seemed empty, even though my two humans were there. I curled up into the lap of my female human feeling lonely. While she petted me, my purr motor failed to start. I already missed Grandma and the little Tiger kitten.

Tale 48 - Observations

Without Grandma and Tiger being here, there wasn't much around to keep me busy. After all the extra attention from Grandma and playing with the kitten, life seemed empty. I decided it was time to check out the neighborhood again. When my humans left for work, I tagged along while they went through the door. The female human was busy with the baby and didn't notice me sliding past her when she opened the garage door.

The big tree in the front yard was a great place to start. I could see all around. It was still early, and the activity centered on humans getting in their cars and driving off. A few kids looked like they were walking like zombies, heading off for another gathering. Some were more determined with full backpacks like they were marching off on a hike. As the sun rose higher, I could see other activity. A young man was tossing pieces of paper on the steps of everyone's home. My home had the same treatment, and I watched carefully to make sure he did nothing other than drop the trash on my porch. If he had lingered, I would have needed to scare him off.

Next up was the bird man who was delivering bills to everyone's house. I figured out his pattern and waited him out as he deposited more bills in the box for my humans to fret over. He left peacefully, lucky for him.

Next came the street sweeper. Some pieces of paper the young man was throwing about had blown into the street. They would sweep these up along with leaves and grass trimmings. After he passed, I noticed two small trucks. A guy on one had this long stick with a net at the end. I knew he wasn't the dog catcher as he went straight to the backyard of the neighbor across the street. The other truck had equipment on it they unloaded. Those machines made a lot of noise when they cut the grass. When he was through cutting the grass, he used another noisemaker to blow the trimmings into the street. The lawn man came too late for the street sweeper. The trimmings would now leave a mess until the sweeper man came by again. If the lawn man came earlier, the street would be clean, at least for a while.

Coming down the sidewalk was a woman walking her dog. I was high up the tree, hidden amongst the branches so the dog could not see me. However, the nose of the dog pointed in my direction several times before its owner pulled him along. It was a good thing the dog was on a leash. Otherwise, it might have found trouble if it had come near my tree.

The man with the long stick returned to his truck and left. The man blowing the grass into the street left too. I then saw another female human pushing a stroller with a small child walking with her. When the child ran up near the flowers in my yard, the mother scolded the child and pulled him back to the sidewalk. She was protective of her young, which is how it should be. Who knows, there might have been a vicious cat living here.

My legs hung down over my perch as I catnapped between the comings and goings as the sun moved across the sky. Some morning zombies returned. They seemed more awake now yelling and pushing each other as they moved down the street. A few stopped and waited as they could hear the ice cream truck with its loud sounds a block over. I knew what this meant; they would buy the treats and then throw the papers into the street. I wondered if it would be faster if the street sweeper followed the ice cream truck and the men blowing the grass into the street. That certainly would be more efficient.

I spotted my female human driving up. As she approached our house, the big door opened, and she drove in. I gave myself a big stretch and climbed down from my tree and ran inside the garage. As she bundled up the baby and moved into the house, I scooted in along beside her. I was thirsty from a hot day.

She didn't notice me until I was lapping up the water. She said "My Thomas. You are thirsty. You must have laid in the window's sun all day." Little did she know I had been outside checking out the neighborhood.

That evening, I jumped up into the lap of my male human. He had retrieved the bills from the box in front and was looking through them. I could feel his tension. His hand petted me, and I could tell he was relaxing. I wondered if I should take those bills out of the box and drop them into the street. Then the street sweeper would take them away. With that thought, I started my purr motor.

Tale 49 - The Vet

I wandered around the backyard again exploring my kingdom. It had been a few weeks since I ventured out due to the wet weather. I waited for a nice sunny day before I began my inspection tour. Besides good grooming, I need more exercise, and this was a wonderful day to do just that.

I weaved in and out between the large weeds, listening as I patrolled the back forty. The sun was bright on this cloudless day, and I should find something stirring. Up ahead, I saw movement around some rocks as I approached. A lizard climbed onto a large rock, probably to soak up the heat. If I took two long leaps, I could catch him. I hunched up, ready to spring forward and then jumped. On my first leap, when my front paws landed, there was a painful sting. Something was wrong as my right paw hurt. I rolled over to take the weight off my front leg. My concern for the lizard vanished along with him.

A huge sticker patch surrounded me and one of those large thorns stuck between my toes. When I tried to lick it, the sharp barbs scraped against my tongue. I bit and pulled on it until a part of it broke off. My paw bled a little as I worked more at trying to remove the thorn without luck. I rose and balanced on three legs while holding my front right paw up. My paw throbbed as I limped back to my house. The heat from the sun and the licking of my paw left my mouth dry.

My female human saw me limping up to the door. She pushed open the door, reached down for me and picked me up. She looked at my paw and said, "Thomas, you are hurt. Let me check your paw. We may need to take you to the vet." She inspected my paw, and when she did, the pain increased. I let out a cry and she rushed me to the garage and put me in the carrier. She made another trip back in the house and returned carrying the baby. We were all loaded into the car and away we went. I continued licking my paw, but it didn't seem to help.

We arrived at the vet, and she examined me. She used something to poke at the spot, and I screamed as it hurt so much. The vet said, "It appears something like a sticker has embedded itself between the toes. We will have to sedate Thomas and remove it when he is sleeping."

The last thing I remember before going to sleep was being placed in this large cage for a while. There were other cats in cages around me. None seemed to recognize that I was a king. Then again, I was not looking too regal with my fur all a mess and my paw held in the air. When I awoke sometime later, I was in the same cage, only this time, there was this big bandage wrapped around my front paw. After a few licks, I knew it would not slip off and ignored it for a while. I found I could put weight on it without the pain I had encountered earlier.

Being stuck in the cage, I put the time to good use. I groomed my body the best I could even if the bandaged paw failed to work properly. I needed to show the world that a noble feline was present and it required a regal looking body. The trip into the back forty had caused a lot of little sticky things to cling to my beautiful fur. It took quite some time, but I cleaned myself up. With all this work, I developed a big appetite.

A young human placed a bowl of food in each cage. I waited for my turn, hoping he would deliver my favorite food. Disappointment set in immediately when he placed the bowl in my cage. It was not something I cared to eat. I lapped up the water and then curled up and tried to sleep. The sounds of barking interrupted my relaxation. Cage doors banged opened and closed, perhaps the dogs were complaining about their food too. Then again, what could one say, they're dogs.

The next day, they changed my bandage along with my food bowl. My paw got the better part of the deal. My stomach was growling. Didn't they know a king has a special diet? Later that day, my female human came and picked me up. I wanted to purr, but only a little meow surfaced. The trip home in the carrier was uneventful, except the baby's jabbering was music to my ears. This was a welcomed relief from listening to the dogs barking while at the vet.

When my food was set down at dinner time, I savored it. I ate and relished in delight over the small things in life. That evening, I jumped into my female human's lap and snuggled up to her. My purr motor started up. I was thankful for my injured paw being fixed and my scrumptious food being set before me. The purr motor was in high gear.

Tale 50 - Super Cat

I started a relaxing day in the big room where the sun was warming the carpet. I guess my idea of some natural warmth wasn't a secret. My female human brought the baby in and laid it on the floor next to me. As long as those little fingers don't grab my hair, I'm all right with it. After a few minutes, my female human returned with a blanket for the baby. When she spread it out, it covered both the baby and me.

I relaxed absorbing the warmth from both the blanket and the sun. I then realized I was wearing a magic cape, and I had turned into Super Cat! With a quick turn and a leap, I could catch flies sitting on the ceiling, not that I wanted to though. I raced through the house with lightning speed and checked for anything different. Nothing had changed. My next stop was the tree outside. The window screen slid away and I dropped out the front window and raced up the tree to see if there were any big bad birds there. I was out of luck.

My eyes surveyed the entire front yard to see if any dogs were on the loose. If so, I would chase them away. Today was their lucky day. I then thought about my big backyard. With a huge leap, I moved from the limb of the tree to the edge of the roof. Here I could see all around me. I hadn't been on the roof before. I remembered the day when the cable guy came by. He had climbed up here several times. I couldn't see anything of interest, so I looked out over the backyard.

In the distance, I could see movement in the trees. The shape was fuzzy, too far to see clearly. I moved closer to the back side of the house and stared out. The sun was in my eyes, and it was difficult to focus. I then realized I had super vision and zeroed in on the prey. The animal looked like a dog but had a strange tail that curved upwards. I knew this was a dangerous animal, but then, it was no challenge for Super Cat!

I leaped down from the roof and rushed to the back of my yard. The animal saw me and started its approach. I let out a deep growl, one I had never heard before. My ferocious roar made the animal stop and look at me again. Under my cape, my hackles stood up, almost making the cape wave. My claws looked like daggers. Another deep growl, this one even louder than the one before. I took a step towards the animal, and it turned and ran. Chalk another one up for Super Cat.

I then felt my magic cape coming loose. Without it, all my magic powers would disappear. I turned, trying to see what was causing this CAT-tastrophe. I awoke and found the baby rolling over and pulling the blanket away. The dream was so real, but now I was back in the big room and all my superpowers faded away.

The baby was crawling around, and I needed to provide ordinary protective services once again. I scanned the room, but I had lost my super vision. The baby moved toward a pencil that had fallen on the floor. The race was on, but not with the lightning speed of Super Cat. I tried letting out a warning growl, but all I could muster was a little whimper of a meow. As the baby reached out, my mouth clamped onto the pencil as I flashed by. With the pencil in tow, I leaped onto the desk and dropped it. Looking down, I saw the disappointment in the baby's face.

It was nearing dinner time and I was hungry from working up an appetite protecting my kingdom and my humans. My female human opened a can of my favorite food and set the bowl down for me. It was a feast for a king.

That evening, I wanted to snuggle up to the baby. Maybe the magic cape would cover me again, and I could extend my adventures. I climbed into the big cage with the baby and curled up. When my female human came in, she covered the baby and picked me up. I lost my chance to be a Super Cat again.

Together, we returned to the big room, and they held me while she talked to my male human. The company felt good, and I dozed. Super Cat was in my dreams, and the purr motor was working overtime. This time, I was being rewarded with kudos from all my fans. They had heard about my accomplishments throughout the kingdom.

Tale 51 - Cat Show - The Leash

I was relaxing in my window enjoying the morning sun when someone knocked on the door. My female human answered the door and chatted with the visitor. I think she called this person Sally. She has been over several times and always gave me some attention. I didn't want to look like I was begging for it, so I played it cool and waited my turn.

While Sally and my female human were talking, I heard several words repeated many times, including my name, Thomas. Something was being said about how good I looked. Naturally, being a king with a royal body is recognizable by many. Sally came over and paid homage with gentle strokes over my head and down my back. The window was the right width for me to stretch out and enjoy this appreciation.

I then heard the word leash several times. I did not know what that was but was to find out soon. Sally took my lightweight collar off and put a heavy collar on me, which didn't feel good. She then attached a long cord to the collar. I had about met my limit on this new collar and jumped down to leave the room. As I did so, I felt a quick pull on my neck. I spun around and tried to pull my head out of the collar. Sally was talking with my female human during this time, but I concentrated on pulling my head out of this noose. I stopped fighting it and laid down to catch my breath and analyze the situation.

Sally was holding the end of the leash and was lightly pulling on it. I had already sunk my nails into the carpet, and the tugging on the leash was stretching my neck. My female human came over and picked me up, hugged and then petted me down my back. She said, "It's okay Thomas. Sally wants to teach you to walk on a leash." She then set me back down on the floor.

Sally pulled the leash and I extended my nails into the carpet once again. It was a standoff of sorts. Sally then let go of her end of the leash. The tension on my neck eased. I waited a few moments and then backed off a little. The leash trailed behind me.

I thought maybe if I tried running, this collar and leash would fall off. So that is what I did, I ran out of the room, down the hall and into the bedroom. I crawled under the bed and then ran back out to the hall and into the nursery. The leash followed me wherever I ran. Maybe the baby could help me get rid of this thing. I circled under the crib, and the leash caught on one leg of the crib. This stopped me real fast, but not without jerking the crib at the same time. It was enough to wake the baby, and the crying started.

My female human came running into the room, but instead of helping me, she picked the baby up and walked out of the room patting the baby's back and making soothing sounds. Sally came in and petted me and then unhooked the leash. I rushed out of the room. I did not need this torture treatment.

My female human was sitting on her bed, and I crawled under it. This has always been my safe zone. I then saw and heard Sally come into the room. She said, "We need to train Thomas with a leash if we're to take him to the cat show."

My female human said, "Well, you just saw how that worked out. Thomas is independent and putting a leash on him would be like putting chains on you or me. Thomas will probably keep away from you now. You need to make it up to him."

Sally called my name several times, but I did not move. If she thought I would come out after being tied up, she had another thought coming. They both left the room, and I napped, secure in the thought it was safe being under the bed.

Most of the day had passed, and I was feeling a rumble in my stomach. I ventured into the kitchen to see if my food was ready. Sally stood there with my food bowl. I waited for her to set it down as I looked around to see if the leash was anywhere close. As she bent down, I backed up, giving her plenty of space. I then let her back away before I approached my food bowl. With a wary eye, I ate.

That evening, after Sally had left, I jumped up into the lap of my female human. I rubbed the collar against her several times until she took the hint to remove it. She then massaged my neck and gave me gentle strokes down my backside. Things seemed to be back to normal. The purr motor started up and created a pleasing sound.

Tale 52 - Cat Show - The Walk

The next day, Sally came back. I hoped she had forgotten about the torture device she called a leash. Instead, my female human and she teamed up and put that hard collar and leash on me again. I was ready. My nails extended into the carpet and I prepared for battle. However, Sally picked me up, and we all went out to the front porch where a cement walkway extended out to the sidewalk. She set me back down, and she then pulled the leash. I extended my nails, but the hard surface prevented me from holding on. The cement acted as a nail file as she dragged me along.

After a foot or two, they would stop, call me, and then pull again. I would take a step or two to release the tension on the leash, but they would then pull it again. I realized if I kept moving, the tension would lessen. Maybe I could beat them at this game, so I ran in front of them and tried to pull them along. While I am strong, they were stronger and I had to walk at their pace.

It took a while for me to get used to this as the stress levels peaked. As we walked, I noticed other things. I was outside the house walking on the sidewalk. This is the same sidewalk where I see those smelly dogs walk by on their leashes. It is also the same place all those pesky kids throw their papers. We stood in front of my house, so I held my head up high to show pride. Both Sally and my female human seemed to praise me, but I was breathing hard. We then went back into the house, and Sally released me. I headed for the window to cool off and take a nap.

That afternoon, we repeated the whole process. It took a few steps for me to go along with this, but I managed. When we finished, Sally brought out a brush and groomed me. I can manage this process myself, but the brush felt good, and she talked to me all the while. The nail trimmers were another story. I didn't like that, but my nails were in bad shape after being dragged across the cement several times. I relented as both humans held me and trimmed the nails. My majestic good looks were shining.

Next, Sally pulled out a royal collar and placed it on my neck. I know this because of the diamonds and rubies embedded in the leather. A new lightweight leash was then hooked up to this. We paraded around the living room, showing off my new shiny collar. I held my head and tail up high.

The two women were chatting about how good I looked. It felt great being recognized for my stature, beauty, and brains. Another quick walk outside and I could strut my stuff to the great outdoors. If there were any other cats around, they would have to bow down.

Sally set my food out that evening. While she was training me with the leash, somehow, she received training on timely nutritional requirements. While I didn't particularly like the leash part, I guess it was in trade for the food. I was glad when she left.

After a long day, my female's lap looked inviting and I curled up in it. She said, "Thomas, Sally will take you to a cat show. I know you will do well. You are so smart and beautiful."

I listened to all this, but I did not understand where the cat show would be held. Maybe I would have to ride in my carrier again. I prefer to just look out my window and watch the cats and dogs parade up and down the street. Why do I have to go somewhere to watch other cats?

My human continued petting me with long strokes. The extra brushing had made my coat silky smooth. The purr motor was engaged, and I was along for the ride.

Tale 53 - Cat Show - The Show

I won't say Sally is a pest, but she kept coming back every day. There was this routine. She would put out my food and water, and after I ate, she put the leash on me. We then walked up and down the sidewalk in front of my home. I held my head high as I strutted along.

Today was different. Sally put out these little fences and encouraged me to jump over them. I was feeling like a trained monkey. However, my regular feedings, along with the special treats, had caused me to gain weight. I knew this little exercise routine would help me maintain my noble looks. It was easy for me to do a little jump and clear each fence. She then raised these to a higher level, and we performed the routine again. My light-footedness allowed me to clear each one without even a hair touching the barriers.

After several days of this, Sally told me, "Thomas, you are such a smart and agile cat. I think you're ready for the cat show."

The next day, Sally set me in my carrier and drove to a place I hadn't been to before. There were big tents and tables all around. I could smell and sense many other cats around. She set my carrier on a table, and I could see other carriers with cats in them on other tables. I wondered if this was the cat show, if so, I was ready to return home.

Sally was gentle as she attached the leash and set me on the table. She brushed me until my coat glistened. I relaxed as I was used to this daily grooming. She then pulled out some kind of special treat. The aroma blocked out all my senses. It smelled tantalizing, not like my normal food. It was just a nibble, but it tasted delicious. I ignored everything else around me as I savored the morsel.

I was then carried into another tent. People were sitting on benches, surrounding a huge ring. A few people with cats were lining up in the center. Sally and I joined this group. One by one, each person set their cat on a small table, and a big man came over and inspected them. When it was almost our turn, Sally waved another one of those fragrant morsels under my nose. I felt hypnotized as I sat on the table. The man ran his hand over my back and up my straight tail. When he wanted to look into my mouth, I resisted. Sally showed me the treat and I opened wide. When the man finished, she gave me the morsel.

She then set me on the green carpet and we walked away from the table. I was glad to move away from the man. We strolled down the carpeted runway. At the end, we turned around, and I saw a series of little fences Sally wanted me to jump over. I hesitated for only a moment until I saw that Sally had another treat. I cleared these fences so fast that Sally had to run to keep up with me. We then returned to the group in the center of the tent. Sally then gave me the morsel I had been waiting for since the fence jump.

We left the big tent and returned to the table where my carrier was setting. Sally was jabbering away as she brushed me down again. Between the extra grooming and these wonderful treats, I knew someone had recognized the royal blood I carried.

I thought everything was over, but I was wrong. Sally carried me back into the big tent where some people lined up again with their cats. We were all set on the floor, and we paraded around in a big circle. The man that had looked into my mouth was there and watched us closely. I kept my eye on him as I strutted with my tail high in the air. I didn't even let it twitch.

After completing a big circle, the man pointed to an orange striped tabby, a long-haired gray cat, and me. The three of us lined up near a judging stand. The man presented a ribbon to each person. There was a lot of noise from the people sitting around the tent. I wanted to get out of there. Sally must have realized this as she picked me up, gave me a big hug and walked out of the tent.

I was glad to be back home where it was quiet. That night, as I curled up in my female human's lap, she told me. "Thomas, you took first place in the show today. You really are a king." The purr motor was in high gear as she stroked my back and gave me a little rub under my chin.

Tale 54 - Ride Along

I knew something was up. There had been a lot of activity around the house the last couple of days. This morning, I saw the suitcases being packed. I didn't pay it too much attention as I was soaking up some early morning sun while lying in the front window. What struck me as strange was they loaded a lot of stuff from the nursery into the car. I should have realized a road trip was on the agenda.

The house was quiet as my male human came into the room and picked me up. He then closed my window and locked it. I was then carried out to the car where he had placed my carrier. I sat next to the baby and could see everything. The baby has grown, and occasionally one of those long legs seemed to wrap around the car seat and bang against the carrier. That wasn't so good, but there wasn't much I could do about it.

My humans talked about tenting the house. That was something new. I thought a tent was something you slept under when outside. They spoke the word termites several times. Seems somehow, they related the two words. Maybe they would give the termites a tent to sleep under.

The steady motion of the car rocked me to sleep. I seem to do a lot of sleeping while riding in the car. I don't know why except there isn't much else to do. Sleeping is something I do a lot of during the day.

My nightly patrol duty has me up several times a night to check on the baby and the rest of the house. When the baby is quiet during the night, I complete the checks quickly and return to my warm bed. My patrol duty keeps everyone safe. In the mornings, I nap in the window, and for my afternoon nap, I lie on the floor in the nursery where the sun shines. Although, with the baby now walking around, I have to be careful to avoid the unsteady steps taken around me.

When the car stopped, there was a lot of commotion as my humans carried things into a room from the car. I heard the word motel a few times. I was still in the carrier until my male human hauled it inside. He set the carrier on a table while they finished unloading the bags. An array of strange smells hit me, some not too pleasant. I hoped we would not stay here too long. Once the room door was closed, my human opened the carrier door, and I stepped out onto the table. I hoped there weren't any termites here, but I didn't know what they looked like.

My female human assembled the jail the baby sleeps in. I was thinking it might make a safe place to rest while my humans were racing about unpacking suitcases and other stuff. When the baby was corralled inside, I looked for another place to avoid all the traffic. I checked out the underside of the bed, but it was blocked off. The bed pillows looked to be out of the way of traffic, and I laid down there. I could see all around the room.

There was one big window, but the edge was too small to fit on, and there was a big noisemaker blowing cold air underneath it. The combination was not one I wanted to venture over to. I like a small breeze, but the machine was like a windstorm coupled with heavy vibrations and noises.

After a while, my stomach grumbled which reminded me I was due for a meal. The humans had stopped along the way and picked up food. The baby seemed to like the little pieces of chicken followed by a cup of milk. Actually, the chicken and milk sounded kind of good right now.

I let out a small meow to let everyone know I was still here. That triggered my female human to say, "Thomas, I bet you're hungry!" Yes, I trained my humans adequately, but they still need reminders.

She unloaded my bowls from a box along with a can of one of my favorite foods. I think there must be chicken in it too. She set my water and food bowls down in the bathroom. I wasn't too happy about that, but when there are only two rooms, there wasn't much choice. I slowly wandered over to my food bowl so my humans wouldn't think I totally depended on them.

That night, after my female human laid the baby down to sleep, I curled up to my humans in the middle of the bed. Their warmth compensated for the wind tunnel created by the noisemaker. My humans were taking turns stroking my sleek body. They were talking quietly to avoid waking the baby. I stretched to have my chin rubbed. Lying there, I guessed I was along for the ride but enjoyed their company and hands that ran over my head. The purr motor was engaged.

Tale 55 - Tiger Visits

The house was being cleaned. I know because the big noise maker was being pushed all around the house. There wasn't a safe place for me to hide except in my front window which I was occupying. It seemed every time they used the noisemaker, we would have more humans come to invade my home.

It surprised me to find out Grandma was coming. She is a loving human. My humans greeted her at the door. It was another surprise to see her holding a cat carrier. I couldn't believe it. Tiger, the little kitten I rescued from the wilderness area behind my home, was in the carrier. When Grandma opened the little carrier door, Tiger strolled out. I hardly recognized him. He was a little taller than me and longer too. I let out a meow in recognition, and he responded with a deep meow. Obviously, Grandma had been feeding him so well he grew out of that little kitten body.

I'm not much into toys but remembered Tiger liked to play with the little red mouse. Now, where was that toy? My humans kept a few toys in the corner of the bookcase. I ran over there, found the mouse, picked it up and ran back to Tiger and dropped it in front of him. Maybe he had forgotten about it as he wandered around the room as if he had never been here before.

The humans were all taking this in, watching with interest to see what would happen. My female human commented on the mouse and said, "I don't think anyone has played with the toy mouse since Tiger was here last."

Grandma said, "I think they need time together. Tiger hasn't been around any other cats since being with Thomas."

Tiger walked into the kitchen and sniffed my bowls. He stuck his paw in the water and then shook it, shaking drops all around. I couldn't figure it out, maybe he was checking to see if it was hot or not. He repeated this a few times before he bent down and lapped up the water. It was almost like he was in a foggy daze, trying to find his way around. He then wandered around exploring other rooms. I waited Tiger out and went back to my window perch where I could observe him.

I had been dozing for a while, and my tail must have drooped down within easy reach from the floor. Tiger found it an easy target to attack which brought me quickly out of my sleep. Tiger was on the floor looking up at me. If I didn't know better, I would say he had a mischievous smirk on his face. I jumped down, and as I did so, Tiger threw his front legs around my neck. I rolled, and my paws came up under Tiger's body, and I pushed him away. We then chased each other through the house, under the bed, around the kitchen, and back to the big room. My playful Tiger friend was back, quicker than ever.

While he went for a drink of water, I hid on one of the bookcase's shelves. When Tiger came back into the room, I sprang from the alcove and landed next to Tiger knocking him over. Then I ran, and he chased after me. We continued this play for most of the day.

The humans had fixed a big meal, I know because there was a lot of heat coming from the oven. That is a rarity here as most of the food seems to come from boxes they bring home or boxes they pull out of the cold storage. It smelled good, maybe some chicken was being baked.

When they all had finished their meal, Grandma called both Tiger and me to the kitchen back door. She asked, "Have you two been good little kitties? I have something special for you." With that, she opened the kitchen door to the backyard and set down a large chicken bone for each of us.

I remembered when I had to scrounge for food and chicken bones were a delicacy. The smell brought back a lot of memories of my younger days. It made me grateful I had my own home and two humans to bring me food every day. I saw Tiger pick his bone up and turn his back. I then went to work on my bone.

After that special treat, Grandma prepared to leave. She gave me a big hug and rubbed under my chin. I licked her hand. Grandma placed Tiger in his carrier and waved goodbye as she drove away.

That evening, I laid in the laps of my two humans sitting on the sofa. Tiger tired me out from all the running around. My humans were giving me a slow petting, and my purr motor was running. I was so relaxed, I fell into a deep sleep.

Tale 56 - A Day of Terror

If I had only known what the day would bring, I would have hidden under the bed the entire time. On most days, the sun shines, and sometimes there are dark clouds. Today, we had the dark clouds, and I wasn't enjoying my window as much as usual. I decided it was a good day to check out my yard and see what the birds were up to.

I sat by the back door until my human opened it and then I walked out to the porch. There was a slight breeze in the cool air, but my beautiful fur coat kept me warm. The big tree in the front yard was my destination. There are lots of limbs to crawl out on to get a view in every direction. My sharp claws made simple work of climbing as I raced up the tree. The first big branch allowed a view of my home, and everything seemed normal. I went up high to another branch, and I could see across the street.

A sudden gust of wind swept through, and I could feel the big tree sway. It was over in an instant, but my claws were dug in for safety. I could hear a loud noise from the house across the way. Something big on their roof was swaying. The skies had darkened, so much so I thought it was nighttime. The black clouds hid the sun, and a chill blew in with the wind.

Another big blast came through, and I felt my tree bend way over before snapping back. Then it happened again. I was near the top and felt like I was being shaken like the way I used to shake mice. This was bad, and I didn't dare try to move for fear of being thrown out of the tree. And then the rain started.

My furry black coat collected water, soaking me, and making me shiver. I didn't think this outing could get any worse when lightning lit up the sky. For a moment, it outlined everything around me in a dark gray and then fizzled to blackness. The wind, the rain, and now lightning. I was cold, wet, and feeling hunger pangs. My house was not far away if I could only climb down without being slingshotted across the yard.

Another huge gust of wind grabbed the tree and bent it way over. I could see the roof of the house come close and then the tree would spring back, nearly tossing me from my perch. My claws were getting tired from hanging on so tight. Again, the wind bent the tree over, and I felt I might jump to the roof, but it was too dangerous to let go, even for an instant. My paws seemed frozen and they were unwilling to let go. They were stiff, sore and wet. It was all I could do to cling to the big branch.

This seemed to go on for a long time. I was dizzy from the constant swaying of the tree. That big noisy thing on the neighbor's roof tore loose and flew away. All the trash thrown in the gutter along with other papers were flying about in big circles. Lightning strikes were coming so fast I didn't need the sunlight to see. The storm scared me and I hoped I could get back inside my house soon.

The wind attacked my tree again, bending it way over. I heard a crack and thought it was the lightning making more sounds, but the tree shuddered as it bent way over. The wind kept attacking, and the tree curved over in an awkward position. My branch was now pointing down, and I was still high in the air. The tree was still shaking as it bent even further. This time, the crack was even louder, and I could feel the tree losing the battle. The ground came up fast, and still, my claws remained clamped to the branch.

The tree went down, and to my surprise, the end of my branch was touching the ground. I scampered down the branch and then dashed off. My female human must have heard the cracking and opened the front door to see what caused it. I saw the door open and rushed inside.

My female human picked me up and said, "Thomas, what were you doing outside in the storm? You're all wet. Let me dry you off." The towel felt good as it absorbed the water from my coat. I could only provide a small muffled sound of thanks.

After my coat dried and my appetite satisfied, I curled up into the lap of my female human to thank her. I turned on the purr motor even without having a hand petting me. I was thankful for not being out in the storm for even a minute longer.

Tale 57 - A Winter Holiday

My humans were all bundled up. There were so many clothes on the baby it restricted all movement. All three humans left the house, and I was free to enjoy the quiet. When they returned, they brought with them a big tree with pine needles. I remembered they did this last year and knew to stay away for a while. It was nap time for the baby, and the nursery was a good place to hang out.

I soaked up the afternoon sun and rested my bones. When the baby got up, I did the same. The baby headed for the big room where the tree stood. You could see the baby's eyes grow big looking at the tree decorated in bright colored balls and shiny garland. The lights made the entire tree glisten.

I watched as the baby grabbed for one of the shiny ornaments on the tree. My female human was fast and stopped that. The baby turned and found another ball and hung on. The whole tree wobbled for a moment before the hand released it. There were lots of giggles coming from the baby. I knew my humans would be very busy this year teaching the little one not to pull on the tree or any of the ornaments.

The toy with wheels on it distracted the baby. The baby could push the toy back and forth, and sometimes it would slide across the room. It looked like a little car. I had to have a watchful eye when the baby plays with toys like this. The baby made some of these small toys fly, and I would have to jump to avoid them. One time, my tail was in the wrong place when the baby pushed a big toy over it. Wow, did I ever let out a loud and long meow.

My humans placed some colorful boxes under the tree with curly ribbons draped around them. When the humans went into the kitchen to eat, I checked these ribbons out. One red curly ribbon hung down the side of a box. I swatted it twice and watched how it swung from side to side and bounced up and down. This was entertaining, and I did it a few more times.

The box was under one ball that hung from the tree. I gave it a swat and watched it swing from side to side. These were all great play toys I would have to come back to as I heard my female human say from the kitchen, "Thomas, it's dinner time."

After dinner, the baby was running around in the big room a
female human was busy keeping the baby's hands from pull

the tree. I watched the ball at the bottom swing back and forth and couldn't resist from running over and giving it a swat.

My female human didn't think it was funny and looked at me while saying something. I retreated with my tail high in the air. My tail attracted the baby, and I could hear the quick steps behind me, and I knew I was being chased. I walked with dignity but had to increase my pace. The baby has figured out this walking and running activity, and I have to be quicker than ever before. I held my head high as I strode out of the room and turned a corner, moving out of sight. I then ran for one of the kitchen chairs and hid on the seat of one, out of sight. The baby came around the corner looking, but couldn't see me. This hideout worked once again.

While my humans were preparing for bed, I checked out the tree again. That big colorful ball hanging at the bottom was so enticing, I had to play with it again. A quick little swat started it swaying. This only goaded me to give it a bigger swat, and it flew off the tree and across the floor where it rolled along. I chased after it and tumbled over it. I picked the ball up between my paws, and rolled over and then twirled it around in the air. It was the most fun I had in a long time. I was getting tired and gave the ball one last bat. It flew across the room, landing in the tree.

I headed off to find my humans in bed under the warm and comfortable covers. They were talking about the decorated tree and how much fun the holidays can bring. I had to agree with the fun part. The pretty ribbons and the colorful balls are fun to play with.

At the end of the bed, I found a spot and laid down. I was thinking about all the new toys hanging on the tree. I needed to reward my humans for bringing me these presents, so I started my purr motor and settled in for a grateful night.

Tale 58 - Home Alone

I was up early and waiting for the morning sun to warm me up. The house seemed colder than usual. Yesterday, my humans were very busy moving stuff out to the car. I assumed they would place me in my carrier and take me along. Nope, this seemed like a rush job. After they drove off, I thought maybe they forgot about me. Then again, they leave most days and return by evening. Meanwhile, I had the house to myself.

I wasn't too concerned until dinner time, and there wasn't anyone around. I checked my bowl, and they filled it with these dry crunchy bits that tasted like cardboard. My stomach was growling, so I ate a few to keep the noise level down.

The next day, while looking out the window, I was hoping to see my humans return and provide me with a feast. The sun rose to the mid-day height and still no food. Maybe my humans were trying to give me a hint it was time to move on. The rumbling in my stomach proved too much for me, and I ate a few more pieces of cardboard.

That evening, I heard a key in the door, and a stranger entered. I hid by the bookcase so I could scope things out. The person looked young and carried a backpack which he dropped by the front door. The person called out, "Thomas. Thomas. Where are you?"

I guess they weren't a complete stranger if they knew my name. The person went into the kitchen, and I heard the can opener. Afterward, I could smell my favorite aroma whiffing through the air. I couldn't resist and strode into the kitchen with my nose and tail high in the air. The person scraped the food from the can into my bowl and set it down. While I was savoring each bite, he cleaned and filled my water bowl.

After licking the last remnants from around my mouth, I went to find this young person and thank him. I found the person, along with the backpack, on the sofa reading from a book. When I felt safe to do so, I hopped up on the sofa. He kept reading his book as I walked over to his lap and laid down. A hand reached out and stroked the top of my head and down my back. It felt good, and I turned on the purr motor for this welcomed petting.

He turned the pages every so often, and I dropped into a slumber, warm in his lap. I guess he finished, as I woke up when he moved me onto the sofa cushion. I watched him pick the backpack up and place the books inside. The person turned off the lights and left. It was now dark both inside and outside. It was so quiet, if a mouse had run across the carpet, I would have heard him.

My eyesight allows me to see in the dark. I prowled around, checking the bedroom and the nursery for any people. While I like it quiet, this was spooky. The bedroom bedcovers provided a comfortable place, and I curled up for the night. I still had this strange feeling, I think they call it loneliness.

The next morning, I found the bowl with the wood chips in it and ignored it. Maybe that young man will come back and work his magic with the can opener again. I waited in the window.

The man in the blue shirt with a big bird on it brought more bills. I could see the box he put them in still stuffed with the ones from yesterday. From my window, I hunched my shoulders and stood my ground, but he turned away after leaving more bills. I thought maybe I would slide out my window and shred all that paper, but decided against it.

Since the big tree in the front yard fell down in the storm, there is more sun in my window. The big birds don't come around anymore either. I guess I scared them all away. My humans planted a new tree in place of the old one. It is too small for me to climb, but the little birds seem to like it. They sit on the branches and chirp to each other.

My stomach was deciding which rock band to mimic, one with a lot of drums. The evening was approaching, and I was hard-pressed to figure out what to do about the food when I heard the garage door. My humans had returned!

They came in and out several times carrying stuff from the car. They held the baby's hand while taking short steps. Once inside, the baby raced over. I think I must have been in a stupor as I did not jump out of the way in time. The baby grabbed me around the middle and held the grip tight for a few minutes.

My female human came into the kitchen and looked at my bowl filled with these tasteless brown chips. She said, "Thomas, it looks like you don't like crunchies very much." She then picked up the bowl, dumped the contents and then made the can opener sing my favorite tune.

That night, I curled up on the warm blankets between my two humans and gave thanks with my purr motor for being there and providing for me.

Tale 59 - Looking Pretty

It was early morning, and I laid in the front window basking in the sun when I heard my humans rustling about. On schedule, they filled my food bowl, and I ate my fill. My female human had left the kitchen, so I went to investigate. She is constantly doing something, and it can be entertaining.

I found the baby in the bathroom doorway watching my female human doing something to her hair in the bathroom. I jumped on the bed so I could watch too. She brushed a part of her hair, squeezed liquid from a bottle onto it, and then wrapped the hair in foil. She must have done this several times because all the foil sticking out made her look like an antenna or maybe an alien. I could see why the baby was so engrossed.

I heard a familiar ring come from the other room. It must be a magical sound like the pied piper because this makes her drop everything and rush to the little talk box. The same thing happened now as she hurried out of the bathroom, through the bedroom, and down the hall. That ring must have also been the starting bell for the baby too.

The baby wanted to see what the mother had been doing with all that smelly stuff she was putting on her head. Standing on the toes, the baby can just reach about everything on the bathroom counter. I knew this was a dangerous situation and unless I intervened, it could spell dire circumstances for the baby.

I dropped from the bed and rushed to the bathroom where I leaped up onto the counter. The baby was already pulling a jar towards her by the hose and bulb attached. The baby squeezed the bulb, and I got a nose full of a very strong odor. It made me sneeze and blink my eyes. My reaction made the baby laugh as there was loud high-pitched laughter echoing in the small room.

I reached out and tried pulling the little jar back from the edge. The baby gave the bulb another squeeze. I turned my head enough to avoid another snoot full. Seeing how I didn't react the same way, the baby's interest changed, and the little hand reached for something else. I extended my paw and dragged the jar back from the edge to prevent further danger.

The hand found another squeeze bulb attached to a tube. My front leg and paw held it down while the hand closed its grip. Some stinky stuff squirted out onto my other leg. The mess covered my beautiful black leg with the white boot. I let out a horrendous meow, intended to either scare the baby away or at least alert my female human there was trouble.

The baby giggled while I held on to the tube. I have made loud meows before, such as the time the baby pushed one of the big toys over my tail. Then there were other times when I was being carried, and the baby would hit my head against the door jambs when moving from room to room.

At last, I heard the footsteps of my female human. She saw me on the counter first, and from her expression, I was in trouble. The baby's hand was still gripping the bulb and squeezing it when she spotted the problem. She rushed in and picked up the baby, checking that none of that smelly stuff had dripped down on the baby.

I was about to escape this torture chamber when my female human picked me up. On my face, I had this strong aroma which was creating a fuzzy feeling in my nose. I felt another sneeze coming on. On my leg, was this goop that smelled bad. She said, "Thomas, you need a bath, really quick."

The torture never seems to end sometimes. She brought the baby into the bathroom and closed the door. There was no escape, she trapped me. She pushed all the stuff on the counter back and filled the basin with water. From under the sink, she brought another container of some smelly stuff out. My female human pushed me into the sink and tried to drown me. As if I hadn't had enough stuff sprayed and splattered on me, I had more dropped on me from this new container.

At first, this was agony, but my female human seemed to understand and took extra care on my face and then additional scrubbing on my leg, still soaked and stinking from the goo. She held me in the sink when I tried to escape. The baby must have thought this was funny too as I heard more laughter as soap bubbles surrounded me.

When dry, I saw discoloration on my black fur along my front leg. It looked like my white boot was growing up my leg. I didn't like it and shook it, hoping it would go away.

That evening, I was lying across the laps of my two humans and heard my female human say, "Thomas was a hero today. He kept the hair chemicals from falling into the baby's hands." Maybe that is why I was getting extra petting. Regardless, my purr motor was in high gear.

Tale 60 - Office Life

After eating breakfast, I noticed the routine of everyone rushing about. There were several trips in and out of the garage, and I followed my male human before the door closed, to see what the fuss was all about. He had started the car and then rushed back into the house one more time.

I jumped into the car and sniffed around. I checked the back seat. There didn't seem to be anything special since my last trip in the carrier. I was about to leave when my male human came rushing back, jumped in the car and backed out. The car's rolling from side to side tossed me around with a series of quick turns, and then everything seemed to settle down. The gentle vibration and swaying rocked me to sleep.

I must have dozed off as sudden braking threw me off the back seat and onto the floor. I let out a big meow in protest of this treatment. A moment later, my male human looked back at me and said, "Thomas, what are you doing here?"

I could tell by the tone of his voice he was unhappy. After more turns and bumps, we stopped. He said, "Thomas, I can't leave you in the car. It will be too hot for you. You will just have to come into work with me."

He picked up the baby blanket next to the car seat and wrapped me in it. He carried me past a lot of cars and into a big building. We then crowded into a small room and the door closed. Being this close to so many people made me think of sardines in a can. The room moved upward, and I felt a strange feeling like being pushed down on the ground. I didn't like it, and when the door opened, I was glad to leave.

We continued down a hallway and through another door. There was the sound of a lot of humans talking, but I couldn't make out what they were saying. There were many smells I was unfamiliar with too. These strange noises and sounds frightened me and was glad my human held me close in the blanket.

Finally, we entered another small room that had windows, and he set me down on a table next to one. He folded the blanket into a square and set it in a box lid, making a perfect bed for me. My male human said, "Thomas, you need to stay here today and not wander off. I'll call home and let them know you're here and get you some water later."

I settled in with the blanket comforting me. It had the smell of the baby along with me. I could also watch my male human busy at his desk. That thing my humans keeps calling a mouse was being wiggled from time to time.

I stared out the window, and while it looked warm outside, I could not feel any heat coming through it. It didn't look like someone could open it either. How were you supposed to enjoy a nice breeze if the window doesn't open, I thought?

Another human came into the room and talked to my human. I tried to ignore this as I was about to doze off. The human saw me and sauntered around the desk and over to where I laid. I could see the hand coming. Bright sparkly baubles hung from her neck and ears. The sun reflected light all around these. I wondered if these were her toys as she patted me. Her hand bounced up and down on top of my head as if my head was a ball. "What a cute cat!" she exclaimed.

Eventually, she walked away and left me dizzy from the patting. Maybe she wanted someone to beat on her head. I closed my eyes again and tried to rest, hoping the sun would warm me. I was curled up trying to stay warm.

My human brought me a small bowl of water, and I lapped some of it up. The room had a dryness to it that made me thirsty. I stretched out with my front legs and let out a quiet yawn and then rearranged myself on the little blanket. I figured I could rest for the remaining part of the day, but that wasn't to be.

Another person came in and walked straight over to my box and stroked my sleek body. I couldn't resist the pleasant strokes, and my tail gave it away. It went up when he stroked my back. He said something about me being majestic and I knew this guy had it right.

My male human packed his briefcase, and I knew the day was over. He once again wrapped me in the blanket and carried me out to the car. The trip home filled me with joy.

That night, I snuggled up to my male human and licked his hand. He earned a big thank you for bringing me back home. The trip answered my curiosity about my human and I won't check the car out again. A little purr was deep in my throat as his hand rubbed my ears.

Tale 61 - Puppy Love

I could tell it was the weekend as my breakfast was late. My humans like to sleep late on the weekends. However, the baby makes for a good alarm clock, so I knew they would feed me.

Today, my female human bundled up the baby and placed it in the push-cart. I had my leash and collar on and assumed we would walk around the neighborhood. I looked forward to these little trips because I can strut and show off my nobility, after all, I'm a king. My male human accompanied us.

We passed a few houses where the dogs made a lot of noise. I know they all wanted to be out and walking free like me. They were just complaining about it.

We approached the little park with the swings. The baby loves to swing back and forth in them. I found this was a great time for me to jump into the push-cart and observe. When the baby tired of the swinging, it was time to run. The baby runs to the end of the fenced park and then turns and comes running back, giggling all the way.

I saw the baby stop near the bushes at the far end and bend over. I couldn't quite see what was happening. My male human ran across the grass to where the baby squatted. He bent down and looked at something. I would have investigated too, but they had tied my leash to the push-cart.

The two of them strolled back. My male human was carrying something that seemed to wiggle in his arms. I then heard the cry of a little puppy. I knew this would be trouble.

My female human petted it, and the baby wanted in on the action too. They ignored me, and I hoped they would put the puppy down and leave, but that was not happening.

We all started back to the house. More dogs barked as we crossed the walkways in front of their houses. Maybe they sensed the puppy was there and was invading their territory.

The puppy was dirty, and my male human found a brush and worked it to get the burrs and dirt out of its fur. It was brown with shaggy fur. My female human poured milk into a bowl and offered it to the puppy who kept drinking until emptying the bowl.

I heard my humans talking about the puppy quite a lot, and I found a tranquil spot in another room. The nursery window was up enough for me to squeeze into and had a little sun to warm me. My eyes closed and I snoozed.

I had forgotten about the puppy when I awoke. When I went to check on everyone, I found the baby playing with the puppy in the big room. How could this day be so turned upside down? This is my home.

The baby seemed to have a good time, and I could observe the dog a little closer. Its shaggy fur had hidden a little collar, on which there was a little silver tag. Its paws were big compared to the rest of him. When he opened his mouth, I could see sharp little teeth. I would have to guard against him biting the baby.

The puppy resembled the big smelly dog that comes into my backyard uninvited. That dog is big and has a mouth with lips that hang down, and it drools a lot. I wondered if this puppy would grow up like him.

I could see the puppy was getting tired. It was moving a lot slower, and the baby was losing interest. It was nap time for the baby, and my female human reached down and picked the baby up and headed for the nursery. The puppy saw me and walked over and laid down next to me.

At first, I wanted to leave, but I held my ground, as this was my house and I'm the king around here. The puppy's eyes took one last look at me and closed. Sleep came quickly. The little furball wanted companionship, so I let him lie.

Both the baby and the puppy ended their naps at about the same time, and the two played again. Then there was a knock on the front door, and my male human went to answer. A child was talking, and I heard the words puppy and lost several times. My male human picked the puppy up and held it out to the little girl at the door. I heard a warm high-pitched thank you and she left.

The sound of the door closing with the puppy gone was music to my ears. I rubbed against the legs of my male human to let him know what a great job he did in getting rid of that dog.

That night, my purr motor worked overtime. I had my house back and family intact. I was in the lap of my female human and had my fur stroked.

Tale 62 - Sick Time

The winter always seems to bring out the worst in humans. Both of my humans slept late, and I didn't get my bowl of nourishment on time. My female human was carrying a box around with tissues hanging out. Every few minutes she would sneeze and pull another tissue from the box. Even the baby seemed to experience a runny nose as my human pulled tissues out to wipe the baby's nose too.

My male human kept me awake last night with his heavy coughing. I was sleeping peacefully when the whole bed shook. He startled me, making me think the house was coming down. I had about fallen back into a slumber when it happened again. This time, the cough was so violent, it threw me out of bed. My female human seemed to sneeze between these coughing episodes. I found a quieter room and ended up on the far side of the house curled up on one of the padded kitchen chairs.

Between the coughing and sneezing, there wasn't any peace in the house. I figured it would be a good day to be outside. However, when the door opened, a freezing breeze came through that reversed my thinking and steps.

I went into the big room and made use of the scratching post. My nails needed a good trimming. Next, I made my way up to the penthouse of my cat tree. The carpeted tree house held my warmth. I could watch all the activities in the big room from there. The window looked too cold to lie in.

The baby was up and had toys scattered all across the floor. My female human was trying to keep an eye on the baby while lying down on the sofa with the tissue box next to her. I could see she would need help today.

The baby liked one toy in particular where a small car started at the top and went around in circles and then came out at the bottom rolling fast. This was entertaining for me too. Sometimes when it rolled out at the bottom, I would swat it as it crossed my path. The baby would giggle at this and rush to put the little-wheeled object back in the top slot.

Today, I watched from my loft as my eyes tracked the progress of the toy. I saw it run all the way over to where the bookcase stood. When the baby went to retrieve the toy, there was a long pause before picking it up. The baby stood there longer than normal, so I jumped down to investigate.

I walked past the baby and over to the bookcase and stared. In a small web was a brown spider. Most of the spiders I have encountered are harmless, and I ignore them. I was unsure of this one. It would be best to keep the baby away.

The baby spotted a small ball and raced back, placing it on the track at the top. It went around and around and came shooting out straight at me. At the right moment, I batted it away with my white booted front paw. The baby squealed in delight. The laughter was enough to wake my female human lying on the sofa. I wanted to get her attention, so I let out a meow. She ignored me and laid back with a smile and took another tissue to her nose.

I heard my male human coughing as he walked down the hallway to the kitchen. I ran in and let out a meow at him. It seemed he was trying to get a glass of water. Once the glass was full, he wandered back towards the bedroom.

I went back to the big room and watched the baby. This time, one of the riding toys was being put to good use. The baby would push it along making the red fire truck scoot across the floor. The baby would then turn it around and scoot in the other direction, this time towards the position I was guarding. I let out a big meow followed by another.

I saw movement on the sofa, so I did it again. Finally, my female human wobbled over towards the bookcase to see why I was using my loudspeaker. From the other room, my male human came stumbling in. I let my siren run one more time. I think my humans saw the spider at the same time. My female human picked the baby up and my male human hurried into the kitchen and came back with a can and sprayed the spider. I backed away from the smelly spray and watched as the spider pulled its legs in tight and then stopped moving.

Once they cleaned up the spider and its web, my female human hugged and kissed me. I would have started my purr motor, but the coughing and sneezing were too much for me. I jumped down and retreated to my penthouse suite.

Tale 63 - Beyond My Backyard

It must have been one of those weekends again. The big noise maker was being pushed all around the house. The back door was open, and I stepped out into the warm air. My kingdom is large, and I need to keep tabs on it.

In the backyard, my humans set the old barbecue and picnic table up, so I knew there would be more humans coming later. Most likely, there would be little humans running around that would want to either squeeze the life out of me or pull my tail. I figured I could avoid them and check out the hill behind my house.

There were trees back there, some with sticky stuff on the bark. The trees smelled good but had too much goo on them for climbing. Some of that stuff had rubbed off onto my royal fur one time, and it seemed to take a week of grooming to remove it. I continued past those trees. My house now was only a little speck in the distance.

I found this rather large log that provided a great perch to rest on. I could see trees and big rocks all around me. The forest was quiet, except for a few birds, high in the trees. I couldn't see them, but they made a pleasant enough sound. The log seemed to vibrate a little, and I didn't know what was going on. I looked around. My padded paws were silent as I traveled the length of the log. I saw dirt fly out from under the log, felt more vibration, and then saw more dirt fly.

I jumped down so I could see better. There was a pile of soft dirt that had been dug out from under the log. When I stepped closer to sniff, a cloud of dirt shot out of the hole and caught me off guard. While I shook most of it off, it perturbed me as it ruined several days of grooming. I moved to the side to see who or what was doing all of this. A furry head with big ears and teeth peeked out from under the log, turned and went back under. He didn't look friendly, so I moved on.

Up ahead, there were trees with large leaves. The sun was shining through as most of the leaves were on the ground. I pounced on some and rolled around. I envisioned the furry animal being one of the big leaves and it was being taught a lesson in manners. The leaves flew everywhere as I batted them about. Feeling vindicated, I continued my little journey.

There were more big rocks ahead where the sun shined. One of those rocks would hold the heat from the sun and had my name on it. I found a big flat rock where I could stretch out and enjoy the warmth.

I must have dozed off as I hadn't heard the slithering sounds nor the hissing near me. My super cat senses must have awoken me as my eyes stared right out at the head of a snake. I hissed and jumped back, slipping off of the big rock. The snake wiggled around the rock and had me cornered. It was staring at me once again. Maybe it wanted to dance as I heard it shaking a rattle at the end of its tail.

The snake's head came straight at me. My lightning reflexes brought my front paw up with the spikes out and gave that snake a roundhouse. It came back up and hissed again. As it shot out at me, I countered with another paw with sharpened claws slamming the snake's head to the ground. Another paw came up and dragged along the snake's head. I reached down with my open mouth and sank my teeth into the snake's neck. The rest of the snake wiggled all around, but another bite and claws sunk deep into the snake seemed to finish him. The snake's body continued to twist, but I knew the fight was over.

I now had some serious grooming ahead to make my once beautiful sleek body worthy of its regal heritage. The flat rock provided the platform to allow me a make-over.

The sun was going down as I finished and there was a little rumble in my tummy. I have trained my humans to set my food out and if I didn't hurry, they might forget to fill my bowls. I have spent too much time training them and didn't want to start all over again.

My home was at least a mile away, so I bounded through the forest, over rocks, and past the big log. On the rise overlooking the neighborhood, I saw my backyard. I continued down the hill and wandered into the yard and looked around. My humans were cleaning up the picnic table and carrying the last remnants into the house. I followed them in.

My human must have noticed me sitting by my empty bowl. She cleaned and filled them. I knew all the training had paid off. That evening, I curled up next to my humans and thought about the adventures I had today. When a hand came down and stroked my back, a little rumble started in my throat. This was the purr-fect ending for a wonderful day.

Tale 64 - Something Fishy

I was enjoying the morning sun while lying in the front window and watching people walk by. A few kids were playing ball in the street. It was close to the time when the man wearing the big bird patch would stuff more bills into the box. I was used to this, but still alert for any sneaky stuff.

I saw a young girl carrying a box. She opened the gate into my yard and walked up to my door. I heard a soft knocking. My humans were quick to see who was there. When the door opened, there was an exchange of chatter. I heard the words fish and vacation several times. My female human took the box and carried it into the kitchen. The young girl followed her in. My curiosity made me follow along as if we were in a parade.

I saw a big bowl removed from the box along with some small containers and other stuff. At first, I didn't see the movement, but then something moved inside the bowl. I jumped up on the counter to inspect closer. Almost immediately, the young girl screamed. It was so startling, I jumped down, thinking something dangerous was about to happen.

My female human told the girl, "It's okay. Thomas won't hurt your goldfish."

I asked myself, was that quick glimpse a goldfish? What is a goldfish? I looked up and saw the girl glaring at me. I stood my ground and lifted a paw and cleaned it, just to show her I was ignoring her.

It was soon after that the girl left. It was my turn to inspect everything. I jumped back onto the counter and stared at the big bowl. It appeared to contain water, and something swam around inside. I stood there trying to figure it all out. I dipped my paw into the bowl. When it touched the water, I yanked it out. I sniffed at it and then licked my paw. It didn't seem as fresh as my drinking water, and it smelled strange. I dipped my paw in again, and the little fish darted around as if on a merry-go-round.

My female human came in and watched me for a short time and then said, "Thomas, we will watch this fish for a few days. You need to be on your best behavior and not bother the fish. Can you do that?"

Hmm. My female human confirmed this was a fish. It didn't look like any of the fish I had at the sushi place where I used to hang out at. It also didn't smell like any of the special canned fish I like so well. I figured I could watch it later, so I jumped down and walked out of the kitchen with my tail high in the air.

I should have stayed in the kitchen because when I rounded the corner heading to the big room, the baby ambushed me. The baby reached down and grabbed me and held me over an arm where I hung like a damp dish towel. The baby must have finished the daily nap and took advantage of the situation.

When the baby holds me, there isn't much I can do. If I try to get away, I could hurt the baby. I find it best to wait. The baby carried me into the big room where I hoped to escape. There, I would run to my big window, but no such luck. The baby carried me around through the dining area and into the kitchen. The baby stopped and let out a loud squeal. I'm sure everyone heard it as the baby let go and I fell to the floor. The baby sounded hurt, but my claws were tucked in, so I couldn't understand why the baby cried out. I turned and saw the baby pointing to the big bowl where the fish was swimming around. Why would the baby scream?

The baby reached high and could just touch the bowl. The fish darted away to the other side. Another squeal came out as the fish turned and swam in a circle. The fish had the complete attention of the baby. The little hand came up again, and the bowl slid towards the edge of the counter. I jumped up and placed my body between the bowl and the edge, preventing it from sliding any further. The baby's hands continued to push the bowl, crowding the space I was in. I let out a big meow.

I heard the steps of my female human coming and let out another big meow. As soon as she saw what was happening, she said, "Thomas, you rescued the fish!" I jumped down and headed for the safety of my window.

I got to thinking if this was a fish, and I like to eat fish, was this a special treat for me later? Maybe my humans were making this a surprise. I didn't want to spoil it for them, so I spent the late afternoon watching more people walk past on the sidewalk and some little birds chirping and flapping their wings.

That evening, my water bowl was cleaned and filled. I inspected it to see if the fish was swimming in it, but it wasn't. I waited for my food bowl, thinking they would treat me to fresh sushi. Instead, my regular food filled my bowl. I wasn't too disappointed as I liked my food a lot. The fish in the bowl would have to wait for another time.

My humans sat next to each other on the sofa watching the moving picture on the wall, and the baby played with toys on the floor. I jumped up and found a lap to lie in. After a few well-deserved strokes, my purr motor started up. I enjoyed having regular meals even if it wasn't sushi.

Tale 65 - Baby Walkabout

It was another one of those weekends. My two humans were in the house taking care of some chores. The baby was in the big room playing with toys, and I was in the window enjoying the warmth from the sun. I was dozing when I heard the mailbox open, and the man with the big bird patch on his coat was depositing more bills into it. I guarded the house in case he did something devious. He must have known better and left. I checked the baby, and there was no noticeable reaction to the minor noise, and everything seemed normal.

I had just closed my eyes when my male human came into the room. The baby looked up, but then kept on playing. The man opened the door and stepped out to retrieve the bills. He seemed engrossed, and I heard him say something about taxes. He was still looking at the bills as he pushed the door closed. I did not hear the distinctive click when he did so. With his head down, he walked into the other room.

The baby seemed bored and walked around the room, touching everything within reach. When the baby came to the door, the little hand pulled on the knob, and the door opened. I stood up on alert as the baby never goes outside without one of my humans. It only took a moment for the baby to disappear around the door. A low rumble and small meow came out of my throat. I coughed, trying to clear my throat.

I jumped down and raced to the door where I could see the baby turning around backward and stepping down the porch steps. A much louder meow sounded, and I needed to decide between running to find my humans or going outside to protect the baby. When the baby stepped onto the flat walkway, I ran to the other room where my male human was and let out a meow, followed by another. I didn't wait for a response as the baby's safety worried me. I turned and ran to catch up with the baby.

The baby was inspecting the flowers along the walkway. There were brightly colored yellow ones, and they seemed to attract a lot of buzzing bugs that can sting. I try to stay away from those. The baby's hand reached in and grasped the stem of one flower and pulled, snapping it off. The baby thought this was funny and giggled. There weren't any bees on this flower. The baby sniffed the flower and giggled more. The flower was then dropped, and the small hand reached again into the planter and pulled out another flower. As the flower was being brought up for another sniff, I saw a bee in the flower's center. I leaped up and snagged the flower from the baby's hand and sprinted across the yard where I dropped it and ran back.

The baby had lost interest in the flowers and was now moving across the lawn. Where were my humans, I wondered? I ran to the front door while keeping the baby in my sight and let my meow siren run for a few moments. As I turned, I noticed the front gate was partially open and the baby headed for it. I'm sure that pesky man delivering the bills left it open on purpose.

I raced down the walkway as fast as I could to beat the baby to the gate. It was unlatched and the baby could easily open this and walk out to the street. With only inches to spare, I slammed my body into the gate forcing it to close and latch. The baby was right behind me trying to pull it open. Hitting the gate bruised one of my ribs and made me dizzy.

The alarm I sounded must have worked. My male human rushed down the walkway towards the baby. The baby saw him and ran across the lawn, laughing and thinking this was a game. He picked the baby up and gave a warm embrace. I stared up at him, and he said, "Thomas, thank you for warning me the baby was in the yard." He carried the baby back into the house, and I followed.

That night, I found a lap to snuggle up into. They stroked my smooth black fur, thanking me for letting the early warning siren blast. Now I was warming up my purr engine as a rub under the chin felt so good.

Tale 66 - The Farm - Jake

I knew something different was up today. After breakfast, there was a lot of hustle and bustle going on. They packed suitcases along with a lot of baby stuff and carried it out to the car. When they brought my carrier in, I knew I was going along for the ride. I let my male human pick me up and place me in the carrier. As he loaded me into the car, my male human said, "Thomas, we will spend a few days out at my dad's farm." He set the carrier next to the baby's car seat.

I didn't know what a farm was, so I knew this would be a new adventure. I have learned wherever the family is, that would be home, and I would continue to look out for them, provided they met my nutritional requirements.

My male human drove and chatted with his mate. This might have made the trip enjoyable for them, but it was long. I tried to sleep even though the baby wanted to use my carrier as a kicking board. The car seemed warm, and I curled up the best I could and snoozed for most of the trip.

The bumpy road caused the car to jar me awake as we went down a rough patch. I learned later this was the driveway to the main house. Once there, my humans exchanged greetings and hugs with an older human they called Dad. Even the baby got in on the act after a few minutes of hiding behind my two humans. After chatting a little longer, they carried my cage and the rest of the luggage into the house. There were a lot of new smells in the air.

It was late in the day, and my stomach was growling. I heard the opener grinding and knew my food was being prepared. When they let me out of the carrier, I found my familiar bowls with food and water waiting for me. It was then I spotted another set of bowls close to mine. I wasn't sure what this was all about, but I didn't let it stop me from eating.

I was doing my best to clean my face with my wet paw when I spotted a cat. It was grayish orange striped with bits of fur missing here and there. I could see he walked with a distinct limp in the back. I watched as he lapped water from the other bowl. He didn't seem much interested in me. I heard the Dad say, "This here is Jake. He was a real mouser in his day. Now he moves a lot slower."

I moved through the house, checking everything out. I could see a lot of the baby stuff placed in one of the big rooms, and the suitcases and other stuff sat in another room. A few doors were closed so I would have to check them out later. Everyone seemed to gather in the big room, and the baby had everyone's attention.

I found Jake lying on a small rug near a scratching post. I made use of the post while checking out Jake. He seemed content just watching everyone. I laid near him for a while.

That night, I was on alert due to all the new sounds and smells. It sounded like a mouse scampering around. After I rose, I could see Jake was on alert too. Together, we headed to the kitchen on silent paws.

I think we spotted the mouse at the same time. Jake ran across the floor, but I could see he did not have the speed necessary to catch the mouse. Jake let out a big meow as the mouse turned in my direction, I leaped to cut him off. The wood floor was smooth, but not so slick as to prevent me from turning without sliding. My aim was good, and my paw reached out and held the mouse down. Jake pounced down with a lethal blow and let out a mighty meow over the victory. I heard human steps coming and let Jake have the glory and left the kitchen. I heard the Dad say, "Good job Jake! You're still a good mouser!"

I felt good about Jake being recognized for eliminating that mouse. Maybe Jake and I can become good friends. Tomorrow will be another day on the farm and there will be plenty of things to explore. I found my humans resting in bed. I jumped up and found a warm place near their feet. A small purr of contentment seemed to ooze out.

Tale 67 - The Farm - Big Animals

I'm usually awake early and today was no exception. However, Jake and Dad were both awake and preparing to go outside. I double checked my food bowl, and it was empty. What a way to start the day. I followed them out, Dad leading, Jake right behind, and me at the end. I had seen little of the outside as I was in the carrier and brought into the house before I could explore.

We walked over to a large building and went inside. Dad had said something about going in the barn so that must be the name of this big building. I halted due to the stinky smell I encountered. The other two kept going, but I moved a little slower trying to figure out why they would go into a place that smelled bad. I heard Dad say, "Jake, are you ready for some fresh milk?"

Dad sat on a small stool next to a big animal. It was larger than him and he was working underneath it. Soon, I saw squirts of milk drop into a pail. Dad kept working and more milk came out. He then squirted some onto Jake who sat at the ready a few feet away. The milk hit Jake in the face and mouth. I could see his face was all white as he worked his tongue around. I sniffed at it, and it smelled good.

Dad then gave me a squirt. While I wasn't expecting it, the warm milk had a pleasant aroma. I licked the milk on my face, enjoying this appetizer. While I cleaned my face of the creamy milk, Dad moved to another animal and continued working his magic to get the milk. Only when I had finished, did I notice he was further down the line of big animals. I walked down closer to him and avoided the long legs of the animals. He said, "Thomas, did you enjoy the milk from the cow?" In response, I licked my lips.

When Dad finished the milking, the cows were all released to move outside where the grass was growing in a big fenced yard. There were some big containers of water for them too. They made a strange sound like moo. Dad closed a gate to keep them in the yard.

The next stop was a big cage with funny looking birds in it. I heard Dad say he had to feed the chickens. The chickens all pecked at the ground where Dad threw the chicken feed. I thought about the big black birds that gave the little birds a hard time, but these chicken birds all seemed to get along. There were even baby chicks following their mother. When finished with the chores, we all headed back to the house. All this hard work had made my stomach growl. I hurried along back to the house where I hoped they would fill my food bowl.

After breakfast, Jake and I wandered around the farm. There were a lot of things to sniff and learn about. There was some tall grass, and we played hide and seek for a while. Jake moved slower than me, and I could see he tired easily. We patrolled all around the farm, even chased a lizard under a rock. The trip tired me too and I was ready for a nap.

Jake led me over to a small shed. He jumped up onto a box, then on top of a fence, and then onto the roof of the shed. I followed him up and found the metal roof very warm. From this vantage point, I could see the house, the big building, and the chicken coop. I laid down, and the warmth made me feel so relaxed, I fell asleep in no time.

Late in the day, I heard the barn doors open again. I didn't want to miss out on any of that milk, so I jumped down and scampered over to follow Dad into the barn. I wondered where Jake was. He must have woken up and left silently.

I saw the cows walking towards the barn. A couple in the back were making those funny mooing sounds. As I watched, I could see Jake behind them running back and forth. It was almost like he was chasing them. Soon, all the cows were in the barn and had their heads bent down into a feeding bin. I then saw Jake come in with his tongue hung out a little, and he laid down and watched Dad.

Dad began the milking process again. This time, he had a small bowl with him which he filled and gave to Jake. He must have been thirsty as the milk disappeared fast. I waited my turn, and Dad filled the bowl again and set it down for me. Like Jake, I didn't waste time in lapping up the contents.

That night, I curled up next to Jake. He worked hard on this farm and earned his keep. I hoped his male human rewarded him for that.

Tale 68 - The Farm - Night Sounds

After all the work Jake and I did, you would think I would sleep soundly through the night. It was dark outside, and there were unidentifiable sounds my cat senses detected that caused the fur on my back to rise. I let out a small growl which alerted Jake. He listened and then also let out a small growl in acknowledgment. I jumped up to one window to look out but could see nothing.

Jake moved to the back door and pushed. A small door opened, and he was out. I tried the same thing, and I was out in the dark with him. There was a little moonlight which we could see by. We listened more and then heard a soft scream, like the one we heard earlier. I wasn't sure, but I remember encountering a fox once, and that is the sound he made.

Jake headed to the big cage where the chickens lived. I was right on his trail, not knowing where he was going. Up ahead, I saw this furry animal which looked like the fox I had seen in past days. I knew foxes preyed on small animals, and birds were one of their favorites. Of course, if we weren't lucky, we might be the fox's dinner.

I figured Jake was protecting his home and as long as I lived here, I would protect it too. The fox was digging along the side of the big cage and dirt was flying everywhere. Jake came up and snarled at the fox. I was a few paces back, and the fox did not see me. The fox turned and faced Jake and let out one of his screams. The two took turns lunging at each other. I could see Jake was slower than the fox and was in danger.

I approached from the side of the fox and let out a growl. The fur on my back stood on end. I hunched my body up making me look as big as possible. It surprised the fox to see me but held its ground. The fox lunged at me, and I dropped back, never losing eye contact. I hissed and lunged, and the fox dropped back. Ever so slowly, the fox kept backing away when suddenly, he leaped towards me, and we tumbled over and over. I felt a deep pain in my shoulder while sinking my teeth into his neck. We broke it off and then went at it again. This time, when the fox came at me, Jake jumped in and attacked. He sank his teeth into one of the fox's ears and hung on. All three of us rolled over and over until the fox called it quits and ran off. Before he did, Dad and my male human came out of the house, saw us fighting, and yelled.

We both limped over. At first, my male human thought we had been fighting each other, but Dad had seen the fox and knew what had happened and explained it to my male human as I heard the words fox and fighting it off several times.

Dad looked Jake over and then me. He saw my shoulder was bleeding and said to my male human, "We need to take Thomas to a vet, and it wouldn't hurt to have Jake go too." My male human rushed into the house and in a few minutes came out with the carrier. They placed Jake and me inside it and then loaded us into the car.

I remembered the bumpy road on the way in, but this trip felt like a roller coaster. I think my male human made the car go extra fast. Dad was in the car too, and he was telling my male human which way to turn. Jake and I kept bouncing against each other in the carrier as the car swayed and bumped as we went.

Seems every time I see the vet, I get the worse end. This vet was a female human and seemed to understand my concern. She rubbed my head and talked to me, hiding the fact she pinched me on my back. That's all I remembered until the next day. I was back at the farmhouse feeling sore all over, and this big bandage prevented me from walking fast.

I took another look at Jake and now understood why he had so many clumps of fur missing. Life on a farm is challenging, and he's worked hard to protect his kingdom. I now have a battle scar to show my worth too. I bet my humans won't take me to the cat show now.

My female human wanted to hold me, and the baby wanted to pull my tail. I wanted to get something to eat, so I jumped down and sat by my bowl and let out a little meow. She received the message and filled my bowl without further ado.

After eating, with my shoulder stiff, I wanted to curl up and sleep. I didn't think my purr motor was operational anymore. Maybe it broke during the fight.

The next day, I had to say goodbye to Jake and Dad. When I saw my humans load up the suitcases, I knew we were leaving. I brushed by the legs of Dad several times, thanking him for the milk. I gave Jake a small meow, recognizing him for the tough job he does.

We traveled over that bumpy road one more time, and then I slept the rest of the way. It felt good to be back home. I didn't have to worry about any foxes here. I only had to worry about a man delivering bills.

Tale 69 - Home Protection

It was night time, and I looked out the front window pondering the most recent events. My injuries from the farm were healing, and my leg and shoulder were better. At the vet's office, he removed my bandages and said: "Most of the fur will grow back, but it might leave a bald spot on the shoulder." I'm not sure I look like royalty now, but at least I have a scar of one valiant in battle.

I saw two young men snooping around outside, and I wondered if I would have to be valiant again. They trespassed into the yards of the humans across the street and now peeped and checked out my front yard. My fur, except for the bald spot, stood erect. I was about to let out a wild roar, but something made the young men leave. Maybe I sent out bad vibrations.

The next night, I was on patrol again, sitting in the window. My male human left his car parked on the street. Usually, he parks it in the garage where the door leads into the house. I then remembered that a delivery truck dropped several big boxes off and they pushed these into the garage. Maybe there wasn't any more room for the car.

How could I forget the boxes? I was hoping my humans would open the boxes so I could play in them. The baby loves to play in boxes too. Sometimes we play hide and seek in them.

Regardless, looking out the window, I saw the same two men from the other night. The moon lit up the sky and I could see them clearly. One man carried something that looked like a stick, only it appeared heavier. He used it to smash the window on the car across the street, and I heard the glass shatter.

These men must work for the evil warlord and are carrying out his wishes. I am the king and responsible for protecting my kingdom. They must not advance and harm anything or anyone. I let out an awful sounding screech. My royal trumpet blared.

I ran to the bedroom where my humans were sleeping and pounced on the bed. As I walked back and forth on the covers that were keeping them warm, I started a serenade of meows. You would have thought the band led by John Phillip Sousa would march through the door.

My male human said in a groggy voice, "Thomas. What are you doing?"

My meows kept up the pace as I jumped down from the bed. I tried leaving the room, but the humans ignored me, again. How many clues do they need to follow me? I leaped back onto the bed and used a deep hiss to get their attention.

My female human said, "I think Thomas is trying to tell us something. Let's follow him."

At least she received my message. All of us headed to the front window with me in the lead. I hopped up and looked out just as one of the car alarms started up. I hissed for good measure. My female human ran back to the bedroom and came back with her little talk box. She rattled off something, and after a pause, she said, "The police are on their way."

The men were about to run because of the car alarm, but I didn't want them to smash the window on my human's car. I leaned on the screen and pushed it out, dropping into my yard. The gate was closed, but I leaped over it while rushing out to our car. I hid under it so I could get a good view of what was happening. I will push these evil henchmen back until I defeat them.

In the distance, I could hear sirens and the men ran down the street. My male human came running out in his bathrobe calling my name. The police arrived and looked around. I saw where the men were hiding down the street and let out a meow. My male human said, "There you are Thomas. Time to come inside."

This time, I ignored him and trotted down the street near where the offenders hid. I then let out one of my wild screams, and my male human, followed by one of the police officers came running. My scream frightened the two men and flushed them from their hiding spot. I watched as the men fled down the street.

The police officer chased them at which time I finished my noble duty. My male human held out his arms and I leaped up to him. He said, "Thomas, I can't believe the things you do."

As we walked back up the street, he petted me. It felt good, and my old purr motor remembered its purpose and started up. For the rest of the night, I snuggled up with my two humans in the warm bed.

Tale 70 - Hot Dog

Today, we were in the backyard. My humans had dragged some big boxes out of the garage and opened them up. They pulled out parts for outdoor pieces of furniture, and my humans were working on making them all fit together. I was more interested in the boxes, and the baby was too.

The boxes were great entertainment. I hopped in and out of two small boxes and the baby crawled around in another. Each time I peeked out of a box, the baby would giggle. I felt we were defending the kingdom and our forts protected us from any would be foes.

While we played, I heard a lot of grunting and groaning from my humans. Today, being a playday, I couldn't understand why my humans seemed so tired. As soon as my humans would assemble one chair, they would sit down in it. It might take them the whole day to build all the chairs if they continue sitting in them.

Finally, my male human finished the furniture assembly. He then towed the new barbecue out. I was glad it was a new one as I remember when the old one blew up and hurt my female human. I wouldn't want that ever to happen again.

My male human must have known what the baby liked because he grilled meat on the barbecue and gave it to the baby. He called it a hot dog. While I don't like dogs, this didn't seem right. It worried me to think he might have a hot cat. I decided it might be best if I kept my distance for a while.

I found that sitting on the fence between the neighbor's house and mine gave me a whole new perspective on life. On the one side, I could see my family having a good time relaxing. On the other side, there was this yapping dog who must have thought he could catch me. Maybe this dog would be a good candidate for the grill. I could lead him over to my yard, then again, who would I tease?

I left the fence and followed my humans inside. Maybe I would get a treat although I'm not sure I wanted any of that hot dog they cooked. I was in luck; my female human must have gotten the message as I rubbed her legs with my soft black fur.

Except for the bald spot, I looked like a king. Maybe kings need a battle scar to show the world they can defend themselves although I think I would rather have fur there. She rewarded me with one of those tasty treats like the kind I had during the cat shows. They are yummy and taste so good.

There was a knock on the front door, and my male human went to see who it was. It was the little girl who had brought the fish over to spend a few days while she was vacationing. Just when I thought I would have sushi, she showed up and took it away. I was looking to see if she brought a fresh fish, but alas, her hands were empty. I heard her say "I want to play with Thomas. Can I take him for a walk?"

It was a beautiful day to go outside, but I wasn't sure I wanted to be with this little girl. Who would trust someone that carried potential sushi around? Then I thought about the hot dog. Maybe being out of sight, my humans wouldn't think about a hot cat.

I sat down at the front door while my male human attached a leash to my collar. Once we started down the walkway, I felt better. The little girl was trying to be friendly, and I was only thinking about food. I raised my head up more and strutted down the street. How else should a king parade?

At the end of the block, we turned around and proceeded back the way we had come. All was well until I spotted someone coming toward us, walking a dog. I can always avoid a dog unless I'm on a leash. I slowed my pace hoping the dog would cross the street. The little girl pulled on the leash to make me go faster as I had come to a complete crawl while I eyeballed the invader up ahead.

There was a big tree growing in the walkway, and I was about to climb it when the walker pulled the dog across the street. The dog had spotted me and strained hard on his leash. He snarled and displayed his teeth. I thought he might make a good candidate for a hot dog.

The danger passed, and we again made our way down the street, but I kept a sharp look out for the dog. We arrived back at my home, and it relieved me to have the leash unhooked. The girl mumbled something that sounded like thank you and left.

That evening, they filled my food bowl on time, and I ate with enthusiasm. I was thankful it was the food I liked, and even happier it wasn't some leftover hot dog. I turned on my purr motor once I was curled up in the lap of my female human.

Tale 71 - Trapped

I consider myself of sound mind but whatever got into me today makes me question that self-analysis. The day started out normally, and I figured being a warm day, I would stroll around the neighborhood. When the back door opened, I scampered out.

My first stop was to sit on the wall separating my yard from the neighbors. It was an easy jump, and the top was flat enough to have a firm footing. The small dog in the yard did its normal yapping. I have yet to figure out why dogs bark long after the effect of it has worn off. Long ago, I didn't have much to do and perched myself so a dog could see me but couldn't reach me. That dog barked until all I could hear was a hoarse cough. Oh well, it was time to explore other yards.

From the backyard, the hill ran along behind all the houses, and it was an easy track to follow. A few houses down I leaped to the top of a corner fence. On one side was a beautiful green lawn, the type my small bird friends would love to play on in the early mornings. On the other side was a large pool of water. If I had to, I could swim, but I avoid water as it makes my sleek fur have a non-royal look. Still, the poolside looked inviting, and I jumped down on the hard cement surrounding the water.

There was a slight breeze that traveled across the water, creating a cooling effect. I stood there for a few minutes taking all this in. An equipment box was near the side, and it was large enough to cast a small shadow. I found some of that shade and stretched out. How often do you get to lie around the pool and do nothing?

While the sun moved overhead, I caught forty winks only to find when I opened my eyes, there was another set looking at me. It was a child, a little bigger than the baby that runs around my home. I backed up, and the fence prevented my retreat. A second child showed up and blocked my side escape. Fingers from both kids now pointed at me, and the noise level from their jabbering reached new heights. They trapped me!

A sticky hand reached down for me, and my first reaction was to show them how sharp my claws were, but I thought better. I tried to wiggle around and slip between the two kids, but the little hands squeezed me tight. Within moments, they carried me into the house, and behind me, I heard the door slam.

"Mommy, look what we found in the backyard," screamed one girl in a high-pitched voice.

The mother looked down and with some sage advice said, "You better let him go. He might scratch or bite you."

"No, he won't. He likes me."

The mother bent down and rubbed behind my ears and found the little tag attached to my collar. She read it and said, "His name is Thomas. I will call the owner. You two can play until they come."

All I wanted to do was get out of there, but the doors were all closed. One girl said, "I bet he's hungry," as she carried me into what looked like the kitchen. The other kid said, "Let's give him some Cheerios!"

One girl held me tight while the other found a bowl and poured stuff into it. They then poured milk into the bowl. The dirty hands pushed my whole body up to the bowl. When she released me from the tight hold, I sniffed at the bowl. I wasn't sure what this all was, but the milk smelled good, and I let my tongue lap at it until I devoured it all. I built up a thirst from being in the sun most of the day, and the milk tasted good.

"See. He was hungry," one girl told the other. "It's my turn to hold him now." A new pair of grungy hands gripped my body. I knew I had to wait them out. It might take a day of grooming to get my good looks back.

The two girls took turns petting my head and long body. One tried to pull my tail when it when up, but I twisted to prevent further abuse. One girl found a comb and ran it through my fur. Where the sticky stuff from their hands rubbed off on me, the comb stuck. I tried to clean the spots myself. The girls tried to be friendly.

It seemed like forever before there was a knock on the door. One girl rushed to open it. My male human stood there. I can't remember feeling so good about seeing him. When I got the chance, I dashed over and leaped into his arms.

That evening, I didn't hurry to have my bowl of food because my stomach was full from drinking the milk earlier. When my male human sat down, I jumped into his lap. Without even a single petting stroke, I started up my purr motor to share my thankfulness for rescuing me. I think I will avoid fence sitting for a while.

Tale 72 - A Cry in the Night

Last night I awoke to a faint, unfamiliar cry. It didn't last for long, and it came from outside. This morning I investigated to find the source. After breakfast, I snuck out onto the front steps, warm with the early sun. The warmth enticed me to stay, but I wanted to find what woke me up.

I hoped the cry would repeat itself so I could zero in on the location. I listened carefully to no avail. It was time to peek into the neighbor's yard. Not the one with the dog in it, the other one. I would not antagonize the dog today as concern filled my heart.

For whatever reason, I rarely go in this direction, so I needed to keep my wits about me in this unmapped territory. The yard was large, much like the one in my kingdom. The house was smaller than mine, and there wasn't any place to hide a car at night. I figured the reconnaissance should not take much time.

I started my stealthy search in the front and worked around to the side of the house. On the far side, I found a small air vent screen missing. It was large enough for me to stick my head in and look around. It was dark under the house and nearly impossible to see. I might need to come back to this hole if I hear any sounds but completed my inspection by circling the entire property.

There was a tall tree in the backyard, perfect for a lookout, I scrambled up the trunk and found a long limb overlooking the yard. The view was great, and I wondered why I hadn't checked this yard out before. The branch provided a perch where I could wait, enjoy the fresh air, and listen for any strange sounds. I dozed off, bored from waiting so long. A small cry woke me.

My head snapped around so my ears could pinpoint the location. The sound was weak and I wasn't sure, but it sounded like a cat. The cry came from under the house. Down the tree I ran and then leaped the final distance to the ground. I dashed over to where the screen was missing and listened intently.

It would be risky to crawl inside. What if another animal was in there and waiting? The small cry sounded again, and I crawled inside, moving cautiously. The soft earth masked any sounds I made. As I progressed, my eyes adjusted to the darkness, and I made out shapes.

From the center of the house, I heard a soft whimper and moved in that direction. A young cat laid still on the cold ground. I sniffed around, but there were no other smells to identify another cat's presence. Maybe the mother abandoned the kitten, or it crawled off on its own and became disoriented. This helpless feline needed my help.

I gripped the scruff of her neck and proceeded to the screen opening. The opening was small, and I worked hard to push the kitten through the hole. Once outside, it was only a short distance to my backyard. My humans always have a bowl of water on the back porch if I need it. I dropped the kitten next to the bowl, hoping it had the energy to drink.

The sun had moved around to the back and was now warming the porch area. Its warmth provided energy to the cold body, and I sensed movement. The head rose and dipped into the bowl where she lapped up water.

Here in the sunlight, I could see the true colors of this kitty. It was gray with straight black and white stripes running down the back. With all the dirt covering her, she would not win any blue ribbons. I licked her head, letting her know my concern.

It was a while before my humans returned. I let out a few loud meows to let them know I was on the back porch. My female human opened the door with the baby standing next to her. I stood by the kitten and looked up.

My female human said, "Thomas, is your friend okay?" as she reached down to pick the limp little tabby up. My human carried her into the kitchen and offered a warm bowl of milk. There were a few laps of the milk, a pause, and then more.

The baby kept looking, amazed at the small size of the cat. My human said, "Thomas, where did you find this little stray?"

After drinking about half the milk, the little kitten curled up in a ball and fell fast asleep. My human found a small towel and wrapped the kitten up and placed it in a shoebox. She said, "We will have to take the kitten to the vet tomorrow. She can sleep here tonight."

My tail waved in the air from helping this frail waif of a cat. At least I won't hear any unfamiliar cries in the night. My purr motor was running as I laid near the kitten to keep it warm and comfortable. I wondered what will happen tomorrow.

Tale 73 - A Vet Checkup

I didn't sleep well last night as I frequently awoke to check on the little stray kitten found the day before. My fears were unfounded as the baby kitten slept like a log in the small box, wrapped in the dish towel provided by my human.

This morning, my human warmed milk in a bowl for the kitten who gingerly lapped it up. My human filled my bowl with my favorite, and I consumed it rapidly. After my female human finished her morning chores, she placed the kitten and me into the carrier and moved it to the car. She bundled up the baby and lifted the baby into the car seat. I knew we were off to see the vet as my female human said so the evening before.

The trip was uneventful other than the baby's foot knocking against the carrier for a while. The kitten shook in fear. I licked her head a few times to let her know all was well.

My female human placed the baby into the stroller and pushed it with one hand while the other hand held the carrier. The vet's place was always scary, but I always seemed to be in good hands. In the waiting area, a big dog strained at his leash trying to reach my carrier. The dog distracted me from the strange smells I usually encountered. Once the dog left, I relaxed my guard until it was our turn.

I was sure the visit was only for the kitten and surprised when I was the center of attention for the first few minutes. The doctor, with her soft and firm fingers, checked me. My leg and shoulder had healed from the fight with the fox.

She said, "Thomas has healed nicely, and you shouldn't need to worry about him." She then checked on the kitten with those same fingers. "The kitten is malnourished but healthy otherwise. She will need a few shots which we can administer today. Typically, we don't recommend a bath at this age, but she needs one. We can take care of that."

My female human nodded with a grateful look. I went back into the carrier while the vet took the kitten to another room. We spent our time in the waiting room until the kitten was ready to go. She joined me in the carrier. What a difference. She smelled good, not like the dirt from under the house next door. Her color was bright, and she felt soft.

Back at home, the kitten had enough energy to bat a small ball around. She tired and found the box with the towel. After curling up, it was lights out for her and free time for me, at least for a little while.

My female human fed and changed the baby. With renewed energy, the baby was ready to play. I didn't realize until too late that I was the intended target. The baby can move fast on two legs and can now reach most of my window ledges. I ran to the big room, and up the cat tree. It wasn't safe there as I could feel the tree lean over. I jumped before the tree came crashing down. I raced to the kitchen and then to the big table to hide. The chairs were close to the table, and I hopped up onto a chair seat hoping I would be out of sight. The baby came around the corner at one end of the kitchen and then ran toward me, turned, and went back to the big room. I was safe, for the moment.

I needed to rest while hiding from the baby. My eyes almost closed when I realized the kitten might be in danger. I ran to the bedroom where the kitten's box lay and was just in time as the baby was about to enter the room. I rubbed my smooth black body against the baby's legs which distracted the baby from attacking the tabby. As the baby reached for me, I backed out quickly, and the chase was on.

I figured the nursery would be a good room to start in. Unfortunately, with the window closed, the ledge was not wide enough for a firm footing. I then ran for the stack of soft plush animals. Maybe I could hide under them. My tail must have given me away as I felt it tugged. I peeked out, and two arms wrapped tightly around me. The baby half-carried and half-dragged me into the big room. The baby must have thought my head was a ball as the hand tapped on my head. My head moved up and down, but not from bouncing.

I wondered if it was worth the effort to save the little kitten. My male human arrived home, and the baby ran into his arms, saving me from further torment. For a tiny moment, I felt a tinge of jealousy. Then a wave of happiness came over me. My whole family was home, and safe plus a little kitten was sharing our home. If we kept her much longer, we would have to give her a name. Maybe something that would recognize her good fortune in life, like Lucky.

That evening, I was in the lap of my male human and Lucky was on the lap of my female human. My purr motor was humming along, and I hoped Lucky would learn to start hers and show thankfulness for the home protected by me.

Tale 74 - A New Home

My home life has transformed with Lucky, the little kitten, running around. Several weeks have passed since I rescued her from the house next door. Her abundance of energy wears me out. As part of my daily routine, I'm up several times a night to protect my kingdom by patrolling the house for unusual sounds and smells. After breakfast, I'm ready to stretch out in the front window where the sun shines in and take a catnap. Do I get to rest? No. Lucky is wide awake attacking my tail trying to engage me in play. I play for a while, but the lack of sleep leaves me exhausted, and I try to find a quiet place to rest.

Today seemed different. I heard my humans talking about Lucky. If I heard them right, one of them said, "We need to take Lucky in and have her fixed."

I didn't know Lucky had anything broken. Maybe I played too rough with her. The baby carries us both around, maybe Lucky broke something from playing with the baby. I guess I need to take it easy on her.

My female human placed Lucky in the carrier, and I heard her say she would drop Lucky off at the vet. The house seemed silent without the little kitten running around. My male human was home along with the baby, and the baby made up for it. Usually, the baby plays with the kitten and without her around, the baby chases me.

It was a whole day before Lucky returned. She seemed groggy and wanted to sleep a lot. Maybe she was building up her energy to attack me later. I let her rest. It took several more days before her energy returned.

When Lucky had her energy back, I received all her attention. Even the baby had a hard time catching up to Lucky. Another week passed, and the little girl from down the street came visiting. She's the one that tried to tempt me with the sushi swimming around in a big bowl. Anyway, she wanted to play with me again, but when she saw Lucky, all interest in me disappeared.

She exclaimed, "Oh what a pretty kitty. What's her name?"

My female human placed Lucky in her hands and said, "Her name is Lucky. We rescued her."

My tail swished in the air as the girl wanted to play with Lucky. Even the baby wanted to play with the girl and the kitten. I went to the back window and found the sun shining in, and I took full advantage of the peacefulness.

A few days later, the girl was back. She brought red yarn and something tied to the end. She dragged it in front of Lucky, and she chased it all around. I climbed up my cat tree and sat perched at the top so I could see all the action. It surprised me how fast Lucky could turn and chase the toy. She was learning how to use her claws when making a quick turn.

The girl pulled out a small ball from her pocket and tossed it in front of Lucky. The gray striped tabby scrambled after it and then rolled past it when trying to stop. She made a fast recovery, and the ball was in her paws, tossing it into the air. The little girl grabbed it and tossed it again. Lucky chased it again with similar results. I tired from watching all the action.

At last, Lucky was too tired to continue, and the little girl said her goodbye. My humans saw the little girl wanted to have a companion all her own. My male human said, "Do you think your parents will let you have a cat?"

The little girl said, "I don't know. Can I have Lucky?"

My male human said, "Talk to your mother and father and then come talk to us tomorrow."

That evening, Lucky and I played, and the baby joined in. The baby pulled my tail, and Lucky attacked my whiskers. I knew I wouldn't last long with these two.

It was on the afternoon of the next day when the little girl and her mother came over. The mother looked at me and said, "So this is

Thomas. I've heard many wonderful things about him." Naturally, I strutted back and forth a few times. It's not every day someone recognizes my royalty.

The girl picked up Lucky and held her. The mother and my humans sat down and talked for a while. My male human placed Lucky's bowls in a sack with some food. The little girl carried Lucky, and the mother carried the sack.

I looked around the house and realized Lucky had found a new home. It was a sad day for me and a happy day for her. While I enjoyed having a furry little playmate, I still have the baby to chase me.

That evening, the stillness set in and I jumped into my female human's lap for company. The soft hand stroked my long sleek, beautiful body. It felt good, but different from the way Lucky and I played. I had trouble making my purr motor start. I missed Lucky already.

Tale 75 - Yard Sale

My humans were busy this morning. They were up early and moved a lot of boxes out to the front yard. The big door to the garage was open, and they carried more stuff out. It was a good thing they didn't forget to feed me with all the commotion they made.

My female human fenced in the baby under a big canopy and had a chair next to it. I heard my humans talking about a yard sale several times. Why would they want to sell the yard, I wondered? I didn't want my kingdom to shrink.

People in cars came and looked in the boxes and picked things up from a display table. Many people came! There was an exchange, and people took items with them. There were two long pieces of wood I heard them call skis, which a short man carried out. Some people leafed through the books and carried a few away.

With all these things on display for sale, I hoped no one wanted the baby. I have grown a strong attachment. Some people stopped and asked about the baby, and I stood guard a few paces away, hidden from view. If someone reached for the baby, they would end up with my teeth and claw marks on their arms.

Some big items took two men to carry. I'm not sure what they were as they came out of the garage. I wondered why my humans were getting rid of all this stuff. It seemed there was enough room in my house for everything. Then I worried. It was only a few weeks ago that Lucky, the rescued kitten moved out. In that situation, a bag with her bowls and food left with her. Maybe my humans would move. I trembled at this thought.

Around mid-day, the number of people stopping by slowed to only one or two at a time. My male human packed stuff on the tables back into the boxes and moved them into the garage. My female human carried the baby back into the house.

The next day, the ruckus started again. They set the tables up, and the boxes from the garage were unloaded. People drove up and stopped in front of the house and walked all around my yard. No one removed any grass or dirt so I felt safe my kingdom wouldn't shrink.

One woman took a whole rack of clothes. She talked a lot, but I couldn't understand anything she said. At one point she appeared to use sign language to talk to my female human. Another woman helped her carry all the stuff to her car.

Another man came, and he took the old patio chairs. We didn't need them because my humans had bought some new ones recently. The baby and I liked playing in the boxes they came in.

It was just after mid-day and my male human loaded a few of the smaller boxes into his car. I heard him say, "We can donate some of this to the Salvation Army."

I wondered what an army would do with some old baby clothes, but then they are human, and I need to expect the unpredictable. Finally, the yard looked normal again, and the baby was free to roam around. They disassembled the baby fence and stored it in the garage. My tail swung back and forth as no one took the baby.

The car was backed up near the remaining boxes and my male human loaded them into the car and then drove away. My female said, "Thomas, let's go inside now." She took the hand of the baby and I followed them inside. It was time for the baby's nap and mine too. It's hard work looking out for everyone.

When my male human returned, he said, "Pizza's here." This strange food seems to be a favorite for my humans. Even the baby likes to pull the sticky stuff off and eat it. I like to stick to my special food.

The yard sale still concerned me. The yard remained the same size even though they had a yard sale. Maybe no one wants to buy any part of my kingdom. There is more space to move around and fewer boxes. Maybe my kingdom was growing? Were my humans preparing to leave this place? I guess only time will tell.

That night, I checked on the baby. The baby rested peacefully in the bed with the surrounding bars. It is a safe place for the baby to spend the night. I then found the laps of my humans. They liked to sit on the sofa and watch the moving pictures on the wall. Their laps were warm and I laid out across both. My male human's gentle hands rubbed my head and my female human ran her hand up my tail a few times. I relaxed, and my purr motor rumbled.

Tale 76 - Catnip

I wanted more excitement in my life, so today I wandered out into the backyard. There have been many adventures starting from this point. I remembered previous adventures with the skunk, the kitten named Tiger, and the snake. I wasn't looking to repeat any of those today.

Something in the air drew me in a general direction. I don't know why, but the aroma had something special. It was a faint smell, but my sniffer kept drawing me closer and closer. I came upon this small plant, and its smell overwhelmed my nose with the fragrance to the point I felt drowsy. A nice bed of leaves looked inviting, and I laid down.

I'm not sure how long I dozed, but I woke up refreshed and ready to battle, but no one was around. Energy abounded within me, and I ran and leaped over dead tree branches lying on the ground. I felt I had super cat abilities and even raced a squirrel back to his tree. He came in a close second. I then ran the length of a fallen tree, weaving in and out of the branches blocking my path. I was a terror racing about.

All this exercise made me thirsty. I knew I had a water bowl on the back steps and meandered back there. I wondered what caused all the craziness that occurred. After lapping up the water, I went back to where that special scent arose. Several little green plants grew in the area, and I found the little bed of leaves where I rested. I then located the plant spewing out the fragrance and bit into one leaf.

The taste was terrible, and I spit it out, but the smell drove me crazy. I acted like a dog and wanted to chase my tail. Lucky for me, these movements took me away from the plant, and after a few minutes, I returned to normal. Me, acting like a dog? No way did I want to do that again.

I had enough of this and headed back to the house. I wondered how the baby was getting along. Maybe it was nap time, and I could sleep in the window and keep the baby company.

I wasn't so fortunate. The baby was already running in the house, saying something I couldn't understand. My female human saw me and said, "Thomas, you better be careful. The baby is showing what the terrible twos are all about."

I didn't understand what she said, but I could feel the warning in her voice. Maybe I could still find a window to lie in. When the baby moved to the big room, I darted for the nursery window. The window was open, and I crawled up to enjoy a peaceful afternoon.

My eyes closed, and while I was dozing, the baby came in. The window was low enough for the little hands to reach me. A firm grip wrapped around my body and the baby spun me about the room. Around in circles, we went. I felt dizzy as this continued, perhaps the baby became dizzy too as we fell to the floor. The grip on me released, and I wobbled to the big room.

Little feet and giggles followed me, and I turned and ran to the kitchen. I saw the legs of my female human and hid behind them for a moment. The baby turned the corner and slipped a little, falling by the chairs. The fall brought on crying and tears. My female human went over to comfort the baby. It was my exit cue.

I found shelter under the big bed. I could rest and ponder the events of the day. The smell from the plant earlier made me crazy. The baby is experiencing the terrible twos and crazy moments. I wondered if the baby had found some of that plant and chewed on it?

Later, I found the baby playing with some wooden blocks in the big room. The baby placed one block on top of another until the stack fell over. The baby re-stacked the blocks again and again, and each time, they fell over. I watched with interest and joined the action when a top block rolled away from the others. I chased after it, pouncing on it and rolling over with it in my paws. After letting it go, I batted it back toward the baby.

My female human saw this and said, "Thomas, you are acting strangely. Have you been eating catnip?"

I raced up the cat tree and looked around. Catnip? Acting strange? Is that what I found in the big backyard? I acted weird after I smelled and chewed on it. I think I will avoid that plant.

After the baby settled down for the night, I crawled into the lap of my female human. She seems to understand more than I give her credit for. I started my purr motor to give her some extra credit.

Tale 77 - Lost Part 1 - Truck Ride

I yawned and stretched after a good night's rest. My humans were up and provided my morning meal. I was in a happy mood and went out to the front yard and watched all the comings and goings. A pretty butterfly distracted me as I wandered down the street.

A man was loading up some noisy machinery that cuts the grass. As I watched the man, a big dog barked and then rushed toward me. I ran fast as he had an evil look in his eye. The only place I could go was up into the back of the truck with all the smelly grass cuttings. I hid behind one barrel where the dog could not reach me.

A minute or two later, I felt the truck move. I tried moving out of my hiding spot when my collar caught on something. The barrel pressed against me as I pulled and pulled, but I couldn't free myself. The truck stopped and started several times, jerking the barrels and equipment around. The barrel squeezed me as I tried to squirm out of the collar. I exhausted myself from trying to gain freedom. The truck turned several times, and the barrel moved away from me. Just as I pulled at my collar again, the barrel swung back at me and my neck strained against the collar. The collar broke off, freeing me.

I had to jump out as soon as possible for fear of being crushed. I waited until the truck came to a stop and then made my move. With quick dance movements to avoid the machinery, I was at the back of the truck and leaped to the street. Another car was there, and I darted to the side in time to avoid it. I made it to the safety of the sidewalk. The only problem I had now was I didn't know where I was. That big dog scared me, but being lost was unsettling.

I had no clue which way to go. I looked up and down the street. Lots of cars moved back and forth. I wandered around, hoping to see something I recognized. While crossing a street, a car came by fast and almost ran me over. His horn blasted and it frightened me more. As the day wore on, I became hungry and thirsty and looked for water.

I walked down an alley which reminded me of my early days. In those times, I would check out the dumpsters looking for food. I thought I might have to do this again. I found a puddle and lapped water from it. It tasted terrible, and I dreamed of my bowl with fresh water waiting for me at home.

I needed a place to rest and think about what to do next. I liked to rest in trees but didn't see one, so I continued down the alleyway. A car came speeding down the alley, and I hid behind a dumpster. It smelled bad, but I felt safe. My black fur was a mess. Besides the grass and dirt from the truck, I now had grease and smelly stuff coating it.

Toward evening, my shock of this misadventure lessened and reality set in. I was on my own to get food, water, and shelter. The ugly memories of my early life returned, like a nightmare, and I needed to fight them off.

A grumbling stomach made me move. I left the alley and followed my nose. There had to be a place I could find food. The road seemed long before I smelled something that might tempt my appetite. The smell was something like the barbecue with the hot dogs, but different. A lot of cars moved around this place, and some humans sat outside eating. Maybe I could approach one and beg for food.

I wasn't successful on the first two tries. The first person waved his hands and yelled scat and the second person stomped his feet. After these people left, I tried again. A young girl who looked a lot like the little girl who lives down the street from me, saw me and said, "Are you hungry?"

She pulled part of her food apart and tossed it at me. I grabbed it and ran back a few paces. I could hear her humans scolding her for tossing the food. The food wasn't something I would relish, but I was hungry and ate it before anything could happen to it. I watched others and waited my time. A female human gave me some of her food, and she said some kind words.

Tired from this journey, I now needed a place to rest for the night. Further down the street, I found a grassy area with a few trees. I'm glad my nails were sharp as I climbed the tree with ease and found a wide branch to perch on. The branch was nothing like the lap of my female human, but it would have to do. The purr motor was quiet for the night.

Tale 78 - Lost Part 2 - The Little Boy

I woke up lying on a tree branch. The activities of the day before came rushing back, the dog, the stuck collar and becoming lost. I looked around and recognized the place as a park. These were places humans came to play in. It didn't look like the park where my humans took the baby. If this were my park, then I would know where I was. My stomach grumbled, and I needed to find food.

All I saw around the park were small birds. I think of them as friends. If I saw a big bird, then I might have different thoughts. I climbed down and started toward a street that had food smells.

The early morning people differed from the evening. At the first food place, everyone seemed to hold a cup in their hands. The aroma of coffee drifted in the air, similar to what my humans made. People brought their cups to the small tables and chatted. Some had their computers open and played on the keyboards. I waited for people to sit down and eat, but the cups and the big black cars surrounding the place were all I saw. Frustrated with this lack of food, I moved on.

The next place smelled of candy. I tried something sweet one time, and it made me sick. More smells kept me wandering down the street until I found a place where people were eating sandwiches. I sat back and analyzed the people. One man looked like my human with a small mustache. I sat trying to look pitiful, which wasn't hard to do in my situation. He watched me, maybe hoping I would go away. He was down to his last few bites when he pulled the meat out of his sandwich. Wiggling the meat in his hand, he said, "If you want it, come over here."

I was not sure whether to trust this man. He sounded sincere, so I walked over. He continued to hold the meat out, and I took it. I held my ground while I ate it next to him. When I finished, he reached down and patted my head. With sadness, I watched him leave.

My belly had nourishment, and I needed to work on finding my way home. I didn't know where to start. When I hid in the back of the truck, I couldn't see where it turned. Somehow, I needed to retrace my steps, and this would not be easy.

I started my journey, not knowing if I was even traveling in the right direction. After traveling for several blocks, something inside me made me stop and look around. I didn't know why but I felt an urgent need to move in a certain direction.

The constant traveling made me tired. I came upon another park and found a water fountain dripping. I stood on top while twisting my head around to catch the drips. The water tasted good.

I noticed a young female human with a small boy walking. It reminded me of home. An empty picnic table offered shade beneath it, and I needed to rest. Maybe I sensed the impending danger. I could just see the boy in the distance and the female human sitting at a bench with something over her ears. The kid played on the climbing equipment and was near the top when I saw him fall. He didn't move, and I dashed over to get a closer look. He needed help, and when I looked over at the female, her eyes were closed and she swayed back and forth on the bench. With those things covering her ears and her eyes closed, she didn't see or hear what happened.

With all the speed I could muster, I ran straight at her. I started my meow siren but figured it wouldn't help. I jumped into her lap which startled her. She yelled something as I hopped down and ran back to the child. Her eyes followed me and then she ran toward the little boy screaming, "Danny, Danny." It was all I could do and time for me to leave. I hoped the boy would be okay.

That strange feeling I had disappeared as I continued my journey. A new feeling took its place, a desire for more food. The small amount of food taken in would not keep me strong. I would need food soon and I let my nose guide me along. The desire for food distracted me from seeing a big a man come up behind me with a long pole and a rope at the end. As the pole came into my field of vision, I ducked to the side. The man tried to chase me, but I took off at high speed, evading the man.

Before I knew it, I was at least a block away, panting hard. I looked back and could not see him. Some of my instincts must have faded from lack of use. I needed to keep my wits about me if I'm ever to find my way home.

That evening, I found a flat roof behind a house. The warmth from the day felt good until the coolness and dampness set in. I curled up tighter and waited for daylight.

Tale 79 - Lost Part 3 - Grandma

The night on the roof was cold, and I was stiff from all the extra running and movements from the day before. Hunger pangs reminded me of not having an evening meal. Food would be a priority this morning.

The chilly night air stiffened me up, and I tried stretching. It hurt to move, but I needed to find food. A fence was near the roof and I used it as a step to reach the ground. I landed awkwardly and my back leg twisted outward. I looked around the yard to set my direction. As I did so, the back door opened and an older female human stepped out. She saw me as I limped down the driveway. She called out, "Kitty, kitty."

I stopped and looked at her. She patiently stood there. She called again and said, "Here kitty." I limped over closer. She went inside, and I waited. I wasn't in any great shape to run but prepared myself in case a big dog ran out.

The female human came out with a small bowl. She said, "I bet you're hungry. Come over here and eat."

My nose sniffed the air and led me over to where the bowl sat on the back porch. Having missed dinner, I gulped the food down and licked my lips to make sure I got every morsel.

The human then set down a second bowl filled with water. I didn't hesitate and lapped at the water. In my haste, I caused some of it to spill. When I finished, I looked up to see the kindly face. She reminded me of the woman called Grandma that came to visit my humans.

The human said, "You look cold and tired. Would you like to come in and rest for a while?"

I didn't fully understand what she said, but she held the door open for me. If my leg had felt better, I would have left. As it was, I gingerly walked in. The warm house felt good, and the lady put a towel down, making a bed for me. I couldn't resist.

Being in this house with this woman made me feel so secure, I slept for several hours. When I awoke, I saw the lady on the sofa with some yarn in her lap she worked with some sticks. Feeling better, I groomed myself. As I did so, I found my rear leg still hurt. I would need to be careful with it and hoped I wouldn't need to move fast.

There was a knock on the door, and the lady answered it. There was a conversation that sounded frantic. I heard her say something like "Mom, can you watch Danny today? Yesterday, he fell at the park. I can't trust the sitter anymore." A small child with an arm in a sling entered the house. I recognized the boy from the park. He had fallen from the play equipment.

The mother left, and grandma hugged the boy a few times. He then saw me and came over to where I laid. I backed up, but my leg was stiff. The boy said, "Look, Grandma, his arm hurts like mine." He reached out and stroked my head and back. This felt good, and I lost my fear of him. I was glad the boy seemed okay.

Grandma pulled out a small ball of yarn from her bag. She tied it so it wouldn't unravel and then tossed it over to where the boy and I laid. I saw the boy's arm still hurt some, and he needed cheering up. I ignored my leg pain and chased the ball, batting it over to the child. He tossed it back. We played together, and I forgot all about my leg. Maybe all the movement helped the leg feel better. The boy giggled and laughed. Grandma watched with a smile on her face.

It was late in the day when the mother returned to pick up the boy. He wanted to stay and play more, but I was glad he left. The playtime with the boy tired me. At least my leg felt better.

Grandma opened a can of food for me. It wasn't one I'm used to at home, but it was better than begging and getting strange pieces of food. It wasn't right for a king to beg.

I felt like my old self again. My grooming revealed my true royal self and my stomach was full. It was time to reward this grandma for her kind generosity. I jumped onto the sofa and crept onto her lap. She must have known what I was doing as her hand ran down my back with gentle strokes. I started up the purr motor and let it run wild. I still missed my home.

Tale 80 - Lost Part 4 - Homeward Dreams

The human I've been calling Grandma was kind and provided food and shelter. This came at the time I needed it most, right after hurting my leg. She has proven that humans can be affectionate. My humans have shown this trait too although it took a lot of training to teach them which food I like. If I ever get home, I don't think I will be so picky with my food.

Grandma said "Kitty, you must belong to someone. I will call around and see if anyone has reported you missing. You are too well behaved to be an alley cat. I'm sure we can find your home."

I heard the word home, and that funny feeling inside me told me I needed to find it. What were my humans thinking in my absence? Who would look out for the baby? It was my kingdom, and I needed to return to protect it.

I looked up at Grandma and thought she might need help and protection too. Without my coaxing, she provided me with food and water along with a place to sleep. I had mixed feelings about whether I should leave.

The little boy came back today. He appeared much better and had more energy. He even took the sling off and moved his arm around. We played with the ball. When his mother came back to pick him up, he raced over to her and said, "Mommy, can we take the kitty home with us? I can take care of him."

The word home, made my ears perk up and I felt homesick. The mother and the grandma talked together. It sounded like grandma was telling them she was looking for my home, but she felt the mother could take me for a few days.

Remember when Lucky had her bowls packed up? This time, grandma packed my bowls. The little boy, with a firm grip around me, carried me out to the car. The trip wasn't too long, and I tried to look out the window as we went. I hoped to see something I recognized.

The boy carried me into the new house, and the mother set the bowls down in the kitchen. She said, "Kitty, this will be your new home until we can find yours." She then put fresh water into one bowl.

The smile on the little boy reflected his happiness to have me as a playmate, and I appreciated having someone to treat me kindly and feed me. However, I still missed the baby and my humans. I had to make the best of a bad situation.

Several days passed, and I heard the word party used several times. If I understood it right, the boy was having one of those birthday parties. Those are the ones where there are a lot of balloons and noisy kids running around and trying to pull my tail. I would need to find a good hiding spot when the time came.

On the day of the party, I frantically searched for a place to hide. I tried the big bed, but there was no way to crawl under it. There was a pile of soft toys in the little boy's room, and I worked hard digging down and then wiggling into the middle. Maybe I could wait out all the humans from this position.

There was a lot of noise coming from the big room. I heard several balloons pop. I felt good hiding from all the noise. My good fortune did not last long. The little boy wanted to show me off to his friends. Two young girls came into the room with him, and he moved the soft stuffed animals away, one by one.

I laid frozen, hoping they wouldn't see me. One girl reached out and put her hands around me. I could feel the stickiness of the hands. I looked carefully at the two girls and recognized them. They were the girls that lived down the street from me. They had captured me and kept me trapped until my male human arrived. This thought excited me, and my eyes shone brightly.

The first girl said, "He looks like our neighbor's cat. Hey Sis, what was his name?"

The sister said, "I think it was Thomas."

"That's it. This looks like Thomas." She then asked the boy where he got me.

The little boy said his grandma gave me to him. The girls petted me and rubbed more of that sticky stuff into my fur. They then went out to play with the rest of the kids.

The last time I was with these two girls, my male human showed up to save me from them. Hope was in the air, and my tail swished back and forth. Someone knew who I was and the wait would be hard. At least, the little boy now called me Thomas instead of Kitty.

That night, I slept at the end of the bed with the little boy. There wasn't anything to ignite my purr motor, but at least I was warm and loved. I dreamed of my return home.

Tale 81 - Lost Part 5 - Home Again

I was at the little boy's house for several more days. Only the little girls knew I was here and I needed to find my home. The urge was strong and I needed to start my journey again. I ate a full breakfast and then waited for the door to open. My next move would be to follow my instincts. The little boy no longer wore the sling, and he would be okay. I could leave without feeling guilty.

About mid-day, the doorbell rang, and I ran to the door to make my escape. I concentrated on running right through all the legs standing in the way. As I darted out, a familiar smell touched my nostrils. I turned and looked around. The male human at the door looked familiar, and my female human was sitting in the car at the curb. The baby sat in the back seat, jabbering loudly. With lightning speed, I ran and leaped through the car window and into the arms of my female human. I could not measure the joy in my heart. I nestled up to her neck, and they could hear my purr motor for blocks around.

Happiness filled my heart now that my humans found me. My purr motor kept running uncontrollably, and I wanted to stay in their arms forever. Even the baby chasing me around the house was tolerable. My humans took me to the vet for a check-up and found my leg, while sprained, was healing nicely. I even received a new collar to replace the one that broke in the truck. A little tag hung from it with my name, Thomas, etched on it.

For the next few weeks, I didn't venture out. My lost adventure is not something I would want to repeat. I only went outdoors when my humans went. Today, there was a big party planned. I know this because they carried balloons into the house. The bright colored tablecloth covered the backyard picnic table, and the barbecue warmed up.

I thought I might hide under the big bed instead of wandering off, that is until I heard the voices of the guests. The first guests were the two girls from down the street with the sticky hands. I guess if it wasn't for them, I might still be out on the streets. The next voice was from the little boy that had fallen from the play equipment. I stayed at his house until my humans found me. Another voice was from the grandma that offered me refuge from the cold and provided shelter and food. All these people were kind during that terrible time when I was lost.

My spirits rose from listening to them, and I strutted out to the backyard, showing off my majestic bearing and good looks. My kingdom never looked so good. Good grooming paid off.

The girls with the sticky hands ran over to hug me. This time, the hands didn't seem sticky. Maybe they washed them before coming over. It was a welcomed relief.

The little boy named Danny was happy to see me and sat down for a few minutes on the porch with me. He gently rubbed my head and said, "I miss you, Thomas."

Even Grandma came over and stroked my head and back. She looked at my collar and tag and said, "Thomas. It's lovely to meet you formally."

The baby wanted to get in on the action. The baby picked me up and carried me around, drooped over the arm. This was an uncomfortable position, but what could I do?

Having all these people over, that I call friends, who helped me return to my kingdom, made my purr motor run, even if it was in silent mode. I didn't want my friends to think I was a push-over for all this sentimentality.

Later, the barbecue was cooking something. I think I heard the word hamburger used several times. Unless it was that dog who chased me, I hoped not to hear the word hot dog.

The baby carried a bun and must have been looking for a hamburger. Those were still on the grill cooking, and I saw the baby eyeing these. I worried the baby's hand might get burned when reaching into the barbecue. I moved between the barbecue and the baby, leaning heavily against the legs of the child and letting out a loud meow. The baby fussed as my male human looked over. He understood what I was trying to do and led the child over to the picnic bench away from the danger. I knew then my kingdom still needed my protective skills.

That evening, I spent time in both of my human's laps. The party had been for all the people who came into my life because of my disappearance. I wanted to thank my humans for everything they did for me. I snuggled up around the neck of my female human and gave her an up-close serenade of my purr motor.

Tale 82 - Cookies

I'm feeling a lot better these days. I know my family needs me and by helping them, they provide for my needs. Take the other day for instance. Remember the little treats they give me once in a while? They are in a sealed container on the counter, I know, I tried opening it. The baby saw my female human give me one the other day. Like mommy, the baby then wanted to give me a treat too, but the jar was too far to reach.

The baby has learned the art of climbing. The baby pushed a chair over next to the counter, and from there was trying to open the treat container. While I would have enjoyed another treat, the baby could fall and get hurt. I worried about this and set off my meow siren, and it was enough to alert my female human to come to the kitchen and prevent an accident.

I received a nice pat on the head from my female human and because of this, the baby wanted to pull my tail for the rest of the day. No good deed goes unpunished is how the saying goes to fit this situation.

Today, a friend of my female human came over with her little bundle of joy. I think they called her Samantha. We all went into the backyard, and the two small humans set out cups and saucers for a tea party. I sat on the bench next to the baby. The baby pretended to give me a cup of tea. There was a lot of giggling and laughter. Even the big humans glanced over and smiled a lot.

I heard the baby say, "Thomas, we need crumpets for this party." I did not understand what those were and ignored the situation. The baby seemed insistent and said, "I know where they are."

While the rest of us sat on the bench, the baby went into the house. I should have known better. When the baby leaves my sight or the sight of my female human, something goes wrong. My internal warning signal was going off, and I looked around. My female human was still chatting with her friend and the baby wasn't in sight.

I ran for the back door which hadn't latched. My front paw pushed at the edge of the door, working it open. When I could squeeze through, I did so and found the baby in the kitchen with a chair next to the counter again. This time, the baby stood on the counter and had the cupboard door opened. The baby looked unsteady. Looking down at me, the baby said, "I found the cookies!"

I was about to start the meow siren when a box tumbled out of the cupboard and down on top of my head. The baby saw it hurt me and yelled "Thomas. Thomas. Thomas."

I suppose my female human heard this as she rushed through the door and saw the baby standing on the counter. She then saw me lying on the floor with the heavy box next to me. She reached for the baby and held her tight for a moment before setting the baby on the floor.

My female human then gave me some attention. The box hitting my head must have stunned me as I slowly focused my eyes. I stood up and with some erratic steps, wobbled off to the big room. My female human watched me and then picked me up and carried me to the cat tree. The top perch was probably not the best place to rest in my condition, but I needed a break. This protection racket is exhausting.

I heard Samantha and her mother say their goodbyes and leave. Hopefully, my female human will watch the baby, and I can rest for a while longer. My head hurt.

Later that evening, I was feeling better. It was near dinner time, and I didn't want to miss that. I was thinking about what the baby had said; the party was missing the crumpets. I think I now know what they are. They are the things that crumple-pets. The baby didn't pronounce the word clearly. Next time, if I hear the word crumpets, I will run and hide. I didn't want to be crumpled again.

I enjoyed dinner and looked for a lap in which to rest. My humans were watching the moving pictures on the wall, and it was a good time to snuggle up next to them. I relaxed in my female human's lap with my eyes closed. My ears perked up when my male human said, "Honey, would you like a cookie? I will get them out of the cupboard."

Cookie I thought? Another word for a crumpet? I leaped out of my human's lap and ran for cover under the big bed. I've already had my crum-pets today.

Tale 83 - Porch Pirate

My male human sat at the computer keyboard, tapping on the keys. I watched as he moved the mouse. I tried moving the mouse for him a few times, but each time, he picked me up and set me on the floor. Now, I sat on his lap and watched his hands sweep across the keys. He said, "Thomas, I think you will enjoy what I'm ordering for you."

I could see the screen with pictures of dogs and cats. There were various items shown including collars, leashes, and brushes. They used all these items on me when I was in the cat show. I didn't want these things, but happy my human thought of me to buy something special. The idea thrilled me.

The next day, I was sunning myself in the window. Because I was inside when the man carrying the bills came by, it saved him. I slipped outside and sat on the front porch. If he came back, I was ready for him. I watched as he delivered bills to the houses across the street. He was efficient, pushing a cart stuffed with bills and only taking a handful to each house.

Some people drop trash onto the porches. Leaflets, flyers and business cards seem to be popular. These people walk the street like the bill carrier but are messier as they don't put the paper in the boxes, just the porch and screen doors.

When the ice cream truck comes around making music, the kids line up. They eagerly wait for the truck to buy the paper wrapped products. The kids tear the wrappings off and toss them to the street within moments of buying it. This adds more trash for the street sweeper to clean up.

Big trucks rumble down the street carrying boxes which end up on porches. Delivery trucks come through once or twice a day on my block. The truck stops, a man jumps out, pulls a box from the truck, hustles up to the porch, sets it down, pushes the bell, and runs back to the truck and drives away. These boxes sit on the porch until the owner comes home and carries them into the house.

My male human told me a box was coming for me. I assumed a truck would bring it by and I waited for this to occur. I wasn't in any rush as the warm porch was a good place to lie, since the big tree which I used to lie in, blew down in a storm sometime back. The replacement tree is too small to hold my weight, not that I weigh much.

In the late afternoon, one of the delivery trucks stopped down the street from me. My excitement was growing over the prospect of having a box delivered for me. I watched the routine where the man carries the box up to the porch, returns to his vehicle and drives away. A weird thing happened next. A car pulled up where the truck stopped and a woman on the passenger side jumped out, ran to the porch, grabbed the package and returned to the car. The man driving the car zoomed off down the street.

I was thinking about this. I didn't recognize the strangers. They didn't live in the house where they took the package. I know the people on my block. My friend Lucky lives with the little girl on that side of the block. The sisters with the sticky hands live on my side of the block. They trapped me one time, and another time helped me find my way home when I became lost. There are several dog owners. Enough said about them.

The next day, I laid on the porch again. The baby had me running around inside the house all morning, and I needed a rest. Outside, the baby can't pull my tail or give me tight body squeezes.

I heard a delivery truck coming down the street, and it stopped in front of my house. Could this be the something special my human talked about? I stepped off my porch to give the man room to put the box down. He skipped the doorbell pushing and hurried back to his truck and drove away. I saw a big paw print on the box and knew it was for me.

The strangers from yesterday pulled up where the truck had stopped. The woman stepped out of the car, pushed open my gate and hurried up to the porch. As she reached for the box, I let out a warning growl. My warning startled the woman who stood up and stared at me. She then bent down again to pick up the box. I leaped onto the box and stared into her eyes. A deep growling and hissing with the hackles on my back standing on end warned her. I even raised a paw like in a stop position.

She said, "Scram. You mangy cat."

She was unaccustomed to my regal bearing and warnings. Her hand reached out again, and my paw caught it with a slight scratch. She tried to push me out of the way with her other hand, and I bit hard into her finger while letting my claws sink into her soft skin.

As she pulled away, the deep claw marks lengthened. Blood dripped on the package and the porch. Her reddened face and narrow slit eyes faced me once again. She tried using her foot but was off balance as the height of the box on top of the step to the porch required a high kick. As she did so, I leaped to her shoulder and set my claws in. My attack was enough to cause her to fall back onto the walkway. I jumped clear in time as she hit the concrete hard.

She looked dazed and then wobbled back to the car. Blood was dribbling down her arm and hand. She was yelling something to the man in the car, but I couldn't understand it.

That evening, my male human retrieved the box from the porch. He pondered a few minutes at the blood stains on the box and the cement. He shook his head and then carried the box in and set it on the kitchen table.

My female human joined us. He said, "Thomas, we got you something special." He opened the box and pulled out two bowls. "We had your name monogrammed on your food bowls." I saw there was something more in the box. He reached in and pulled out a bag of snacks and said, "We can also refill your snack jar." He snapped open the bag and offered me one. One little sniff and I took the snack from his hand. I devoured it and licked my lips.

My humans can be so thoughtful. I love when my humans give me these gifts. My tail swished as I stared at the bright colored letters spelling out my name. Naturally, I would value these bowls more when filled with fresh water and my favorite food. I rewarded my humans with extra purrs that evening.

Tale 84 - An Artistic Touch

I love the summer. The skies are bright, and the sun warms my body. Unfortunately, the warm weather brings out many little flying bugs. A big fly was in the house, and I spent an hour chasing it around. Anything buzzing around my head bothers me.

The baby was up and spent its time chasing me. My secret hiding area is in the bedroom, but the baby still finds me. I jump onto the bed and peer down, but the baby somehow climbs up. When that happens, I race off to the kitchen and curl up on a chair seat. The loud sounds the baby makes when running alerts me, and I tuck my tail in tight. If I'm not careful, the baby will find me.

I noticed my female human gathering up stuff from around the house. She collected some strange items and set them on a tray on the kitchen counter. This is the same tray used to carry food to the backyard whenever there is a party or a barbeque. I wondered if any of these items needed cooking. When my human opened the back door, the baby rushed out. Maybe today I should stay indoors. Then again, when the baby is outside, trouble seems to follow and I have a duty to perform. I left the safety of the chair and followed my female human outside.

I watched my female human putting paper down on the picnic table. She covered the whole table with the white paper. She placed several saucers on the table and then poured colorful liquids onto each one. It reminded me of a rainbow; red, orange, yellow, green, and blue. From a small bundle of sticks, she pulled them out and set one next to each dish. There was soft hair at the end of each stick. I wondered where the hair came from and hoped they had enough. I already have a bald spot from that fight with the fox a few months back.

The baby sat at the table observing her mother's actions. I know they were talking, but I didn't understand what they were saying. My female human dipped one stick with the hair at the end into the gooey red stuff and then handed it to the baby. The baby's eyes brightened as the little hand gripped the stick. A grin grew big on the baby's face as the red goo brushed across the paper.

The baby giggled and moved the brush back and forth. My female human traded sticks with the baby and this time there was blue goo on it. I heard my human say, "You can paint a blue sky with this brush."

That's what they're doing, painting. I know little about painting, but it was fun to watch the baby pushing and then dragging the brush back and forth making colorful designs.

I heard a ringing coming from inside the house. My female human left the table and hurried inside. It seems anytime it rings, my humans abandon everything else to go to talk to the little box.

I enjoyed sitting in the sun while the baby painted until I heard a bee buzzing around my head. My head swiveled about trying to keep it in my field of vision. The bee landed on the table, near where the baby was painting with yellow paint. I eased up onto the table, ready to pounce on it.

The bee raised up and spun around the table. I watched and followed the bee around. As I did so, I felt a little wetness around my paws but ignored it. I jumped into the air trying to bat the bee down. My paws kept trying to swat the bee but missed. The baby giggled while I performed my acrobatic maneuvers trying to rid the area of this bee.

I was victorious and chased the bee out of the area. When I looked down, my paw prints were all over the table. They were red, blue, and green. My furry paws brushed the paint around just as the brushes had. The problem was I now had three of my paws covered with these colors. My royal appearance needed a major repair.

My female human came out of the house and saw me standing on the table looking at my paws. She said, "Thomas, I didn't know you had an artistic touch, but we better wash the paint off your paws."

The baby's hands had paint on them too. My human rinsed the baby's hands in a bucket of water and then afterward, dunked my paws and washed them. After additional self-grooming, I restored my royal appearance, accented by my four white paws.

The baby laid down on the sofa for a nap. I curled up close and let my purr motor sing a lullaby. With me guarding the baby, nothing bad will happen.

Tale 85 - Day Care

Strange things never cease to happen. My breakfast came early today and afterward, my female human placed me in my carrier. They usually tell me if we are going to the vet, but I heard nothing about it. This piqued my curiosity. My human carried me to the car, but the baby insisted on walking and climbing in without help. The baby is turning into a little human.

After being buckled in, my female human drove down the street. I hadn't settled down yet, not knowing where we were going. My female human must have noticed this and said, "Thomas, everything's okay. The baby wants to show you off at daycare. It will be a fun adventure." Somehow, the words fun and adventure never seem to go together well.

Upon arriving at the day care center, it shocked me to see hundreds of little people running around. My female human carried me inside so I would feel safe. We entered a room, and the door closed behind us. There were fewer kids in this room. The baby ran over to the teacher and gave her a big hug. The baby pointed at me and said, "I got my best friend, Thomas, to share today."

I noticed a nod from the teacher to my female human, and she set me down and left the room. Some kids arriving spotted me and reached out to pet me. Most hands were slow and gentle as they crossed my back. Some patted my head, like a basketball only I was trying not to dribble. I spotted a bookcase high enough to stay out of reach. While trying to maintain my royal stature, I crossed the room and leaped to the top.

From this vantage point, I could see the entire room. The teacher was trying to organize the kids and have them all sit on the floor. She handed out plain paper to each child along with some crayons. While doing this, I noticed a very shiny object drop out of her pocket. One kid grabbed it, and another kid yanked it out of his hand. I watched the shiny pen slide under a cupboard, lost from sight.

The crayons and paper occupied the kids for a while, keeping them quiet. After they completed the activity and cleaned up, the teacher said, "We have a special guest. His name is Thomas." The teacher walked over and picked me up. As she sat me down in front of the kids, she said, "Be gentle and don't pull his tail."

The baby was in the back. I weaved around the kids, working my way back there. I have to admit, the petting felt good. One kid pulled my tail, and I almost hissed but thought better. Once back with the baby, the arms encircled me, stopping all the other kids.

The teacher had another activity, and the kids busied themselves with it. One little boy walked over to where a fishbowl sat out of reach. I hadn't noticed the potential sushi swimming around. The bowl sat on a cloth runner hanging low enough for the boy to reach. He tugged on the runner causing the bowl to move closer to the edge. I looked at the teacher, but she didn't see the danger. I leaped over one child and bounded for the shelf where the fishbowl sat. The bowl continued to slide closer to the edge. I set my claws into the runner and pulled back. The bowl slowed its movements toward the edge, but it was a losing battle. I turned on my meow siren and let the kid have it.

My meowing caught the attention of everyone, and the teacher came running, just as the bowl reached the edge. She rescued the bowl and pushed it back on the shelf. The teacher looked at me and said, "Thank you for rescuing the fish." I eyed the fish swimming around and while she rubbed my head and ears, she continued. "Thomas, you can forget about eating that fish."

Later that day, the big humans came and picked up their kids. I wanted to thank the teacher for being kind. I then remembered the shiny pen that dropped from her pocket. Looking under the cupboard, I spotted it. With my paw outstretched, I reached it and slid it out. I picked it up in my mouth and walked over to her, dropping it in her hand.

My female human had walked in and saw the pen drop. The teacher said to her, "I am amazed at how talented Thomas is. I've never seen such princely actions."

Well, at least she acknowledged my royalty, even if she didn't recognize me for being a king. A gentle purr started as I rubbed against the teacher's legs.

Back home, I realized now where the baby goes to work every day, just like my male human. I think between the two places, the baby has more fun. I would rather remain at home, lying in my window and enjoying my kingdom.

Tale 86 - Camping

There was a lot of hustle and bustle today. My humans packed the suitcases and loaded them into the car along with things I couldn't identify. I think I heard the words tent and camping a few times. Only when I saw my food bowls packed up did I know we were going on a trip.

The temperature changed a lot. At home, it was hot, and as the road trip continued, it dropped to a more reasonable temperature. I rode in the back seat next to the baby. This position prepared me for the baby's foot to beat on the carrier, but I guess my humans recognized this torture treatment and put a bag between me and the car seat. All I had to do was survive the bumpy roads as we drove along.

It was almost dark by the time we arrived. There seemed to be a rush to unload the car and set up the tent. The tent was a portable house and big enough for all my humans to lie flat in. They even brought a blanket for me to lie on. Once the tent was up, my male human worked at building a fire. At home, there is a barbecue, and he only has to push a few buttons to make it light. After several tries, he started the fire. As darkness set in, strange shadows appeared, and it was difficult to see well.

They served my food, and I ate hungrily. I noticed they washed my food bowl right after I finished. I guess they didn't want to leave it out with its fragrant aroma. That was okay with me as long as they filled it in the morning. I headed off to the tent and found my sleeping blanket. I had a little grooming to finish before I closed my eyes for the night.

The chilly morning air was refreshing after the heat around home. My humans all looked like they were still asleep while they prepared breakfast. Maybe the hard ground they laid on while sleeping had something to do with it. The baby seemed to be full of energy.

When they had everything cleaned up, my male human pulled out a long pole and said, "Thomas, do you want to go fishing with me?"

I heard the word fish and instantly thought of sushi. I brushed by his leg and let out a small meow. The baby wanted to come along on this adventure too. We walked down to the water. I didn't know the lake was here as we arrived late yesterday. I looked out on a huge body of water. If the fish lived here, there must be a lot.

My male human put a worm on a hook and threw it out into the water. A line attached to it so he could pull it back in using the pole. I watched the baby picking up small rocks and tossing them into the water. Maybe that helps make the fish come. My male human wasn't smiling, but he wasn't saying anything either. The baby moved further down the shoreline, and my human seemed intent on holding his pole.

The baby saw something floating in the water and tried to reach it. It bobbed up and down, just out of reach. I saw the baby's feet go in the water and knew this might be dangerous. I looked back at my male human, and he was busy pulling on his pole. In the distance, I heard him shout, "I got one."

Meanwhile, the baby was still trying to reach this colorful bobbing object. It would only be a few moments before the baby would fall into the water. I let out a big and long meow.

I don't like to get wet, but exceptions always arise. My front paws tested the water as I tried to reach the baby's pants. I made another meow before sinking my teeth into the clothes. The water was cold, and the small waves washed up on my chest. I pulled hard trying to keep the baby from moving any further into the water.

Maybe my male human heard me, regardless I saw him running toward us. He reached out and picked the baby up. I stepped out of the water and shook myself. Most of my body was wet, and the chilly air made me feel cold.

My human, carrying the baby, walked back to pick up his pole. A small fish hung from the end. He set the baby down and then unhooked the fish and tossed it back into the water. I wondered if I would ever have sushi.

We walked back to the campsite, and the baby had dry clothes put on. I found a sunny spot and worked at grooming my wet body. Being out in the open differs from living in a house. I'm not sure why they would leave a warm bed to come out here. I'm not sure if I like this camping idea, but I will have to wait and see.

Tale 87 - Camping - The Campfire

I think my big humans were watching the baby more diligently now since the baby tried to walk out into the cold water. I finished my grooming and looked around. My male human brought wood over to the fire pit. There was enough to have a big fire tonight. My female human laid in a chair looking very relaxed. She had a book and turned the pages every so often. The baby found a stick and pulled it around, creating little grooves wherever the stick found soft dirt.

My male human was preparing a mid-day snack for the family. I figured it was an opportunity to catch up on some well-deserved rest. A large boulder lay near the campsite, and the sun shone on it. That is where I curled up.

I woke up with a start. My male human wanted to attach the leash to my collar. I liked my freedom, but I sometimes understood the need for the leash. He said, "Thomas, we have to go up to the ranger station, and you need to be on a leash."

My family of humans and I walked down the road, leaving the camp behind. While there were bits and pieces of conversation being tossed about, I enjoyed the fresh air and the unique sights around us as we walked.

It didn't take long to reach the ranger station. Someone constructed the building from logs. I wondered, did they chop down the trees in this forest to build it? Inside, there were a few people wearing uniforms, like the pesky mailman, but these were brown. There was a patch that showed a tree which was friendlier than the big bird the mailman wears.

One ranger wanted to pet me. I could tell she recognized my regal bearing by saying, "Wow, such a good-looking cat." She knew how to rub around my ears. If she had continued stroking me, my purr motor would have started up, but she stopped.

We continued walking around inside and came upon some dead animals. One was a bear, standing up tall. There were other forest animals, and the baby had to run to each and point them out. I hoped none of these animals had friends that would visit our campsite.

After we saw everything, we headed back down the road. My eyes darted back and forth, looking for bears. After seeing the one at the ranger station, I didn't want to meet up with any. I know I'm strong and can fight off small animals, but the bear appeared too big to fight. I would need to run up a tree.

Back in camp, I felt better when my human unhooked the leash. My male human worked around the fire pit. He carried more wood over and piled it up. I then saw long wires placed near the ring of rocks. He lit a small piece of paper and pushed it under one log. At first, he wasn't successful but started the fire on the next try. It didn't take long for sparks to jump out and fly around. I moved back and watched from a distance. Maybe the fire would scare the bears away.

A big log lay near the fire ring, and all three humans sat on it. The long wires had weenies pushed on them, and the family roasted these over the fire. The weenies looked like hot dogs, but maybe they tasted better when called weenies. After they ate them, I saw white cubes pushed on the wires. They held these out over the fire while roasting and burning them. The baby held one that dropped into the fire. Another cube took its place on the wire, and the cooking continued.

After rubbing my female's leg, she remembered to feed me. I had worked up an appetite today, first with the tempting thought of sushi, then keeping the baby out of the water, and now eyeballing the weenies.

I licked my face and watched the family have fun. It felt good seeing them all together. My male human walked away, and my female human went into the tent. The baby worked at putting one of the white cubes on the wire and then waved it over the fire. It didn't take too long for the cube to catch on fire. The baby waved the wire around, and I watched the fireball swing in the air until it dropped harmlessly to the ground.

The baby reached for another white cube and pushed it on the wire and soon had a second fireball. This one flew all the way over near the tent. Some stuff from the car sat there, and the fireball landed on it. This was bad. I let out a big meow as I ran toward the tent. I let out a siren of meows as I reached the tent flap. The fiery cube was burning through a paper sack. My female human rushed out and saw what was happening. She kicked at the sack moving it away from the other items and then stomped on it until the fire was out.

She turned and saw the baby lighting another cube and took the wires away. I was glad the danger was over. If the tent had caught fire, my bed would have burned up.

That night, I didn't sleep well. I kept thinking about the big bear in the ranger station and hoped none of his friends would come visiting. This camping out is not my thing.

Tale 88 - Camping - The Hike

The second day of camping wore me out more. There were strange sounds all night, and the baby was restless. I hoped the morning sun would refresh me. My humans remembered to feed me, and there was milk leftover from their meal. I had the pleasure of finishing it.

My male human said something like, "We should hike down to the ranger lookout station." I remembered the word hike from before, and that meant a lot of walking. I couldn't let my family wander off without my protection, so I joined the crowd.

People had traveled the path around the lake many times and it was well worn, but the trail leading up to the lookout was less traveled and covered with growth in some places. My female human led the way, followed by the baby, then me, and then my male human. The four of us stomped on the brush, although, my paws were too light to leave any marks on the foliage.

The lookout was a tall structure made of wood. I checked out one of the corner poles and used it for a scratching post. My male human ventured up the ladder while the rest of us watched. My female kept her gaze on him as he climbed. The baby wandered around the lookout and found another path. I didn't see the baby for a few minutes due to the high brush. My internal alarm went off, and I scurried around hoping to catch sight of the young human.

On the opposite side of the structure from where my female human stood, my super cat senses kicked in. Maybe it was a slight movement in the brush or the baby's scent. Regardless, I trotted down the narrow path.

When the baby wants to run, fast is the only way to describe it. The baby was out of sight, and I needed to take long leaps, racing down the trail until I caught up. I found the baby stooped over and pulling a small lavender flower from a plant. I meowed, hoping the baby would return the way we came down the path. Instead, with the flower gripped in hand, the running down the path continued. I let out a big meow and followed the baby. Further down the path, the baby stopped and pointed. "Thomas, see the pretty kitty."

I looked and saw a black and white animal with a bushy tail. I remembered these creatures have a terrible smell. One time, the stinky dog down the street chased one from my backyard, wow, he got a snoot full. The baby held the flower out in an offering to the smelly animal. The black-and-white striped animal twitched its nose.

I had to get the baby to safety and away from this skunk. The skunk looked at us, and I let out a soft growl trying to scare the skunk away without it becoming mad. A few moments passed before the skunk waddled off toward the trees. The baby tried to step forward, and I blocked the progress. I let out a growl in warning but felt bad about having to do this to the baby. However, I needed the baby to stop going any further.

A strange look appeared on the baby's face. It was a look of bewilderment, maybe from realizing the big humans were not around, creating a frightening moment. I nudged the baby back to the path toward the outpost. The baby's eyes closed for an instant and I saw a tear form. I continued pushing the baby until I could see my female human running down the trail towards us. The baby ran and jumped into her arms.

Further down the path, we caught up with my male human who also gave the baby a big hug. While walking back to the campsite, I never once saw the hand of the little human leave one of the big humans.

In camp, I needed grooming to remove the stickers and burrs picked up from the hike. I found my female human's lap and laid in it while she picked them out. The hike made me famished, and I finished my dinner in record time. The water bowl had a workout too.

I noticed the baby was tired and ready to call it a day. The hike wore both of us out. I didn't even have enough energy to start the purr motor. I curled up on my bed next to the baby and fell fast asleep.

The next morning, there was a lot of movement. Right after breakfast, my humans took the tent down and packed it along with the other stuff. I rode in the carrier near the baby, just out of kicking distance. When we hit a smooth road, I fell asleep. I hope we don't go camping again.

Tale 89 - Cat Door

Most everything around me happens on the weekends. I know what the weekends are, it's when both my male and female humans don't leave the house early to go to work. It's also the time when other people show up. Take today for instance. We had a young man come to the door trying to sell something. My male human listened politely and then said the words "No, thank you" and closed the door. Later, a couple came to the door carrying leaflets. My female human talked to them, and then they left.

Another sign of it being a weekend is all the activity in the house. They run the big noise maker on the floors to make them clean, and the baby runs throughout the house playing hide and seek. I do my best to avoid all this. In fact, weather permitting, I like to wander around outside. My humans must have left, for when I returned, there was no one at home. This was one of those times when I wished I had stayed inside. Meowing at the back door proved fruitless.

Dark clouds blew overhead, and the air felt chilly. The front porch has a roof over the steps, and I moved to take advantage. By the time I walked to the front of the house, the rain had started. I thought the porch would provide cover, but the wind blew the water across and within minutes, it soaked me. The chilly water, coupled with the blowing rain created an uncomfortable setting for me. It has been a long time since I was in a situation like this.

When my humans returned, they opened the big door to allow for the car to hide undercover and I scampered in out of the bad weather. My male human spotted me as he opened the door to the house. He said, "Thomas, you're all wet." He grabbed a towel from the laundry room and rubbed me dry. I can testify it felt good to dry off as he rubbed me down.

I heard my humans talking about me and how cold I was from being outside in the rain. My male human said, "I think we need to install a door for Thomas." There was a mumbled agreement.

The next day, my male human was working on the back door. He was using some noisy equipment and causing dust to fly all about the kitchen. My female human kept the baby in the other room. That was smart as the kitchen area looked like a disaster zone. When he finished, he called me over and said, "Thomas, try out your new door." With all the noise made during the installation, I stood frozen. He pushed the little door open and said, "Come on Thomas. This will allow you to come and go when you want."

This seemed like a good thing. I could see it was sunny outside, so I ventured out. As soon as I did, I heard the door close. My human called me to come back in. It was quieter outside, and I liked the sun. I heard him say, "I have a treat for you." The sun was not as attractive as it was a few moments earlier and I pushed against the door. The flap moved out of the way, and he gave me one of those tasty treats once inside. I have to admit, this gave me more freedom moving in and out of the house. Besides, the treats tasted good too.

The baby was chasing me, and I remembered the door. I headed for the kitchen and lined up to use the door. Before using this, I slowed down as I didn't want to hit my head on the way through. My head was out, but the baby caught up with me and pulled on my tail. I tugged a little harder and squeezed through the door. The escape hatch seemed like a welcomed relief. When I turned back, the head of the baby stuck through the door. I wasn't sure if the baby could climb all the way through, but I didn't want to take any chances. I stood on the porch and let out a long meow, followed by another. The baby's head disappeared inside the house.

I entered through my door and saw my female human holding the baby. My female used her loud voice which made my male human come running. There was a quick discussion and finger pointing at the door. Finally, my male human took a panel and slid it down the inside of the little door, blocking it from being used. He said, "Sorry Thomas."

When they moved to the other room, I pressed my head against the door. The panel prevented it from opening. This was not a good thing. I guess easy come easy go. At least I got a few treats from this exercise today.

Tale 90 - Baby Rescue

I like to watch the baby play with things, some of which my big humans use often. Yesterday, the baby found the talk box my humans speak into. The little fingers were tapping the screen, and the box talked. I wandered over for a closer look and saw pictures moving on the screen. It looked like a miniature of the big screen my humans watch at night. These types of pictures carry no interest for me, and I ignored the play toy and headed to my front window to soak up some warm sun.

The baby found another plaything, a fluffy red ball, attached to the keys used for the car. Besides the keys, a black thing with buttons hung from the ring. I could see the buttons on it being pressed. After a few minutes, the baby dropped it.

I was dozing when those same little fingers sought me out. The baby picked me up and carried me to the nursery. I hung on the baby's arm, draped like a towel. In the nursery, a pile of stuffed animals laid in the corner. With me in tow, the baby ran and leaped on top. I gasped for air as the baby rolled on top of me. I scrambled away, heading out the nursery door. There ought to be a sign here saying, Danger Zone.

I found my female human in the kitchen picking up her opened purse from the floor. She looked around, maybe for the missing contents. I followed her into the big room where she picked up her talk box. Still looking around, she found the car keys. The fluffy ball attached made them easy to find. The baby took all these things from the purse, and now my female human played hide and seek with them. Once she accounted for all the items, my female human picked up the baby and headed to the garage.

This was a routine I recognized. Pick up the purse, pick up the baby, and head to the garage. This meant they would leave and I could wander around without worrying about the baby pulling my tail. With the house to myself, I started my grooming ritual. A king should look good, and I wanted to look my best when they returned. I might even have a catnap.

Later that day, I heard the big door to the garage open, and then the squeak from the house door leading to the garage. My female returned from shopping and carried in a few bags. I hoped she remembered to stock up on my special food.

There must have been a lot of bags as there were several trips in and out of the garage. Then there was a period of quiet. I wondered where the baby was. The door leading to the garage was open, and I strolled out and found my female human trying to yank open the car door. She was nervous and becoming frantic as she ran from door to door trying to open one. Through the partially open back window, she talked to the baby. The opening was small, only a few inches. She said, "Mommy will get you out. Don't worry."

I took a vantage point on a bench near the car. I could see the baby in the car seat eating something from a red box with yellow arches. The baby seemed content watching mom from inside the car. It was then I saw the fluffy red ball in the front seat, still attached to the keys. My female human tried all the doors again. She darted into the house where other keys hung. She returned with a look of desperation.

I jumped over to the warm hood of the car and peered in. I could see my human's little talk box next to the keys. The baby finished the food and got antsy. This was not a good thing. I hopped back to the bench and studied the situation.

The rear window was down a little, maybe enough for me to crawl in. I leaped over to the car and clung to the top of the window. I drew myself up and squeezed my head inside. Within a moment of doing this, some sticky fingers with red goo on them reached for me. I felt the fingers slide across my freshly groomed fur as I jumped down, avoiding further contact.

I maneuvered into the front seat and found the keys. At first, I thought about trying to carry them to the window, but the obstacle course in the back seat made me rethink the idea. There were buttons on the thing attached to the keys. I clamped down on them with my teeth. At first, nothing happened, and then I heard a click.

My female human watched me, and when the click sounded, she yanked open the door to the baby. I guess the sticky fingers didn't bother her as she released the baby's straps and pulled the baby to her shoulder. I heard mumblings as she talked to the baby. She then said, "Thomas, I don't know how you did it, but thank you very much."

I figured it was all in a day's work. Now if she really liked what I did, there would be a treat for me. Inside the house, I worked on my grooming again. While doing so, my female human called me from the kitchen. The baby held out one of those special treats. The baby's hands were clean, so I didn't have to worry about any added flavors.

Tale 91 - A Visit From Lucky

The little girl from down the street surprised me today. She brought Lucky to visit, and it made my tail swish. I remember rescuing her from next door several months ago, and the little girl adopted her. Lucky was almost as tall as me, and the gray stripes were more distinct. Her body has grown, probably from eating well. The little girl must feed her extra.

The timing could not be better to have a play day. My female human took the baby to a class wearing a funny uniform. It was white with a long belt hanging down, just the right length for me to swat. Only my male human was home to answer the door. As soon as Lucky saw me, she jumped out of the girl's hands and ran over close to where I stood. We sized each other up and then rubbed our heads together.

The girl held a bag from which she pulled a little white ball. She rolled it across the floor, and Lucky leaped on top of it and rolled over. The ball popped out of her grasp, and I stuck out my paw and batted it across the floor. The girl must have enjoyed this as she watched while laughing. Lucky retrieved the ball and I once again swatted it away. I'm not one to chase balls often, so I wait until they roll near me.

The girl pulled another toy out of her bag. This one had a stuffed mouse on a string tied to a short pole. She dragged the mouse in front of Lucky who did her best to catch it. The mouse was too fast for her. I watched and waited, and when the mouse came close, I pounced and hung on. The girl tried to pull the mouse away, but I sank my claws deep. My instinct to cling was strong. Lucky came over and sniffed it, and I released the toy.

We must have played for hours because my female human and the baby returned. By then, the constant play had exhausted both Lucky and me. The baby had other ideas and tried to engage Lucky and me with the ball and the mouse. It was of no use. We watched the baby roll the ball back and forth. The baby then dragged the mouse around with the same results.

The baby ran to the nursery and brought back a little blanket and covered Lucky up. I retreated to the cat tree to watch all the action. The baby brought more toys from the nursery, and the baby and the little girl played with them.

The day was hot, and someone opened the front door to let the air flow through the house. A big dog was wandering around outside and came into my yard. His scent put me on guard before I saw him. I jumped down from my hangout and stood in the open doorway. The dog came into view, and my hackles rose. Lucky must have sensed the danger at the same time and walked up next to me. We both watched as the dog came closer and closer to the door.

I checked behind me and saw the baby and the girl still playing with some toys, oblivious to the potential danger. I stood my ground and waited. Maybe the dog would leave. I saw the dog sniff several of the plants along our walkway, and then he saw us through the open door. He let out a low growl followed with a bark. This only meant one thing; he was preparing to charge.

I have learned something about dogs. If you take the first step, they will normally back off. I stared out at the dog and then ran onto the porch and let out a loud hiss while holding my paw up high. If the dog thought he would get past me, he would have to suffer the consequences. The dog growled again. This time, Lucky ran up next to me and offered a strong hiss of her own. With two of us looking the dog in the eye, he backed down and ran out of the yard.

I have to hand it to Lucky. She is learning quickly about defending your home and inhabitants. We strode back into the house with our heads held high. The royal guards defeated the heathens once again. The royal family was undisturbed.

A short time later, the fun and games ended, and the girl picked Lucky up and said goodbye. I hoped she would come back and visit again, sometime soon. I now had confidence in Lucky to defend her home and the little girl that lives there.

That evening, in the lap of my female human, her hand petted me and rubbed my chin. I thought about the good time I had with Lucky and let my purr motor run wild.

Tale 92 - Smoke Alarm

My humans need to pay more attention when I need them to do something. Maybe they need more training. On multiple occasions, I have tried to get their attention, and all they do is ignore me. I have tried meowing, which has escalated to my siren, and the old method of jumping up and down on them. Eventually, I get their attention but the time it takes seems excessive.

My latest attempt, and I'm happy to report it was successful, happened last week. Let me explain. My male human installed a small door for me not too long ago. Once I figured it out, a panel slid down the door and blocked its use. This is because the baby figured out how to stick its head through and it might get stuck. Anyway, they unblock the door sometimes and I can move in and out. This was one of those days.

I was sunning myself on the picnic table in the backyard. While stretched out, I could see everything around me. A few hairs were out of place and I took the time to groom myself. My black fur and white boots require a touch-up to maintain my regal looks. After enjoying the warm sun, I dozed.

My cat senses stirred within me and brought me up to full alert. Nothing seemed unusual around me, and I wondered what triggered them. My nostrils flared, and I smelled it, smoke! Where was it coming from? I stared at my house, and it appeared okay. My humans hadn't dragged the barbecue out so that wasn't it either. I then peered up the hill, not seeing anything. The pungent aroma grew stronger, and I knew danger was in the wind.

I rushed into the house, glad no one blocked the little door. Scampering from room to room, I searched for my male human. My female human was in the nursery, busy with the baby, and my male human was in the big room reading a newspaper. I leaped into his lap and cried out. Jumping down, I meowed again. In return, he asked, "What's wrong, Thomas?"

I ran to the kitchen and turned on my siren and waited for a response. My human didn't follow me, so I rushed back into the big room and flew into his lap. The paper he read crackled as I smashed and crunched it. I hopped down and let out another long meow.

At last, my male human stood up and trailed behind me to the kitchen where I went through the cat door. He opened the door and followed me. I suppose human smell isn't as robust as mine as he took a few moments to catch the smell of smoke. When he did, he rushed inside and picked up his talk box. I followed him in and watched his moves. There was a lot of excitement in his voice when talking. While he talked on the box, he yelled something to my female human. "Honey, there's a fire. Pack a bag for the baby. We need to evacuate. Now!"

It's not too often I see my humans scurry, but this was the day. Typically, my female human takes 10 minutes to pack everything up for the baby. Today, she must have set a record as one hand picked up the baby, and the other hand picked up a few bags. She then beelined it to the garage. My male human pulled a suitcase out and threw clothes in it. He then rushed into the kitchen, picked up my bowls and threw them and some of my special food into a bag. Without even picking up the carrier, he called me out to the garage. The baby was being buckled in, and the bags tossed any which way. I didn't dilly dally either as I jumped into the car.

At least my human secured the baby in the seat. My body slammed against the door as the car rocked back and forth in a series of turns. The car slowed when a fire truck passed us going in the opposite direction. When we reached the safety of the city, we could see a huge cloud of smoke darkening the sky behind us.

That evening, we stayed in a room with two beds. The baby had a bed, and my two humans had another. When the baby fell asleep, my male human called me over. Between my two humans, I think they rubbed away some of my fur due to the extra petting. There were many soft words spoken which I didn't understand, but I knew they were expressing their appreciation. I moved over to the bed with the baby and slept at the end.

We had to spend three days at this place. When we returned, everything smelled of smoke. The fire blackened the hill behind our backyard along with the surrounding area. I'm glad my siren worked to alert my humans, but I wish they would react quicker. Training humans is hard work.

Tale 93 - The Dog

With the morning rituals completed, I made my way to the front window, hoping for a ray of sunshine. Sunny days give me extra energy along with a bright outlook on life. My tail swished with happiness. I have two big humans that take care of my needs and a baby that gives me daily exercise. What more can a handsome cat like me ask for in life?

I watched a man carry a box up to our door. I stood on alert as I didn't recognize him. The box was open, and there was movement in it. The man set the box on the porch, pressed the doorbell, and then left rather quickly. I'm not sure, but it appeared his eyes were watering.

My female human answered the door only to find the box on the porch. By this time, I already slid out beside her and peered inside. I caught the odor of a dog! A young dog sat on a cloth and whimpered. My female human called her partner, "Honey, we have an unexpected visitor."

She carried the box inside with the little dog trying to stand up straight. She pulled out a piece of paper from the box. When my male human entered the room, my female human read the note. I heard the words, "Please take care of Max. I have to move and cannot take him with me."

If I understood this, the dog's name is Max, and he is being left, abandoned by his owner. It's understood that dogs require owners. They're not like cats who can adopt humans. Regardless, poor Max needed a home. As much distaste as I have for dogs, I sympathize with any abandoned pet.

Now, all we have to do is find a home for Max. I gazed into the eyes of my two humans and listened to them talk. My male human said, "We could keep him until we find him a home. Maybe he would be good company for the baby."

What? A dog be good company? I had to weigh in on this situation. I meowed several times to let them know this was not a good idea. As usual, they ignored me. I tried to stomp off, but my padded paws were as silent as ever. I retreated to my cat tree to sharpen my nails, I might need them later.

The baby must have discovered the dog as I heard squeaks and squawks coming from the kitchen. I rushed in thinking the baby was in trouble. The baby petted the little dog and made all these funny sounds. It must have delighted the dog as his tail wagged back and forth. I took my exit cue and found the cat door open and walked out.

Outside, I had the quiet surroundings provide a peaceful setting for me to think everything through. I didn't like a dog in my kingdom. Besides, they smell bad. I felt sorry for the dog losing his home. Perhaps the dog would keep the baby busy, and I could rest undisturbed. Now that was a thought! Maybe the dog would only be here for a short time, and my humans would find a home for the animal.

I made my decision, and I would make the best of a bad situation. However, the dog would need to learn its place as there is only one king in this household. The dog will need training, and I've had a lot of practice in training my humans so a canine shouldn't be that difficult.

I went inside to lap up my water. While standing at my bowl, Max came over and tried to stick his nose in my water too. It was never too early to begin the training, and I swatted his jowls. He received the message and backed off. He then approached again, and I swatted him again. Max provided evidence that dogs don't learn as quickly as he kept coming back for more. Maybe I should extend my nails, then again, being a dog, he needs a second chance.

I left with my tail held high in the air. I realized there would be the need for many training sessions. My escape was the front window which allowed me to watch over the big room and avoid the dog. The baby came running in, and the dog followed. The dog's abundant energy almost matched that of the baby. At last, the dog laid down and closed its eyes. It was nap time for the baby too.

That evening, refreshed from their naps, the baby and the dog went at it again. I only had to move my head around to watch them play. Both seemed overjoyed. I realized that the dog, even though I'm not happy with him, would make a good addition to the family.

I later crawled into the lap of my male human, hoping for some petting. He caressed my back and rubbed my ears. I rewarded him with the soft melody of my purr motor.

Tale 94 - Max

I have resigned myself to having a dog around. His name is Max, and with the training I've been giving him, he might become a good companion, within a few years. For now, I put up with his drooling and annoying barks.

The cat door installed for me works for Max too, at least for now. He eats a lot, and I noticed his growth. In another month or two, he will outgrow the little door. I will have fun teasing him when that happens. He likes to go outside whenever the door is open. It's a good thing the front yard is fenced. I think he would wander off if it weren't there. Funny thing is, Max is a lot like the baby. He is always getting into trouble.

Here's an example. Yesterday, Max and the baby were playing, if you can call chasing your tail playing. The baby laughed and laughed as Max turned in circles trying to catch up to his tail. I think dogs are the only animal to try this stunt. Anyway, Max turned around so fast, he bumped into things. First, there was an end table where a lamp rested. The table wobbled, and the lamp leaned. I didn't want Max to get into a lot of trouble, so I jumped on the table to steady it. As the lamp steadied, Max and the baby left the room together, trying to move through the doorway at the same time. Max bumped into the baby trying to be the first through.

Last night, everyone was sleeping well, including me. We all awoke to Max's barking. It was enough to scare the baby and that required soothing from my female human. In the unlikely case Max identified something suspicious, I trotted around the house, checking each room. When I completed my inspection, I found a warm spot on the covers at the end of the bed. In the morning, my humans made grumbling sounds directed at Max. Maybe someday, he will learn to differentiate between everyday noises and those that present a danger to the household.

Today, Max found my male human's slipper in the bedroom. He carried it out to the big room, and the baby tried to pull it away. It became a tug-a-war game with the slipper. Max won the prize and chewed pieces off the slipper. Hiding something like this is hard. My male human showed his displeasure by scolding Max. I was in listening distance, and glad I wasn't the one being lectured.

The baby loves playing with Max. The baby rediscovered the red stuffed mouse my humans brought home for me to play with a long time ago. I let it stay there collecting dust, but the baby had pulled it from behind the bookcase and now tosses it about for Max to retrieve. They play in the big room, and Max lumbers after the mouse. His paws have grown big, and if he steps on the mouse, his paws hide it from view. I watched him do this and then look around dumbfounded trying to find the mouse. He is such a dog. When he picks up the mouse, he romps back to the baby who throws it again.

My male human takes Max for a walk every day. It is part of his training. At first, Max wouldn't walk with the leash on. I remember the days when I went through this training. I would lie down and not move. Max shakes his head and tries to pull his head out of the collar. It seems Max is a slow learner, then again, he is a dog.

Max has short, curly gray fur. His paws are big, and the nails look thick. From the looks, he has the potential for digging deep holes. This might come in handy if we do gardening. He has a long snout with a lot of teeth. I have seen him eat, and he gulps the food down. Overall, he seems friendly, even when the baby pulls his tail.

The man with the bills came by and created noise with the mailbox. This set Max off on a barking spree. I was thinking, if my humans needed an alarm for when the bills came, Max is up to the job.

I was in the nursery where the sun shines in on the floor, resting. Max came in and plopped down next to me. He laid there for a while edging a little closer. He then turned and gave me a lick. I think this was his way of saying sorry. He then laid still and I stood my ground, so to speak and continued to lie where I was. I would need extra grooming to remove the smell, but for now, I swished my tail a few times.

That evening, I found Max in my female human's lap. How could he take my spot? I was about to jump up and box his ears when my male human called me over. I jumped into his lap and received a gentle rub under my chin. My purr motor started up. That's something Max can never do.

Tale 95 - Ride 'em Cowboy

To maintain my noble look, I groom myself daily. Max, being a dog, doesn't seem to care how he looks. His curly gray fur comes down in front creating bangs over his eyes. I don't understand how he can even see where he is going.

Max has grown bigger, and the baby plays with him all the time. I hate to admit that having Max around is a good thing. He's clumsy, and I make fun of him. He comes running down the hall, his feet plopping, and I wait for him to reach the doorway where I hide. When he comes through, I pounce on him and put my paws around his neck. I don't stay long, just long enough to give him a scare. I like this game and have played it several times already. You would think he would wise up and slow down at the doorway. Then again, he is a dog.

Another trick I like to play is King of the Hill. My cat abilities allow me to jump up high while Max has to stay on the floor. When he chases me, which I let him occasionally do, I end the chase by jumping up onto the counter in the kitchen or one of my windows. It is fun to watch his expression of disappointment, like why can't I do that? Sometimes he lets out a little bark in frustration.

Max is now bigger than me. Maybe the way he consumes his chow has something to do with it. They fill my bowl with a good portion, thanks to my training the humans, but his bowl is bigger and filled twice a day. Then again, he has those dry cardboard nuggets to chew on.

My humans found Max likes to wander off, which is typical for a dog. So today, my male human worked in the backyard building a fence. Max was on a long tether, and I had the run of the yard. It didn't take me long to figure out exactly how long the rope was. I would sit just out of reach of the rope with my back to Max. I might even tease him by cleaning my paw. Thinking it was an opportunity to catch me, he would barrel over and then the rope would pull him up short. He would then bark in disappointment.

My male human made loud noises hammering in nails and cutting wood. He seemed to know what he was doing, and I watched for entertainment. He even dug a hole for each of the big pieces to set in. As he walked by one hole, he slipped, and his foot went into the hole, causing him to fall. He must have hit his head because he didn't move. I knew he was in trouble and ran over to him. His eyes were closed and he wasn't moving.

I ran to the back door, but they blocked my cat door. Maybe the baby was trying to escape again. I rushed to the front and found the front door closed and the big garage door closed. Somehow, I needed to alert my female human and quickly. Racing to the back again, I checked on my male human, and he still hadn't moved. Back on the porch, I stood with my meow siren blasting away to no avail. I needed to get my female human's attention.

I needed something louder, so I ran over to Max and meowed at him, hoping he would bark. Max looked at me with his tongue hanging out. I jumped on him and hung on tight. He didn't like it and bucked and barked. His thick fur prevented my nails from hurting him, but it hurt his dignity enough to make him bark. He turned in circles like he was chasing his tail, but I clung to him like paint on a wall. I felt I was in a rodeo riding a bull.

The twisting, turning, and barking was wearing Max out when my female human opened the door to see what all the barking was about. I hopped off of Max and started my meow siren again. She said, "Thomas, what is all the racket?" I then ran out to where my male human laid and increased the volume. My female human saw me and rushed out to help.

That evening, both humans sat on the sofa. My male human said to my female human, "Honey, tell me again what Thomas did that caused Max to bark so much." Max laid on the floor, part of his training as he is too big to sit in the laps anymore. That's a good thing as I now have both laps all to myself. While they talked, my purr motor hummed right along.

Tale 96 - Can You Dig It?

Two weeks ago, my male human hurt himself while building a fence in the backyard. He is okay now and finished the fence. Now Max can run free in the backyard without being tied up. Even the baby can now roam about without extra supervision.

So here we were, the baby, Max, and me, taking advantage of the fenced in open space. I'm more careful now that Max can run free. I think he still wants to get back at me for riding him like a bull. A tree in the backyard provides shade during mid-day, and the baby sat at the picnic table with paper and crayons. I sat on the table watching, and Max had to settle for lying on the grass.

When it was nap time, my female human took the baby inside. I thought about going in, but something nagged at me. It was a hot day, and Max stretched out, trying to keep cool. What was it that bothered me?

A faint shrill carried in the breeze. Where was it coming from and what was making the sound? Max was not helping as he dozed off. I padded over to the fence where I sit to annoy the neighbor's dog and leaped up. I listened, trying to zero in on the sound. Nothing.

I dropped to the ground and headed to the newly built fence along the back. The new wood had a forestry smell to it. I perched in the corner and listened again. A high-pitched shrill came from a distance. The fire burned most of the big trees a while back, but a few survived. I jumped down and made my way through the blackened remains. In the distance, I saw a surviving tree with fallen timber surrounding it.

The sound was intermittent, but louder now. I moved forward and then found the source of the cry for help. The log trapped one of those furry animals under it. There wasn't any way for me to help. If I was to save the bunny, I would need help.

I hurried back to my yard where Max was sleeping. He didn't know it, but he was the help needed to rescue the bunny. He woke up fast after I batted his ear a few times. This caused him to chase me, and I led him to the back fence. When I stopped, he stopped. I think he has figured out not to bite as my paw can stop his jaws fast.

Max needed to be on the other side of the fence, and the first step was to have him dig under it. Max's training has come along nicely, even if he is a dog. Next to the fence, I pawed the ground where I wanted Max to dig, trying to get him to do the same. He got the idea right away and dug. The ground was still soft from trenching for the fence. When the hole was big enough, I slipped through so he would know what to do. He had to dig a little more before he could crawl under too.

I ran to where the bunny was, and I knew Max would follow. Once there, I had to get Max to dig under the bunny without hurting him. I'm sure Max thought this was another playmate, but I had to watch him. I pawed the ground trying to engage Max. It took several attempts before he understood.

Max's big paws worked at the dirt which flew under his back legs. When Max dug enough dirt out, the bunny wiggled loose into the hole. The bunny sat there, exhausted from trying to escape. I knew if the bunny ran, Max would chase him, so I had to lead Max back home.

I caught Max's attention and ran to the fence, sliding under using the hole. Max was so intent on catching me, he squeezed himself under the fence and into the backyard. It was a big job trying to move the dirt back into the hole, but I pawed enough to slow any attempts at escaping. If I left the hole the way it was, Max might try to leave, and I knew my humans wouldn't like that.

When my male human saw the dirt on Max, he walked the yard and found the hole. He covered the hole and put bricks down to prevent further digging.

That night, I laid down next to Max. I wanted to thank him somehow for helping save the bunny. Sometimes, good deeds go without recognition or reward. The only thing I could think of was to start my purr motor. He turned and gave me a big lick. That was the last straw. I didn't want to smell like a dog, so I jumped into my human's lap. At least they don't lick me.

Tale 97 - Ghost Image

With Max settling in and learning his place, the household is running well. He sleeps in his own bed, which is in the bedroom where the humans sleep. I sleep on top of the bed as royalty should. The baby now has a big bed, and they moved the bed with the bars to the garage.

I trained Max not to go near my food when I'm eating. At first, he kept trying to stick his snout in my food, but my paw with the nails extended continued batting him away. I delivered many swings along with some hissing before he learned his place. He is such a dog.

The baby likes to follow my female human all the time and tries to mimic her moves. In the kitchen, the baby needed an apron because mommy had an apron. When mommy prepares food, the baby is alongside wanting to do everything. Thankfully, the humans keep the knives at a safe distance. The two of them were talking today, and I heard the word cake several times. They used a big bowl to put the ingredients in. The baby held a sack of white stuff and tried to pour it in the bowl. Max wanted to see what was happening and stood on his hind legs while reaching up with his front legs next to the baby. The baby turned with the sack in hand and dumped most of the white contents onto Max.

Max sneezed, and the powder blew all over. While the baby was laughing at Max, my female human rushed over and grabbed Max's collar. She then booted him outside. Some of that white stuff had fallen on me and rather than being escorted out, I used the cat door.

Max stood there looking like a ghost, white all over. He shook, and more of the white stuff flew off and fell on me. I blinked to clear my eyes and ran to the picnic table. I had a heavy-duty grooming job to perform. While cleaning myself, Max sat on the porch, waiting for the door to open.

When my male human came home and saw Max, he laughed at the ghostly image. He called Max over to where the garden hose was curled up and washed all the white stuff off. As soon as the washing ended, Max shook himself several times causing the water to fly all around. Some even hit my male human. The wash job didn't improve Max's looks. He was still the gray curly-haired dog I remembered.

When Max was all dry, they invited us back into the house. The baking smells created a delicious aroma. I suppose these enticed Max beyond his control. He paced back and forth in the kitchen with his nose in the air. The baby came in and saw Max sniffing by the kitchen table. The baby said, "You want to see the cake?"

Max's nose followed the baby's hands. The baby picked up the cake and lowered it down for Max to see. He probably thought the cake was for him and sunk his snout into it, taking a big bite. The baby screamed, dropped the platter, and ran from the room, followed by me. I wanted to avoid this disaster.

The baby and I hid in the nursery. I think Max upset my female human as some unpleasant commotion came from the kitchen. I heard the back door slam. Later, I learned that Max had a second bath for the day. My female human came in and picked the baby up and said soothing words. It wasn't long before the baby and I played chase in the house.

At dinner, I had my bowl filled like normal, but they set Max's bowl outside on the porch. I heard the words, "too wet to come in" spoken by my male human. Later when Max was dry, he came back in.

That evening, the baby and Max played with a ball. The baby would roll it, and Max would bring it back. It's too bad he wastes all that energy on fetching a ball. Max needs to learn to do something useful, like scaring the bill man away, although he does bark when the bird man delivers the mail.

And so, it goes. We have a happy family, and they have cleaned Max up. He still smells like a dog, but I guess he can't help that. I laid in my male human's lap and put on an old recording of Purr. He must have enjoyed the music as he kept stroking my back. I appreciated the gentle strokes across my well-groomed body.

That night, we all slept in our own beds, while I kept watch over everyone with periodic trips to check on the baby. I will always protect my family, including Max.

Tale 98 - Max Meets Lucky

It's rare my humans go away, at least not without taking me along. I suppose Max is an added burden. This morning, they packed the suitcases, and I was ready to climb in the car, but my male human did not invite me. Instead, he put the leashes on Max and me, and we walked down the street. I thought this was to give Max and me some exercise before a long trip in the car. The big sack my male human carried gave me concern. Earlier, I saw him pack the feeding bowls and food into the bag and figured he would load it into the car.

I kept my head up, as a king should do, showing Max how to strut. He wanted to stop and sniff every bush we passed. Near the end of the street, we crossed over to the house where the little girl lived along with Lucky. I thought we would say hello.

My male human knocked on the door, and a woman answered. The little girl stood next to her looking down at us. She said, "It's Thomas and his friend Max." Before going in, I heard the words from my male human say "We'll be gone for two days. Their food and bowls are all here."

My male human left, and the woman said, "Jenny, why don't you show Max the backyard." So, the little girl's name is Jenny. She opened the back door, and we all went outside. I looked around for Lucky but did not see her. We played for a while and then moved inside. The woman put our food bowls down and filled the water bowls. It was hot outside, and Max and I lapped up the water.

Lucky hadn't appeared yet, and I wondered why. I remembered Max never met Lucky, and I hoped Max wouldn't scare her. Jenny went into another room and returned with Lucky. Lucky opened her eyes wide when she spotted Max. Jenny had her hands full trying to keep Lucky from jumping out of her arms.

Max didn't help much either. His tongue hung out of his mouth, and he drooled on the floor. He acted like a typical dog, and this frightened Lucky. I needed to act fast and show Lucky there wasn't any reason to run. I walked back and forth in front of Max, making sure my tail dragged around his neck. Max didn't move, and Lucky relaxed. Jenny set Lucky down on the floor. I wanted to nuzzle against Lucky but figured I better keep Max from chasing her.

Max made his move, wanting to sniff Lucky. Lucky hissed at him and put up her paw. Max recognized the warning signs and backed off. I knew everything would be okay after that greeting.

Jenny pulled a ball from the bag they had carried our bowls in. The ball is one of Max's favorite toys, and she tossed it across the room for Max to chase. While the two of them played, I had my chance to nuzzle up against Lucky. Her gray stripes make for a striking appearance. I let her know Max wasn't a threat even if he is a dog.

That evening, Lucky and I slept on Jenny's bed. Max curled up on the floor. The closed bedroom prevented me from wandering around the house, so I had a good night's rest. In the morning, we played in the backyard. Jenny and Max played ball, and Lucky and I performed grooming activities.

Max and Lucky seemed to be okay with each other. Lucky spotted a butterfly and chased after it. When Max saw Lucky running, he took off after her. When Max caught up with her, Lucky turned, hissed, and held up her paw with the nails straight out. Max skidded to a stop and turned around. He realized quickly there were more enjoyable activities than having his face used as a scratching post. He didn't chase Lucky anymore after that encounter.

The next day, my humans came to pick us up. The baby played with Jenny for a few minutes, and my big humans talked to the woman. Afterward, the leashes were hooked to our collars, and we walked back to our house. I was happy to visit Lucky and glad Max met her. If we ever do it again, I think Max and Lucky could be friends.

I relaxed more now that I was home. Maybe my happiness came from having my whole family together again. It might explain why my purr motor hummed when I reached my female human's lap.

Tale 99 - Street Repairs

I'm glad I'm not restricted to the house and backyard like Max. The backyard is nice with a big shady tree, but I love to wander about and see the world. Besides, how long can a cat of my royal bearing hang around with a dog? It might tarnish my reputation.

Today, we finished breakfast, and I watched my male human leave for work. I remembered the time when I slept in his car and had to spend the day at his workplace. The window there didn't open, and he has to sit at a computer all day. I like it when he comes home and gives me a special treat from the container on the counter.

The baby and Max played in the backyard, and I watched until boredom set in. I headed to the front yard and looked around. The morning birds already left and a gentle silence filled the air. I should have known this couldn't last for long.

Two big trucks pulled up and stopped on my street. Several men wearing orange vests got out and huddled around a spot in the street. They unloaded machinery and switched it on. A loud noise erupted as the men prepared to dig in the street. Bursts of even louder noises that sounded like a machine gun interrupted the loud sound. Bits of debris flew all around as the men dug.

The flower beds have some beautiful green bushes growing in them. I hid behind these and watched between the long leaves hanging down. The man with the bills came and dropped off another bundle in our mailbox. I'm used to him but worried if Max ever gets out when the mailman comes, one or both will be in big trouble. I hope the bill man can run fast.

The men in the street took a break and sat down. Someone turned the machines off, and the silence was deafening. The peacefulness almost restored my hearing when the machines started up again. The hole they were digging grew in size.

School let out and kids, carrying their backpacks, walked down the street. Some stopped to watch the men working. The men ignored the kids and kept on digging.

Near the end of the day, the men must have tired as they covered the hole they dug with big sheets of metal. The men loaded the equipment up and drove off. Silence, once again, was the norm.

The ice cream truck drove down the street playing terrible music. It was like the pied piper, and the kids from all around ran down the street chasing it. It stopped right on top of the metal plates covering the hole. I wondered if the truck would fall in.

The kids made their ice cream purchases and threw their paper wrappers down. Maybe the men digging the hole would pick them up when they came back. Then again, maybe the hole was to bury all the wrappers and trash strewn about. As the truck left, I heard an ugly screeching sound come from the metal plates. I walked out to the sidewalk and peered out. One plate shifted, and I could see a dark crevice. I thought if another car or truck drove over this, it might shift more and the car would fall in. Then again, the spacing was not that big. I went back to the shade in the flower bed.

As the coolness set in, I thought about my male human. He should return from work soon. That meant it was almost time for my evening meal. Then I thought his car might get stuck in the hole. I couldn't let this happen.

I hurried out to the sidewalk and examined the hole again. My male human's car might fall in, and I couldn't take the chance. I waited for him to drive down the street and didn't have to wait long. When I saw him, I ran into the street near the hole. He is a good driver, and I knew he would stop for me. He said, "Thomas, get out of the street." There were more words, but I didn't understand them.

I waited until he got out of the car and came over. He then saw the big hole and let out a gasp. I figured he sensed the danger and I could now go into the house and await my dinner.

Inside, my male human yelled into his talk box, describing the hole in the street. My female human listened in. When he finished, he said, "If Thomas hadn't been out in the street, I think my car would have fallen in that hole."

Tonight, they gave me two treats on top of my regular food. They were scrumptious. An additional treat was the extra petting I received. And to think, I didn't even have to turn on my purr motor.

Tale 100 - Past Tense

I woke up in a sad mood. I wasn't my old self. Some old memories floated inside my head causing me to think about things that happened long ago. Back when I had to take care of myself, I got in a lot of scrapes. Sometimes I had to fight other cats just to get food. I even scrounged in the trash cans.

When I was a kitten, my mama would bring me food. It wasn't long before she made me go with her. She taught me where to find food and made me work to get it. One place we went often, was where many people went to get food. We would sit in the bushes and stick our heads out, and people would sometimes throw food near us. I think they called the food chicken. My mama would always get a big piece, and I had to settle for smaller portions. Then again, I was still small and growing.

As I got bigger, I became more aggressive and tried to get larger pieces for myself. There were other cats I would sometimes have to compete against to keep my food.

One day, some men came with long sticks with a net at the end. They captured my mama and several other cats. I hid back in the bushes, and they didn't see me. I never saw my mama again, but the lessons she taught me have lasted a lifetime.

Another place I visited was the sushi restaurant. They would carry the trash out late each evening. The man there got to know me and saved a big piece of fish for me most nights. This was heaven until some other cats crossed into my territory. I learned how to fight in this environment. I lost many battles before learning how to fight well. Eventually, the other cats found out how good I became and backed down most of the time.

I didn't relish this life, but it was the only life I knew. It was a constant bid for survival, finding food, water, and shelter. My search for food expanded and I wandered into some nearby neighborhoods. Other cats and dogs seemed attached to humans who put food out on their back porches. These houses presented a new way to look at life. The animals remained close to the houses and ate when the food was out. They did not have to compete with other animals. Some even had a door they could use to enter and leave the house. I wondered what it would be like to have a regular home and have humans provide me with food every day. Could a life like this really exist? How could I find a friendly home?

These thoughts ran through my head until the day I changed. No longer did I want to be an alley cat. I wanted to be a king and find a better life for myself. I would not let myself be homeless anymore. There were more neighborhoods I needed to scout, but I was positive I could find something.

What made a good home? I didn't want to compete with another cat, and certainly, I didn't want to try moving in with a dog, so I only looked for homes without other animals. This was no easy task.

My search was long, but the home I'm in now was my reward. Two good humans, a baby, and now, even a dog. Fresh food and water provided twice a day. I think I'm in heaven. Of course, I pay my humans for these offerings by allowing them to pet my beautiful body. It even feels wonderful when they do this, and my purr motor serenades them when they do a good job.

Having been without for so long, I don't take my shelter and nourishment for granted. Everything has to work together, so it continues on and on. I protect my home and everyone in it and I won't let anything come between the outside world and my kingdom. When everyone is happy, I'm happy.

So why was I thinking back on this? Why was I in this mood? Then I realized, this was my fifth summer of life. I have spent three summers with my humans. It was a time to celebrate, but how should I do that?

My humans celebrate with friends, cakes and balloons, none of which makes sense for me. Kids pull my tail and balloons pop all around me. I try to find a quiet place outside while the noisy parties take place.

I then realized that I'm the happiest when laying in the laps of my humans. Even being around Max and the baby gives me a good feeling. We are a family!

Looking around, I found my female human resting on the sofa. The baby was sleeping next to her and Max was on the floor. I strolled over and jumped up on the other side of my female human and then snuggled up in her lap. The thought of being with my family primed the purr motor which then started without coaxing.

THE END

ABOUT THE AUTHOR

Dwayne Sharpe has written over 50 short stories in multiple genres and age groups. Topics include Animals, Love Stories, Crime, Adventure, and Fantasy. His background includes computer management and technical writing. Hobbies include genealogy and geocaching. He lives with his wife in Long Beach, California.

Made in the USA
Coppell, TX
09 December 2020